ISAAC'S JOURNEY

Rise of The Intelligence

D.H. SEGAL

First edition

ISBN: 9798282125887

To Isaac and Ava.

May your journeys be happy ones.

Part 1
RISE

My home is gone. I am… alone.

No matter where I go, how many times I try to find hope, it's always the same.

Please, not the machines again.

Elrion

1
Freedom

Grass, Isaac thought. He gazed into the distance. Hills. Endless, rolling hills covered in green. A lone tall tree sat on one particularly large hill. Isaac's attention shifted to his body, thinking about how relaxed it felt for his legs to be stretched out on the soft, yet prickly grass-covered ground. With his fingers interlocked and resting on his stomach, Isaac appreciated every rise and fall of his chest as his lungs filled with the clear, clean air of the natural landscape around him. He closed his eyes.

"*Breathe,*" he told himself, quietly. "*Hold.*" A couple of seconds passed. He then let go of the air he was holding onto, exhaling slowly, with a great feeling of being at peace. He began to open his eyes again, to enjoy as much as he could, while he still could.

The wind blew across the fields, whirling around his head, making soft whooshing sounds in his ears. His eyes shifted to the blue sky above. *Breathe*, Isaac thought, *remember this moment.*

Remember how it feels to be out here. Don't you ever forget what it means.

"GET UP!" A large prison guard shouted.

The smell of the artificially clean and sterile floor filled Isaac's nostrils. The gentle breath of fresh outdoor air was now replaced with breaths of cleaning fluid, of blank, heartless tile.

"IT'S TIME TO EAT!" barked the prison guard as he threw down a few chunks of bread onto the floor in front of the cell's bars.

There were ten or so boys and girls sharing the cell with Isaac, ranging in age from about five to eighteen, with Isaac seeming to be the oldest. They ran over to the food, which was never enough to satisfy them. It was enough to sustain them, yes, but they were always kept a little bit hungry.

Isaac stayed on the floor for a moment. He gave a final, slow breath before gradually rising. Staring at the boys and girls fighting over the food newly dropped, any sense of calm he had was now replaced with contempt. He felt anger against those forcing him and the other children into this life. Whatever their reason, he thought, they had no right to keep them in there, treated like this. Still, Isaac was hungry.

He took in one more breath, readied himself into a sprinting stance, and quickly made his way through the crowd. Amidst the tangle of grabbing, shoving, and clawing, he spotted a torn piece of bread overlooked by the others and snatched it. Only bread was given for now. Protein would not be fed to the prisoners for another few hours, so Isaac walked away from the group, deciding not to waste any more energy, back to his corner as everyone else was still fighting over food that wasn't there. It wasn't much, but the small chunk of bread would nourish him until protein time. He ate, neither quickly nor slowly. If he ate too fast, he might spend more energy than needed. If he ate too slowly, then he could risk creating a craving for more food than he had.

How long had he been doing this routine? How many years? It was hard to keep track of time in there. How he missed the outdoors, the smell of fresh air, the sight of colors, the night sky full of stars. His parents...

Isaac had to stop himself from dwelling too much on the past. *This will not be my end. This will not be the end of my generation*, he thought. *Somehow, I will find a way to stop them, to stop* ***It***. He just didn't know how he could, not yet and not like this.

Ready to let time pass as usual, being ever stuck in this hopeless situation, Isaac let himself grow tired. He would return to the peace of his dreams yet again, back to his fields of green grass, blue skies, and soft fluffy white clouds. He laid down on his back, returning to his thoughts of nature and of freedom. His hands again rested on his stomach, feeling the air entering and leaving his body, ready to wake up to a world outside. The cold, hard floor under him would soon be replaced by grass and earth. Isaac whispered to himself, "*Another morning without freedom, if this even is morning*." His mind wandered back to the fields. That fuzzy state of dreams crept closer and Isaac softly began to smile.

BOOM!

An explosion ripped open a door-sized hole in the wall opposite him. Bricks shot across the space. Some almost hit the other children in the cell. He sprang to his feet, ready for anything that might come through the cloud of dust. Others cowered in curled-up fetal positions, like babies in a crib, hiding in the corners of the room in clusters together.

The shadow of a figure emerged from the haze. The light of the hallway, spilling into the cell from behind them, cast a glow around the edges of their body. As the dust settled, the figure became clear. She took off her black night vision goggles.

"RUN!"

2

Hesitation

Eight years ago

"Isaac, RUN!"

Isaac's mother screamed. Even though he was only ten years old, she knew he was old enough to understand what was at stake if *they* found him. She did not want her son to be taken like all the others down the street. Though she had no idea where they were being taken or what was done to them, she nonetheless feared for the worst. At least if he ran, then maybe he would have a chance.

"I said, RUN!" She shouted again.

"But I can't leave you here!" Isaac retaliated.

She kept focused on what she knew was best. If she argued with him, she would risk losing even more time. "If you stay, you will get captured. We don't know what could happen to you. If you leave now, maybe I won't see you again, but they won't have you. Please, I love you. You have to leave NOW!"

Isaac paused for a moment. He knew she was right. He didn't want to admit it, but she was indeed right. Nodding his head and standing motionless, Isaac stared at the ground as he tried to process his situation. *This can't be happening*, he tried to convince himself. He was not willing to accept the truth—that he had to leave his mother behind. Sure, if he left, he would have a better chance to get away to safety. But what about his mom?

His father trained him well to consider all options, to analyze what was best, and to act immediately. Then again, his father was not there. Of all times, when he was needed most, Isaac's dad was gone. Isaac found himself standing there, frozen in uncertainty. He hesitated. Even if only for a moment too long, Isaac stood still. It was too late.

"Isaac... it's here." Isaac's mother's face was pale in fear.

The front door of their home always seemed so nice and peaceful, with its handful of square glass panes that allowed sunlight to shine in. Now, though, the ominous glow of blue light made its way in, light that shined in from a robot now scanning the inside of their home. This robot, this "Population Controller," or "PC," as people called them on the news and on the internet that day, was looking for children. It was looking for Isaac, and nothing was going to stop it from getting to him.

"Isaac, my body is between the door and you. Maybe, just maybe, its sensors won't see you if I'm blocking the light. Just... slowly... walk backward. Go out through the back." But just then, the doorbell speaker was suddenly taken over by a voice, **"I am here to pick up your child. Please open your door immediately.**

Thank you!" The overly polite tone clearly came from a machine, not a human. They stood up like humans, walked and moved like humans, but they were made of metal, plastic, wires, batteries, and electric motors.

"I repeat, bring your child to the front door as soon as possible. Thank you!" The PC's blunt nature was meant to calm the people it was talking to, to get them to drop their guard, to maybe even believe that, if they cooperated with a PC, they would be unharmed. But even if that were true, if following the PC's instructions meant you would be left alone, what parents could cooperate with machines when told to give up their children?

Isaac's mother wouldn't just let her son be taken without a fight. She had to make a plan. If she did nothing, they would go through her and take him. She wasn't going to just hand him over, though. If she ran away from the door, it would probably break the door down and rush in to take him. She could only think of one thing to do, and it was to do what the PC said, but slowly, very slowly. *Maybe*, she thought, *I can convince Isaac to leave. And if I can't… I'll have to fight.*

So, she continued to walk toward the door, as the PC expected her to. But as she did, she pushed her son to leave. "Isaac, go." She lurched forward slowly, and ever-so-gently lifted her foot off the floor as she began to step toward the door.

"There's two of us, I can help!" Isaac stated firmly.

She shook her head left and right as she placed her first step onto the ground in front of her — one step closer to the PC. "Isaac, you can't do this. You have to *go*. Look, I love you. Please, please go. You can't help me. You're too small. I'm sorry. GO!"

Her voice broke, her eyes starting to water, as she took another step forward.

Knock!

It knocked on the door with a hard thud. Isaac's mother knew it wouldn't stop. She had seen what happened at every other home. PCs knocked once on the neighbors' doors down the street. Then twice. And finally, if they did not open their doors after the second knock, a PC would break it down on the third. Always on the third. They were methodical, unstoppable, and ruthless.

The PC's voice spoke through the speaker system again. **"Open up, please! Hello, Isaac. We have come to assist you in a trip to our children's camp. Ms. Levi, please open the door at this time."**

Did they hear him? Isaac's mother thought to herself. *I thought I was blocking the light. It's okay, if Isaac moved to the back door by now, maybe he's already out. I think I've bought him enough time.*

Still, she couldn't stop moving, or the PC would knock again or, perhaps, it would rush in and try to capture Isaac. She very carefully turned her head while her feet inched toward the front door. Tears streaked down her face. Isaac had not taken a single step. She was so close to the door handle now, the PCs' scanners could likely see Isaac through the glass.

"Isaac. They will knock one more time. Run, please, just run. Maybe they—"

KNOCK!

The second time was even harder. The thick wooden door now had cracks running through it. "Isaac, *please*, you know you have to go. If I open this door or they break it, you will be taken."

Isaac just shot back at her, "I WON'T LEAVE YOU BEHIND!"

Her face dropped in disappointment. "I love you, Isaac." It happened in an instant. As Isaac's mother opened the door, she did so with the least amount of force possible, so as to give the heavy wooden door time to open slowly while she prepared an attack. As the door opened to only five inches, Isaac's mother had already grabbed a baseball bat nearby.

The door was still opening, now 10 inches. Isaac's mother, with baseball bat in hand, held it ready to attack her enemy. She thought to herself, *They will NOT take him!* Every muscle in her body was ready to hit and break any sensitive point she could see, any cameras, sensors, or weak spots this PC might have. The door opened to 15 inches, enough for her to strike.

Isaac had never seen his mom move like he was about to. He knew she was athletic, fast, but he was surprised at just how quickly and aggressively she moved to protect him.

"YES!" Isaac shouted as he saw the bat land on the blue light sensor, the circular frame positioned on the center of the PC's chest. But Isaac's mother had no time to celebrate, no time to waste. The computers in these Population Controllers would likely be able to process the situation and figure out how to stop her almost immediately. She pulled the baseball bat back and moved it straight toward the PC's flat plastic cover on its face, attempting to damage any cameras or other sensors it might have underneath. No matter how strong these robots were, no matter how fast they could calculate their next moves and formulate their attack, they couldn't do anything without the ability to sense their environment.

WHAM

She struck the black face cover as hard as she could. Less than half a second had passed since she opened the door. She had already destroyed its sensor on its chest and had tried her best to destroy whatever tech it had in its head. But, even if only for the briefest of moments, she had doubt in her mind—she wasn't sure she was actually damaging anything in the head except for the cover plate. In a fraction of a second, she made the decision to encourage her son to leave... while she still could. Before attempting another strike, she turned to her son. "Isaac! MOV—"

CRASH!

The PC punched its metal fist forward into her stomach and then drove her body into the stone floor of the house. The PC withdrew its hand and stood up straight, its motors and actuators whirring as it did so. Towering over Isaac's mother, it spoke without an ounce of emotion, without an ounce of regret or reaction of any kind to what it just did. "**Hello Isaac, please come with me. I will take you to the children's camp now.**"

Isaac turned to run, but it was no use anymore. The PC moved so quickly, it was as if he could barely see it move at all. It looked only like a blur to Isaac's eyes. The Population Controller picked him up with a grip that felt unbreakable, carrying him like a bag under its arm.

"Mom." Isaac began to cry. The PC turned and walked back to the front door, stepping right over Isaac's mother. Isaac didn't want to look.

Just as they were about to move out through the door, though, Isaac opened his eyes to look back at his mom one last time. Though painful to see, Isaac told himself he wouldn't look away. He would not forget what the Population Controller, The Intelligence, did that day. With tears still flowing down his face, he looked up at the PC holding him and thought to himself, *No more. Next time, there will be no hesitation.*

3

Run

Present day

Isaac walked from the edge of the prison cell toward the newly created hole in the wall. The others, however, stayed where they were, shaking in fear, huddled in the corners together. The girl who had blasted through the hole saw Isaac walking steadily toward her.

"Hold on," she said to him, "what about the others? You're just going to walk away from them? Aren't they your friends?"

Isaac stopped for a moment, now standing next to her. He turned his head only a little to take a look at his fellow prisoners. His eyes shifted to look at her. "They are just wild children," he said, coldly. "Leave them."

Her mouth dropped open in disbelief at his lack of care. Isaac shifted his weight forward, ready to continue through the hole, but the girl put her hand on his shoulder to stop him.

"Surely, there's still hope for them. Just because they're too afraid to get up, even if we're in a hurry, doesn't mean that we should give up o—"

Isaac stopped her from continuing. "They never learned to speak," he said. "It's too late for them to understand anything you try to tell them..." He paused for a moment and breathed out a heavy sigh. "Even if you pointed and screamed for them to go, I don't think they would know what to do. I don't think they would understand you. They're *wild*. I think most of them grew up in here."

She took her hand off Isaac's shoulder. Her eyes took one last glance at the shivering children in front of her. She slowly turned to go, muttering under her breath, "I didn't know it would be so bad in here." She then looked again at Isaac. "What's your name?" She asked.

"...Isaac," he slowly replied.

They both began to walk through the hole, about to leave behind the "wild" children, as he called them. But leaving them behind deeply bothered her.

"Why don't you care about trying to help them?" She asked. Isaac, trailing only a couple of meters behind her, didn't respond. She stopped in her tracks. Isaac, noticing this, immediately stopped as well. "Answer me. I came here to save *everyone* I could. My parents told me to—"

"Stop," he interrupted, "we don't have time to—"

Now she cut *him* off. "STOP WHAT?! We need every person we can get to save humanity! And even if they can't help us, isn't it right just to help them get out?! You called those children 'wild' because, why? Because they don't know how to speak English?

Because they never had an education? Because they will *probably* struggle to escape or even survive if they get out? Isn't it worth it just to try and save them?!"

Something in Isaac stirred. He lowered his head and faced the ground. She looked at him and was surprised at his reaction. "Isaac, are you crying?" He looked straight up at her, his brow furrowed with anger. Was he angry at her? Was he going to try to escape alone? She didn't even know him. What if he was going to attack her? She did, after all, only just meet him. She had no idea what he was really like or who he was. Then, he spoke.

"You're right. I'm... sorry." How could he let his time in this prison get the better of him? His mind flashed to the memory of the day he was captured. The rage he felt toward the artificial intelligence, toward the Population Controllers that stole so many lives, the PC that stole his family's life. "This will *not* be the end of our generation. We have to put an end to it!" His sudden exclamation, his sudden call for action, surprised her.

She stared back at him. She was stunned that he actually felt like she did, especially after he was so willing to leave the others so easily before. "Isaac," she said, "are you crying?"

"There's no time to waste." He wiped his tears with the sleeve of his prison rags and smiled. "Let's *try* to save them." As he turned around, he respectfully and gratefully told her, "Thank you."

"For what?" She asked.

"For making me remember what was important." He smiled. "By the way, what's your name?"

Her eyes opened wide as she realized how she hadn't actually introduced herself to him yet. "Oh! It's Emma."

In response, he gave a thumbs up. "Great! Nice to meet you, Emma." His attitude was now the complete opposite of what it had been just moments ago, having changed from callously indifferent to positively kind.

She was relieved that this person she just met was actually nice. It was incredible really, to see him so cheerful all of a sudden, considering his situation, considering how long he must have been in that prison, and how he wasn't willing to help the others just moments ago. "Okay, we need to move. Let's get these kids out." But before she could...

"Did you lose your waaay?" A guard creepily spoke, suddenly appearing from down the hallway, slowly walking around the corner. "Did *you* make the hole in my cell? How did you even get into this 'camp?' Are you trying... to take my little friends away from me?!" After his intimidating shout, he started to run toward Isaac and Emma, with a stick-like weapon, a baton, like those that used to be held by police, in his hand.

From the little that the remaining humans knew of these "children's camps," it was believed that prisoners barely had enough food to survive. No one knew if children actually died in these places, but they certainly weren't expected to be living comfortably. She knew that the children would likely be weak and need help to get out. It was her time to protect them, to protect Isaac.

Emma quickly got into a fighting position. She knew combat could be part of the mission after all. This was part of her training. This is what she prepared for. "Isaac! Get back!" But he stood there, just staring into the cell at the scared children. He was unresponsive to Emma and to the sounds of the heavy guard's feet stomping toward them. "Isaac!" She shouted once more. "Get back!"

At that moment, Isaac could hear his mother's voice as if it was hers calling out to him.

The guard was only feet away from them. With his heavy metal baton gripped tightly in his hands, he stretched his arm back, readying himself for a massive swing aimed for Emma. But then, for no reason that Emma could figure out, the guard suddenly closed his eyes and started to fall to the ground.

THUD

It was as if he had just fallen asleep. He simply dropped, and his body went limp, his weapon bouncing and then resting on the hard ground.

Emma turned to look at Isaac, to see if he knew something she didn't, or if his face would show the same confusion as hers. "Isaac?" Emma couldn't believe what she was seeing, or rather, what she didn't see. Isaac was gone. Emma found herself alone and terrified in that moment of silence. She couldn't move from where she was standing, afraid that if she did, she could disappear like Isaac too. *What kind of sick experiments were they performing here?* She had heard about the speed of PCs, that they could move too quickly for a person to react to. But hadn't seen anything. PCs were fast, but not invisible. No sign of a PC anywhere. With so many years since it all began, could there be a new model of PC in the building right now, with even more upgrades, faster than ever reported? If they took Isaac, where did he go? Would she be next?

Then, she heard something coming from inside the cell. She crept up, one gentle step at a time, avoiding noise at all costs. She slowly peered into the cell. "Isaac?"

"I'm trying to help them out. I didn't say anything at first. I didn't want to scare them." Crouching down in front of the huddled group of children, he stood up and walked out next to Emma again. "I don't know how we're going to convince them to leave with us."

Emma was still confused about what just happened to the guard, who was lying motionless on the ground, and confused by how Isaac was so calm and seemingly showing that guard no concern at all. "Isaac, what is happening?"

Isaac turned to face her and put his hand on her shoulder. She looked at his hand and back at him, surprised by his casual sharing of space after barely knowing her and amidst this strange situation. He spoke to her. "I stopped the guard. And now," he took his hand off her shoulder as he smiled, "I think these kids are warming up to me. I think if we start walking..." He turned around and began walking into the hallway, gesturing for them to follow him as he did.

One by one, they cautiously exited the cell. Though their eyes were darting left and right, scared of a new guard who might come and attack them, they were nonetheless making their way and trusting Isaac as they followed him.

Emma was happy to see that her mission to help free prisoners was becoming such a success, though she was still wondering what exactly had just happened. "How did you stop the guard? What happened to him?" she asked, as she walked ahead of the group to help lead their way.

Isaac answered calmly. "Well, I hit him on the chin. He's not dead or anything, just knocked out. When I was a kid, I learned how to box, how to knock someone out. But," he paused as he looked at his hand while clenching it into a fist, "I've never been this fast before. This is all new to me. It was as if the guard was just standing still, even though he was actually running toward you. I can't explain it just yet, but something in me changed after I looked into that cell, when you called out to me to move. I felt my rage, and I felt it finally had somewhere to go."

Emma just stared at him as he said this.

He continued to explain as he put his hand down and looked ahead. "I can do things now I could never do before, that I could never have dreamed of. I just feel... different."

For a few seconds, neither of them said anything. It was as if they both needed to consider what exactly he could mean.

Emma broke the silence. "Turn here, to your right." The hallway split into different directions. *Apparently*, Isaac thought, *she knows where she's going.*

"By the way," he said, "how many years have passed since it all began, since the other children and I were taken here?"

"Eight," she replied.

Emma's answer matched Isaac's estimate, based on the count of the days he kept track of while trapped in there. Or, at least, the count of how many times he went to sleep and woke up.

Before Isaac could say more, they saw the iron bars of a jail cell ahead of them. This time, however, there was a guard standing there. He noticed them and their group of trailing prisoners. He smiled a twisted grin while taking out his baton.

4

Light

Seeing this new threat, who was looking at their group with a cruel smile that showed he wanted to hurt them, Isaac's old prison cellmates huddled together once again in fear. But now, they positioned themselves behind Isaac, as if they now saw him as their protector, a safe person to stay behind.

"This time," Emma turned to tell Isaac, "let me try!" She thought to herself, *I'm the best fighter we have. I know my limits, and I can do this!* "Isaac," she confidently put her hand on his shoulder to assure him and to stop him from joining in, "I can handle him."

"Are you sure?" Isaac was skeptical if this was a good idea. He felt he had to say something. "Emma, why risk it? Just let me do it. I can knock him out, and no one has to get hurt. What if you make a mistake?" Emma stared at him, then at the guard, and then back at Isaac.

The guard butted in. "Are you here to play wi—"

"I'll get to you in a second!" Emma interrupted while maintaining *strong* eye contact with Isaac, ignoring the guard's attempt at intimidation completely. "Isaac, just shut up and watch." With that, Emma turned to face the enemy down the hall.

Both the guard and Isaac stood there frozen in surprise. Isaac's eyes were wide open, stunned by her courage. Or was it foolishness? Emma started walking past him as he looked at her with disbelief.

"Ohhh, little girl thinks she can fight *me*?" The guard taunted. "You're what, 110 pounds? Oh, please." He let out a loud, confident laugh. He was right, though. Emma was, in fact, only five feet three inches and very lightweight—small, actually, compared to many adults, and tiny compared to the guard who was colossal by comparison, maybe over six feet in height and 200 or more pounds. Isaac realized all of this, and it got to him. He was growing scared for Emma.

"Emma, the instant you look like you're in danger, I'm coming in to join you." He offered.

Emma just gave him a smirk as she began to walk confidently toward her opponent. "Funny," she said, "apart from you, *I'm* supposed to be the fastest person alive. Also," she put on her night vision goggles, "unlike you, I've been trained to do more than just punch for knockout. How do you think I got in here?" The guard readied his heavy, metal baton, squeezing his grip around its handle.

Emma focused on the ceiling lights first. Her legs bent slightly. Then, she jumped... ten feet up.

"Woah!" Isaac was taken aback. "How is she doing this? She has special abilities too?!" He was so startled that he couldn't help but say his thoughts out loud to himself. He knew he could probably move like her, or maybe with even more capability, but he was shocked to see it from someone else.

Emma flipped mid-air with ease, landing gently onto the ceiling with her feet. To any normal person, with this one move that lasted no more than a fraction of a second, they would have only seen what looked like a person launching themselves up into the air and hitting a ceiling, but Isaac's eyes could track her movement as if she were in slow motion. He could see the actual precision and intention of everything she did. It was elegant.

As she landed on the ceiling, she punched through a row of tube lights, breaking them and creating darkness in that portion of the hallway. She then pulled her hands back close to her body, preparing for another set of punches. Isaac knew what she was going to do next. *Such skill,* he thought to himself. *Such control!* With her feet planted on the ceiling, she suddenly jumped sideways across the hall, onto a wall, and then jumped once more through the air toward another set of lights on the ceiling. As her body glided across the air, she spun like a drill. At the moment that she was positioned below the next lights, she launched her fists into them and destroyed them too. She continued like this over and over, jumping from wall to wall, spinning and punching, until every light was destroyed along the hall, including, of course, where the guard was standing. He now found himself in darkness.

Isaac was probably the only one who could see everything she did. He realized that, with how fast she was moving, though it felt like a long time to *him*, only a couple of seconds in total had actually passed for everyone else. If the guard knew anything, he would know he stood no chance against this kind of speed. *He should just give up*, Isaac thought.

Then, the guard yelled, "What just happened?! The lights went out?!"

Oy, Isaac thought, *he has no idea.* Although Isaac could not see into the dark, he could hear every movement. Emma had just landed gently at the far end of the hall. Isaac could then hear Emma's footsteps beginning—slowly, at first. *What confidence*, he thought. *She's taking her time.*

A few hundred meters away, she could see what Isaac could only hear: the guard was standing still, unaware of where she was in the darkness, unaware that she was getting closer to him from behind. The guard was still facing the same spot where Emma used to be standing, where she jumped from at the start, assuming she was still there. His baton was readied in his hand as he faced no one but an empty space.

Then, her footsteps stopped. "*Maybe she feels bad for him*," Isaac quietly told himself. But then...

Tap-tap-TAP-TAP-TAP!

She rocketed across the floor with rapid steps, closing the distance between her and the guard almost instantly, and kicked the back of his knee, making him lose footing and collapse onto the ground as she whizzed past. A gust of wind blew across Isaac's hair. Emma was standing right next to him and in front of a crowd of children who were still gathered around him and stunned by the sudden darkness and alarming sounds. She then turned around, without wasting any time at all, and speedily ran right back to the guard, this time kicking him directly in the face. His nose broke.

"ARGH!" By the time he lifted his left hand to hold his face in pain, Emma had already taken the baton away from his right. Isaac couldn't see, but he could hear the sound of the baton's handle leaving the guard's hand and the sound the stick made as it moved through the air. She grabbed it before it hit the ground and prepared herself to strike the guard on the top of his head with his own weapon.

Though he could not see, Isaac could hear every movement so well that he had a clear image in his mind of what was happening. He shouted to stop her. "No! Don't! That could kill him!"

Emma stopped, and Isaac smiled in relief. She froze while holding the baton just inches above the guard's head. Emma looked through her night vision goggles at Isaac. She called out, "How do you even see me?" That was a mistake. The guard heard her voice and, though confused at how, he knew she was now behind him.

He turned around and punched his massive arm into the darkness behind him, toward Emma. She wasn't prepared for that. His fist landed squarely into her stomach, driving her whole body backward a few feet, through the air, and onto the ground. The pain and surprise from the hit caused her to let go of the baton.

CLANG clang clang

The echo of the weapon hitting the floor was clear and close enough for the guard to know where it had dropped. He went on his knees to begin searching for it, his hands patting and swiping across the floor until he felt it, and taking hold of it with his right hand.

Emma was still breathing heavily a few feet away, curled up in pain. Meanwhile, the guard stood up straight, confident now that he would get revenge on the 'little girl.' Thanks to Emma's tactic of taking out the lights, though, he would need time to actually find her.

Isaac yelled, "Do you need help?!" No response. It sounded like she couldn't yet speak up. *Maybe she got the wind knocked out of her*, Isaac thought. The guard shuffled his feet around the space, swiping the air with his baton, not knowing where his target was. Isaac just had a realization. *You idiot!* He thought to himself. *She can't speak or she'll give away her position.* She was clever. Still, Isaac couldn't stand there and do nothing anymore. *Even if she has a plan, I have to do something!*

Bump

"Uh-oh." Isaac just heard the guard's foot make contact with Emma on the floor. "This isn't good!" As the guard lifted his huge leg in the air, preparing to stomp his foot down onto Emma's body, Isaac readied himself to run, to sprint into action, and protect her. But as Isaac was just about to run forward, he heard Emma move and then...

WHAM

Emma kicked the guard in the stomach, hard. The guard let out a big breath of air as his face scrunched up and tears formed in his eyes. And with just as much grace and control as before, Emma planted her hands on the ground, launched herself up into the air, and landed her feet gently onto the floor. Without a moment to lose, she jumped toward the guard with a knee strike across his chin. The move instantly made the guard unconscious, just like Isaac had done earlier. The guard's body fell with a heavy set of THUDS.

"See!" Emma said, panting between her words. "I can—fight—too!" She hunched over and put her hands on her knees, struggling to catch her breath.

Isaac was somewhat confused. It seemed as if she had abilities like him but, unlike him, she was tired. "What is happening here?"

Emma gasped another deep breath and replied, "Hold on. Let's help everyone here see a bit better." She reached into a pouch that sat around her waist. "Here we are." She ignited a flare and threw it on the ground, which created a red splash of glowing light around them. She took off her night vision goggles and slid them down around her neck. Standing up again, her breath relaxing, she continued. "I have what are called 'augmentations.' I have little machines in me that make my body be able to do things better than what people can normally do. I'm fast, like you. Well, not quite like you—you do seem much faster. I also get tired pretty quickly after moving at full speed like that, like you saw. But now's not the time to talk too much. Let's help free some more prisoners and get out of here!"

5 Awakening

"Ask me questions if you want to," Emma said as she patted the pockets of the guard, looking for keys to the cell. "But if I don't have time to answer, it's because we need to focus on getting out."

As they both crouched down and moved closer together to examine the guard, Isaac thought about the outside world, his dreams, and carefully considered what questions he would want to ask her. His mind was racing. There was so much he wanted to know. The first thing that was most pressing on him, though, was his curiosity about his abilities, and Emma's too.

Isaac was trained as a fighter early on, so he'd always seen himself as a strong and fast person. Even throughout all the years he spent underfed in this prison, of growing up malnourished, underweight, and weaker than he probably should have been, he still felt, for that entire time, like he was actually quite the physically capable person. And that wasn't even considering what he could now. He could apparently do things that could only be described as superhuman. He knew that something was most definitely different about him, something that even separated him from Emma's abilities. After all, *he* didn't get tired like her. And, he was pretty sure he could go even faster than her, than what he just saw her do.

"Isaac," she said as she was finishing up checking the guard for keys, "you lost in thought? Look, I can't find the keys anyway, so I think it's time I blow up another cell wall." She picked up the flare from the ground and held it up to the bars, to get a better look at who was inside.

As both looked closer, the red glow of the flare filled up the cell. Near the back, where the light was most dim, they saw them —children holding each other, likely afraid of these visitors who caused such sudden darkness and who fought and won against their intimidatingly large guard.

Isaac knelt down and tried to greet them softly, to help prove they were friendly. "Hi, we're here to help." The children only grabbed each other tighter. Isaac stood back up and looked at Emma. "I think they're wild chil—"

"No, mommy, I don't want to go to school today." The quiet and sleepy voice, colored with a New Zealand accent, came from one of the beds inside the cell, from the only prisoner still asleep on a bed.

Isaac and Emma looked at each other and couldn't help but let out a laugh. Realizing the absurdity and urgency of the situation, however, Emma stopped laughing suddenly and shouted out, "Who said that?!" The children shook in fear. The person who spoke before now wiggled and sat up on his bed.

"Wait..." He paused, slowly opening his eyes and turning his head side to side. "What's happening here?" He looked to his left at the other children in his cell and noticed them cowering. "Hey guys, why are you all so scared? It's almost protein time! Cheer up. Wait, why is it so red in here?" He jumped out of bed and walked over to the other prisoners. "Sally, Rick, Bob, everyone... why is everyone so afraid?" All at once, they pointed over to the front of the cell towards Emma.

Isaac and Emma had the same surprised face and the same thought. *They can understand him?* These children were different from those standing in the hall, from Isaac's cellmates who had never shown, in all their years spent with him, that they could understand him when he spoke. The prisoners in *this* cell understood other people!

The mysterious New Zealander spun around. "Woah! Who are you two? Came out of nowhere, you did. Hey, those are some nice night vision goggles!"

"Uhh. Thanks," Emma replied. She was lost for words.

"He can speak," Isaac said.

"The others understand him," Emma added.

Both were in disbelief. Emma didn't want to wait around much longer, though. She reached into her pouch and took out what looked like a large lump of clay. "Alright, stand back, I'm going to blast a hole in the walls here with this explosive."

The strange prisoner held up his hand, gesturing for her to stop. "No, no, no. Stop that right there."

"*Who is this nut?*" Isaac whispered. "Hey, guy, we're here to get you and your friends out of here. Let us help you."

"Uh, the name is Dennis. 'Guy' is that one over there. Say hi to the nice people, Guy." Guy didn't speak, but he cautiously waved a little wave. Dennis continued. "Yea, Guy doesn't actually talk at all, but he understands us. Sometimes he makes sounds, but it's rare. And you are..." He pointed to Isaac, apparently asking him to share his own name.

"Umm, my name's Isaac?" Isaac said, still sounding like he was gathering himself and trying to understand what was happening.

Dennis then pointed to Emma. "I'm Emma," she stated with confidence, as if feeding off of the comforting and casual energy that Dennis was giving off.

"Okay, Isaac and Emma," Dennis went on, "you blow up these walls and someone is going to get hurt. Not very bright are you? Right, Guy?" Guy nodded in agreement. "I can tell you two are confused. It's okay, let me help clear things up."

Dennis walked over to the bars, placed his hands on two of them and, to the shock of Emma and Isaac, he pulled them apart. The metal rods warped and bent wide enough for people to be able to fit through.

Isaac slowly leaned toward Emma, whose mouth was gaping open. "*What the heck?*" He whispered, in shock as well.

"Alright everyone," Dennis instructed his cell mates, "looks like we should go now. Thanks you two!" He walked through the gap he just made with his clearly augmented strength. "I couldn't do this alone, thanks! Now, come on everyone, hurry up! Hey look at that, our two new friends knocked out the guard! What are your augs then?"

"Our 'augs?'" Isaac asked, unsure of what this word meant.

"Yes, your *augmentations.* You took care of the guard over there. No way you could've done that if you two were normal." Dennis pointed at Isaac first. "Well, *you're* all thin and bony." He pointed at Emma next. "You're just tiny. No offense." He asked again, "You couldn't do what you did, with how you look. So, what are you installed with? What kind of 'augs.'"

Isaac wasn't sure how to answer, since he still wasn't sure himself where his abilities came from. *Maybe the stories Mom and Dad told me were true, that I'm special,* he thought.

Emma filled the silence and answered for him. "He has the best leg, lung, heart, and eye augs I have ever seen." Emma didn't really know what Isaac's story was yet, or where his abilities came from, but she assumed, just as well, that his abilities were like hers, only better. She did her best to name the body parts he must have had augmentations for to allow what he'd been able to do so far.

"I have similar augs," Emma went on. "Legs, lungs, heart, and eyes. All upgraded. They're pretty good for where I'm from anyway. It's a runner's package, but not every part is the best. Not like Isaac!"

Dennis interjected. "So, what's that make of your abilities, exactly? What can you do?"

Emma answered, "Well, we can both run fast, Isaac a bit faster. We have eye augmentations to help us see things quickly, too. My lungs just barely help me keep up with what my legs can do, so I can fight, but I get tired quickly. Isaac doesn't seem to get tired at all, though, so his lungs have better augs." Isaac knew she was making things up, but didn't bother to correct her.

Dennis looked at Isaac. "Sweet as."

"Huh?" Isaac said.

Dennis clarified, "Oh, right. It's New Zealand slang. I guess it means 'cool' as you would say."

"Sweet as!" Emma said enthusiastically.

"That's right!" Dennis exclaimed.

Isaac cut in, "Great. So what are your 'augs,' Dennis?"

"Ah! Skeletal muscle upgrades, whole body! Makes me hit hard! Though, I get short of breath like Emma here if I exert myself too much. That's why I could never just get out on my own. I'd get tired after just a couple of fights and my friends here would be in danger. Couldn't have that." He looked back to the children who were now making their way through the gap in the bars. Guy gave a smile and thumbs up as he passed through. Dennis responded with a smile and thumbs up too before looking at Emma and Isaac, his new potential friends. "Now that you're here to help, though, we can work together to get out."

"Well," Emma replied, "sure! We may as well go together, especially with another augmented person like yourself who can help protect everyone."

With Isaac and Emma leading the front of the now two groups of prisoners, and Dennis staying in the back as if to watch over his friends from behind, they made their way down the darkened hall. Dennis's hands rested on top of his head, showing how relaxed he was. He even seemed to be enjoying himself. He began to whistle.

"*Dennis, shhh,*" Emma whisper-shouted back.

"*Sorry, ma'am.*"

6
Surprise

As they walked, Isaac felt the smooth walls with his hand. The hall was covered with the familiarly unnatural, pristinely clean white tiles. He closed his hand and patted the wall with the fleshy underside of his fist. *I'm finally getting out of here*, he thought. Though he wished he could move faster, he was with a group now who couldn't, and who desperately needed Emma's and his protection.

Emma looked at Isaac and gave a sad yet sympathetic smile for this young man who was going to finally be free, but only after he had spent so many unfortunate years growing up in a place like this. She wanted to say something to him, but couldn't find the right words.

Isaac broke the silence first, whispering to help keep them from getting caught. "*Really makes you think, what was it all for? Why capture all of us? Why bother with all the experiments? Why not just kill all the humans if it wanted to take over the planet?*"

"When we get out of here, you'll find out more when we join up with the others. For now, we should stay quiet and focus on getting out." Just then, Emma looked forward as she noticed another cell in the distance, at the far end of the hall they were currently in. She held up her hand to signal for the group to stop. She leaned over to Isaac and whispered, "*There's some things we know and there's some things we don't know enough about. There's a lot you missed and there's a lot we have learned. You'll find out soon.*"

She turned to the whole group and raised her voice only slightly above a whisper. "Okay everyone, my mission is to save as many people as I can. We're going to save one more cell up ahead and then leave. Isaac, I'll trust you with the knockout. With this many people, we can't take any risks. Dennis," Emma then looked at her new strong ally, "you open up the bars like you did before. I will stay with the group here in case any guards come from behind. I'll take out the lights above our group, so the dark can help hide our friends who can't defend themselves. I'll have my night vision goggles to help me. It also means there will be less of a chance for someone to call reinforcements or sound the alarm. If the alarm rings, the warden could come, the person who leads the whole prison. You don't want to mess with the warden. From the little we've learned about these places, the warden could be augmented."

Wow, Isaac thought, *she really is well trained. She came up with the entire plan on the spot like it was nothing. I wonder what else they taught her, what else is going on out there.* His mind was starting to wander through all the possibilities. But before he could get distracted from the moment at hand, he snapped his attention back to what was happening here and now. He needed to focus on the job he was assigned: take out the guard.

Emma continued. "Though it's my mission to save as many kids as I can, this group will need to be the last that we free. Any more than that, and I worry we are taking on too much risk. Even though I disabled the alarms before sneaking in, if we have too many children with us, there's a greater chance one of them could get lost. If that happens, *we* would be lost. It only takes one prisoner going the wrong way, running into a random guard or the warden himself, for them to come after us. We could get overwhelmed quickly. Still, even though we can't save everyone today, we will save some! Let's move." She looked over at Dennis. "You understand your part?"

"Yea. Easy. Open the cell." He responded with his usual casual tone and demeanor.

"Alright." Emma was ready for them to begin.

The group stood still and kept their eyes on her as she walked to her position behind them. She spun around to face everyone. She shifted her gaze from right to left, looking at each and every person, checking one last time if she felt ready, if Isaac and Dennis were ready. "Ready?" She asked them, to confirm. They nodded their heads. She smiled. "Let's save some lives." She held up her hand, preparing to wave it down to signal the start of the mission. "Go," she told Isaac and Dennis as she gave the signal.

A huge gust of wind swept across the group, dust flying up from the spot where Isaac once stood—the dust from Isaac's rags perhaps. Dennis was still turning his head when Isaac had already reached the guard, half a kilometer away down the long hall. "Oh my—" Isaac kicked the guard down in between Dennis's words

"—gosh!" Dennis started jogging over. He looked back over his shoulder to the group as he ran, "Did you see that, Guy? Who even does that?!" Guy's eyes were wide open and frozen there. He shrugged his shoulders—his gaze still stuck staring at Isaac down the hall and at the guard who was just beginning his tumble down to the ground. Guy started walking to follow Dennis.

"Where are you going?!" Emma asked, trying to keep everyone together. Guy just silently pointed to Dennis. "Ugh, fine. Just don't go wandering off!" Emma jumped up to the ceiling and destroyed all the lights behind them in a couple of seconds. The mouths of all the kids dropped open in shock. Emma emerged from the darkness she just created, night vision goggles on. One of the kids let out a yelp. "AH!"

"Shhh!" She took off her goggles for a second. "It's just me!" She then put them back on and turned around to face the dark, awaiting whoever or whatever might come from behind.

Dennis caught up with Isaac after ten seconds of jogging at a speed he thought was fast. "What the heck, man? Can she do that too?"

Isaac answered, "She's also fast, yea, but she might take a few seconds to do what I would in less than half a second, or maybe even less than that."

"Oh, you won the speed contest then. Congratulations." Dennis then let out a joking applause gesture with his hands.

Isaac laughed. "Sorry, I didn't mean it like that. I wasn't trying to brag or anything. I was just trying to answer your question honestly."

Dennis moved the conversation on. "All good. Let's free some more friends now, shall we?"

"Go for it!" Isaac enthusiastically agreed.

Dennis grabbed a bar in each hand and pushed them apart with his super strength, creating a gap like the one he had made earlier. "Hello everyone. Please feel free to join us. We're escaping. Don't worry about your guard." He twisted his upper body and pointed at the unconscious guard on the ground. "See. Knocked out, right there."

Isaac and Dennis stood on either side of the gap, comforting the prisoners with smiles and pats on their shoulders as they walked out of their caged room.

"Oh hey, Guy," Dennis said. "Glad to see you're here to help welcome our new friends." Dennis gave a wave over to Emma down the hall. Emma looked too focused to pay attention to Dennis, though, as she continued to use her night vision gear to peer into the dark portion of the hall.

Isaac looked over and saw that a few of the newly released prisoners gathered around to look at the guard on the ground. But the way they stood there, emotionless and just staring silently down, bothered Isaac. He walked over to join them. *Maybe they're just in shock and need some support*, he thought. "It's okay. You won't have to see that guard ever again. We'll be out of here soon. The one who helped us out, the girl down there, she knows how to get us all out of here. She's going to get us all free!" He took a deep breath. His eyes began to water a little. "We'll see the outside world very soon." But the children who were just freed from this prison cell didn't respond. Their emotionless faces remained blank. "Oh, sorry... can... can you understand me? Can you talk?" Still, no response. "I'm sorry. I'm so sorry... OW!"

Dennis slapped his hand on Isaac's back. "My fault. I don't know my own strength sometimes. I really thought that one was gentle."

"Yea, Dennis, maybe practice *some more* of that when we get out. Hey, how come the prisoners you spent time with are the only ones who can understand us when we talk?"

"Did you talk to your prison mates?" Dennis asked.

"Yes, but they never said anything back." Isaac was confused.

"Well, did you *teach* them how to talk?" Dennis widened his eyes as he asked, as if what he was suggesting was obvious.

Isaac was stunned. "I... uhh."

"Mate," Dennis stated in disbelief, "how can they learn to talk if you don't try to teach them?"

Isaac was taken aback. "You mean, I spent all these years meditating, feeling like I had to be on my own, and I just didn't think to help the other children *learn* to talk?" Isaac looked down at the ground in sad reflection.

Dennis replied. "Not sure what you're talking about with meditation, but yea. Yes to the helping them learn part." He could see Isaac was upset and put his hands on Isaac's shoulders. "Sorry, mate." He looked around. "Speaking of prisoner friends, let's go help this lot."

"AAGHH!" Someone screamed behind Dennis's back. The sound came from among the crowd that was gathered around the knocked-out guard.

Emma, still a few hundred feet away, shouted out, "What happened?!"

"Hey, strong guy," a creepy voice spoke. "It looks like someone jumped in front of my attack to save you. He must really like you."

Dennis and Isaac turned around. A prisoner with messy black hair hanging down to his shoulders, with dark green eyes, was holding the guard's baton and standing over someone lying on the ground, right at their feet. Dennis looked down and recognized his friend immediately. "Guy! NO! No, no, no..." His hands trembled as he crouched down to look for where Guy was hurt, ignoring that the black-haired, green-eyed man was standing right next to him.

"Now it's your turn." The attacker drew back the baton, as if to get Dennis next.

"ENOUGH!" A powerful wind surrounded them. Isaac's kick landed perfectly on the maniac's jaw. "Fall," Isaac said, with anger in his words.

Except, he didn't. The green-eyed prisoner reached over with his free hand, attempting to grab Isaac's ankle, but Isaac pushed his foot off and landed on the ground before he could get caught. Isaac put himself into a fighting stance, like a boxer's with his fists clenched and guarding his face. "That should have knocked you out!" Isaac yelled.

"Too bad for YOU!" The green-eyed man swung his weapon toward Dennis once again.

This time, though, Dennis grabbed the person's wrist before the baton could land. "You hurt my friend."

THOOM

Dennis's fist drove into this person's abdomen. The black-haired, green-eyed man fell to his knees and breathed heavily.

Dennis let go and turned around to help his dear companion, Guy.

Emma caught up to the group just at that moment. "Woah! What happened? Why did you punch that prisoner? Oh no, Guy." Looking at their friend on the ground, her eyebrows raised in fear that he was injured or worse. She knelt down beside Dennis to see how she could help Guy. Unsettled and angry, she asked, "Is this why Dennis punched that prisoner? Was it him who did this?"

The black-haired man, who had been hunching over, breathing heavily, now toppled over onto his side. Curling up, his breath slowed down. A moment later, his whole body stopped moving, and he went quiet.

Isaac reassured her. "It's okay, Emma. Dennis got him good. Looks like he passed out after getting the wind knocked out of him."

Isaac sat down too and placed his ear next to Guy's mouth to hear if he was still breathing.

WHAM!

The sound of the metal baton hitting Dennis's head echoed through the hall. "I can't believe you fell for that."

Isaac stood back up.

Dennis tried to put his hands up for a fight but lost his balance and wobbled, barely able to keep his eyes open. "I'm sorry—everyone." And with that, Dennis fell unconscious, and his body started falling to the ground.

Isaac quickly dashed under Dennis, extended his arms, and caught him before his body hit the ground. Isaac gently lowered Dennis to the floor as he listened carefully to the baton-wielding prisoner's every movement. As Isaac listened carefully to make sure whether this violent prisoner was going to make another move, he made sure to lower Dennis gently onto the floor.

Isaac felt a surge of passionate anger build up inside. "No more. No more!" He yelled. "No more people have to die! I won't let you hurt anyone!" Isaac sounded fierce, determined to end the fight. "Emma," he called out while not breaking eye contact from the green-eyed man. "Please stay with them and see if you can help them. **I'm going to stop whoever this is.**" His demeanor, the way he carried himself and talked, was completely different from the person she knew before. Isaac's voice was rough, stern, and focused on one goal: **"I will stop whoever this maniac is."**

"Oh, I like that... *Maniac*," the green-eyed man said in his twisted voice. "That sounds so much better than my real name. Call me *that*."

"Whatever, 'Maniac.' I won't let you harm anyone else." Isaac got into his fighting stance.

"And how are you going to stop me? Your strong friend couldn't. *You* couldn't." The Maniac moved forward slowly as if there was nothing to worry about.

Isaac attacked first. In an instant, Isaac kicked the face, the stomach, behind each knee, and the chin. These attacks would normally make anyone fall to the ground and fall unconscious, but The Maniac just kept moving slowly forward, toward Emma and the people on the ground. "What are you made of? How am I not hurting you?!" Isaac exclaimed.

"Who knows? *They* did this to me. I woke up one day unable to get hurt." The man confidently continued to stroll toward Dennis and Guy on the ground while casually talking to and taunting Isaac. "Ohhh, you're all like jelly compared to me. You can't hurt me. And you can't stop me." He was now standing right above Dennis, despite being constantly bombarded by Isaac's attacks. "But," The Maniac swung his baton toward Dennis's head, "I can definitely hurt YOU!"

Isaac moved as fast as he could to save Dennis and Guy—so fast, in fact, that The Maniac looked like he was moving in slow motion. Still, Isaac seemed helpless to stop The Maniac's body from moving. Isaac tried everything he could, attacking every part of the body he could. But, nothing slowed the strike coming from the green-eyed man. The baton, though moving slowly, was moving nonetheless closer to Dennis's head.

Emma's motionless figure started to move. She was using her augmentations and speeding up. Though not as fast as Isaac, she was able to speak and be heard by him. "I-s-a-a-c."

Isaac slowed down, just somewhat, so he could match Emma's speed.

"Isaac!" She pleaded and then, as the baton was just about to make contact with Dennis's head, she screamed, "HELP!"

Isaac's heartbeat pounded in his chest as she and The Maniac froze still. The blood in Isaac's arms and legs filled up dramatically as he felt his heartbeat pulse throughout his entire body. His muscles felt more powerful, his senses more sensitive, his focus and attention to everything around him going beyond anything he had ever experienced. Isaac pulled back his fist.

BOOM!

With a colossal, explosive sound, Isaac punched The Maniac through the floor beneath his own feet. Stone and dust flew up into the hall. Isaac slowed down, and time moved at normal speeds. Isaac looked down through the hole as the dust settled.

He hadn't just punched The Maniac through one floor—he hurtled him down through many, many floors—at least 20, from what Isaac could see. It occurred to Isaac, looking at the exposed scale of this prison, that there were so many more children still there to save. He also just experienced a glimpse of some of the astonishingly terrible harm The Intelligence had inflicted upon the human race.

"Eh, Isaac," Emma stuttered, "where did that come from?"

"Forget that for now." Isaac needed to focus. His friends were hurt, and they needed to leave. "What's the situation with Dennis and Guy?!" He was frantic not to lose one more life on his watch.

"They're okay!" She assured him. "They're alive. They're okay."

A wave of relief washed over Isaac.

7

Carry On

Though the guard was still knocked out, and 'The Maniac' was knocked deep into the building somewhere, Emma and Isaac knew they still had to get the prisoners out of this cell and they needed to leave the prison as fast as they could.

Emma had to keep them moving toward the exit and knew, more than anyone else, just how dangerous it could really be if they took too long to get out. "With so much destruction running down through the building, they will definitely notice," she said to Isaac. "The alarm will ring, and we *don't* want to still be in here when that happens. We do *not* want to face the warden."

"Didn't you say the alarms were disabled?" Isaac responded.

"The automatic systems, yes. Destroying a cell wall would normally trigger an alarm. I turned off that system. That hole you made, however, *that* will get someone's attention, and someone will pull the alarm manually. Just like a fire alarm, there are manual access points. A person could pull a lever or push a button and turn it on—any moment now, as soon as they see the 20 floors you punched The Maniac through."

"Wait!" Isaac noticed his friends were moving.

Dennis sat up first, if a bit woozy still. "Oww." He rubbed his head. "I really got bonked, huh? I must be seeing things... What's that hole?"

Emma answered, "That was Isaac!"

Guy started to get up too. "Uhhhh."

"Guy!" Seeing his friend was okay, Dennis snapped back to his usual self, full of energy. He hugged Guy, tight.

"Uhhh!" Guy cried out.

"Ahem. Sorry!" Dennis tried to apologize as he let go and stood up. "So, what are we waiting around here for? Let's get these new pals running along and let's get out!"

Dennis helped encourage the newly freed prisoners, the ones that shared a cell with 'The Maniac.' "Alright! Let's go. Let's follow Emma out of here!" However, as he spoke, he realized he was actually still feeling a bit dizzy from his hit before. He tapped on Isaac's shoulder. "Oy, you be Mr. Strong Man now, if we need it. I don't think I'm all there yet."

"Of course," Isaac replied. "We'll make sure to help protect your friends."

"Thanks, mate," Dennis responded back. "Actually," Dennis took a hard look at the multiple holes through the building Isaac created using The Maniac's body, "I guess it looks like you wouldn't need me anyway!"

"Alright! Let's get going!" Emma called out.

Isaac attempted to communicate to The Maniac's cellmates using hand gestures and body language. But they just kept standing still. The only prisoners that started walking were those that came from Dennis's and Isaac's cell. They all seemed eager enough to leave.

"Um..." Isaac's voice sounded sad and worried.

Emma raised her hand to signal for everyone to stop moving. "What is it?" She asked.

"The Maniac's cell mates," Isaac explained, "they're not moving. I don't think they understand what's happening. I don't think they know that we're trying to escape. Or, they're traumatized."

Emma walked through the crowd and stood next to Isaac. "Let's try. At least once more, let's try."

So, the two of them tried their best. They walked from prisoner to prisoner, tapping their shoulders and pointing down the hallway, tugging at their rags, saying words like "let's go" and "safety" as they did so. Sadly, they were met with only blank stares. Some of the children would begin to look up slowly at Emma and Isaac, but only for a moment before looking back down or staring back at them blankly. The Maniac's cellmates were completely unresponsive.

Emma whispered sympathetically to Isaac, "*I don't think we can help them. I'm sorry. We have to go.*"

Isaac looked around the hall at each prisoner. He was desperately trying to come up with a plan. *I can't let them stay here. They've been through so much. I have to save them.* He thought.

"Isaac," Emma offered, "I know how you feel. I'm the same way. But we can't help them the way we are right now. The resistance is waiting for us though, outside, in the real world. If we come back later with you and Dennis, with your abilities and other soldiers to help us, we can come up with a better plan to save them, to save all of them. This was just the first mission they planned, meant just to save a small handful and to see how The Intelligence would respond to a small and stealthy infiltration." Emma looked to the prisoners they had already saved and back to Isaac. "Hey, we were lucky to find children who could understand us at all. It's good that we can save even some of them."

Isaac appeared to stop what he was doing. He was no longer looking around the hall, frantically thinking up some strategy for getting them all out. He turned and looked straight into Emma's eyes. His face showed he was serious about something on his mind. His gaze pierced through Emma and caught her off guard.

She inhaled a quick breath, as if surprised by his sudden look of determination. "What is it?"

"Maybe we can't save everyone," he said, "but there is a way we can try." He walked over to one of the oldest prisoners from The Maniac's cell, maybe 10 years old, and lifted him onto his back.

She stood there, taken aback by the obviousness of his solution to the problem and by his heartfelt determination to save the seemingly hopeless children. She then followed his lead and picked up another child, slightly younger and smaller than the one Isaac had picked up.

Dennis, being among the stronger, picked up the largest and oldest children he could find. Though still feeling a bit uneasy from getting hit earlier, Dennis tried his best to manage. Then, soon after, the older kids among Dennis's group began to pick up other, smaller, and younger prisoners. One by one, everyone was picked up. Even a couple of Isaac's cellmates showed understanding of what was happening and helped too.

Isaac and Emma looked at each other and smiled.

"Let's go!" Emma enthusiastically shouted.

"If anyone gets tired, I'll carry more of you myself!" Isaac exclaimed.

As they walked along the hallway, Isaac asked Emma, "How much further are we from the exit? I don't know how long we can expect these guys to carry each other. I don't think they're strong enough to handle it."

"A couple minutes at most." She replied, "Not far. I blew a hole in a wall near here using my explosives. We shouldn't see a lot of guards where we're going—I made my way through the back of the building, far away from the front entrance where a lot of guards were stationed. No one should notice us when we try to leave."

"I hope so. I really hope so. But I'm really surprised the alarm hasn't gone off yet," Isaac stated, starting to wonder how strange their situation began to feel.

Emma agreed with his sentiments. "Yea. It is strange." As they continued to walk, making their way ever closer to the exit, she looked back at their somewhat large group of soon-to-be free prisoner friends. "If we were escaping by ourselves, we could probably handle many more guards on our own, but now that we have others to worry about, to protect, I don't know."

"I'm not worried about the guards," Isaac stated confidently. "We can take them out quickly, even with the group we have with us. The guards aren't who I'm worried about."

"Oh?" Emma turned around and walked backwards for a moment, to look at Isaac as they talked. She also used this as a chance to see past everyone and down the hallway behind them, checking for any children wandering off or guards that could be coming. "What do you mean?" She asked him, wondering who else he could be afraid of besides the guards.

Isaac clarified. "The Maniac."

"What about him? Isn't he dead?"

"No, he's down there somewhere, alive for sure. When I punched him, I didn't see or feel any damage. Sure, he got smashed through some floors. I don't know how many levels of concrete he must have hit on the way down. But his body felt indestructible when my fist landed on him. I don't think we can hurt him."

"Yea." Emma's eyes widened a bit to reflect the concern she shared. "That's pretty scary actually. Well," she turned around to face forward again as she continued to talk to Isaac, "he doesn't move fast and he still has to make his way up a lot of floors to fight us again. Plus, he has to fight a lot of guards too to escape from where he is. I don't think we'll see him again." She tried to move on from the conversation, away from the concerns. "Okay, we're only a minute away now!" She called out to the group. "We're very close to the exit, everyone!"

"Maybe you're right. We're okay." Isaac sighed, a breath escaping his lips. He was tired of seeing people get hurt. Most of all, he was tired of seeing dangers in front of him and not being able to stop them. "I failed before, Emma. I should've been more mindful of who was standing with us. I should have been ready for danger, and I could've stopped Dennis and Guy from getting hurt. I could've—"

She interrupted him. "No. You can't say that. We all thought it was safe with the guard taken care of. Who could've known that a prisoner was so violent and so crazy that a *prisoner*, of all people, would try to hurt us? The guard was taken care of. We all thought we were safe."

"That's true. What about the baton, though? I could've taken it away. I could've stopped someone from grabbing it."

Emma gave a deep sigh, almost as if she was tired of hearing Isaac complain. And yet, the sigh sounded like it was coming from a place of understanding too. "Isaac, let me give you a piece of advice my parents told me when I was young. I've lived by this advice my whole life, and it's made me feel better almost every time I tell it to myself. 'You can only do your best with what you know, right now.' You only knew what you did back then. You did your best with what you knew. We all did."

She was right. Isaac knew only what he did at that moment. Back then, he only knew the prisoners as good people, as victims, not enemies. When the guard fell to the ground, why would he think a prisoner would take the baton to hurt other prisoners? He did his best at the time, with what he knew. That's all he could ever do. "Thank you, Emma. Thank you for helping me see it a new way. That really helps, actually."

They neared the end of the hall they had been walking down, and, as they walked around the next corner, they saw it. "Look!" Emma yelled out. "See the hole! Your freedom is only a couple hundred meters away!"

The alarm rang.

8

The Warden

Dennis looked at his friends with concern. He tapped Emma's shoulder with his forehead, as his hands were busy holding a person on his back. "Uh-oh. How strong is this, uhh, warden person again?"

Emma darted her eyes around them, looking for danger as they hurried to the hole ahead of them. "I don't know, but from the information we've gathered, every prison's warden has top-of-the-line augmentations. No guard or prisoner would be as strong or as fast as the warden." Emma didn't have any more time to explain. "EVERYONE MOVE!"

Isaac helped as much as he could to get them going. "Go for the exit!"

Dennis, Guy, and all of the prisoners ran as fast as they could. Isaac and Emma helped rush everyone toward the exit too, pointing and pulling them along. Though some of the prisoners had been emotionless before, the frantic behavior seen now from

Emma and Isaac had an influence on them. Their blank expressions turned to fright.

Some prisoners were now just about to reach the hole in the wall, the light from the outside world shining in, getting closer, giving them some hope.

"Almost there!" Isaac shouted. He had always thought, these last eight years, that the inside of the prison was a pretty bright place. With lights all along the ceiling and bouncing off the reflective white porcelain walls, Isaac forgot just how much brighter the outside world actually was compared to where he had been trapped for so long.

He was approaching the hole. Many prisoners were already out before him. He leapt through. As he felt the grass under his feet, the light from the sun blurring his vision, he closed his eyes as he ran. Slowly, as the discomfort of the brightness waned, he slowly opened his eyes as he continued running. After he was far enough for everyone else to have space to get out as well, he stopped and stood.

He started to cry. They were surrounded by fields of grass and flowers. A single large tree stood not too far away, reminding him of the dreams he had in the prison.

"Isaac… Isaac! Isaac! Hello!" Emma tried startling him back to focusing on what they were doing.

"Emma," he finally responded, "we're free."

"Not yet! We have to make our way through the fields. A forest lies past that hill in the distance. That's the forest where the rebels are, the other survivors, my allies. We need to take cover in that forest before we get caught here!"

"Understood." Isaac wiped his tears. "Everyone, keep running!" He looked up at the sky above as they moved. "What a beautiful blue. What beautiful clouds," he quietly said to himself. Isaac couldn't help but have the biggest grin on his face. He was happier than he had been in a long time.

As he looked over to Emma next to him though, his smile disappeared. He sped up his focus to slow down his perception of time. The group now appeared in slow motion to him. There, running alongside Emma, was a robot. He recognized immediately the black plastic face plate, the metal body, and the blue light shining from its chest. A PC. It started to move toward Emma—to attack.

Isaac's heartbeat sped up. Everything froze around him as his thoughts suddenly went back to the memory of his mother on the day he was taken. The memory came back to him so clearly as he looked upon the PC that appeared in front of him now. That horrible day from eight years ago began to play back in his mind. That awful blue light shining through the panes of glass in the front door of his home. The banging that followed...

Knock! He remembered the fear of losing his mother. His heart sped up more.

KNOCK! Isaac's veins began to enlarge with a rush of blood. An urge to fight filled his mind. *This can't happen again!* He angrily thought, as he dropped the child from his back.

CRASH! The image of the PC driving his mother into the floor of their home vividly appeared in his mind. His attention snapped back to reality, back to the figure in front of him now, to the one that was about to take away the lives of his friends like a PC did his mother.

Rage.

As the PC's hand reached for Emma's neck, Isaac's fist was already plunged into the blue sensor of its chest. The PC's face turned downward to see what was attacking it. Isaac's eyebrows were furrowed in anger, his mouth spread wide with his teeth clenched hard. The PC pulled back its arm, away from Emma, and prepared to punch Isaac.

"TOO SLOW!" Isaac screamed in a frightful rage. He remembered, in that moment, how his mother went for the chest sensor first, then the face. This time, however, there would be no hesitation. And, this time, Isaac had the power to really damage it. His mind flashed back to the moment a PC drove its hand into his mother's stomach. Now, it was Isaac's fist driving itself into the PC's face plate. It cracked and shattered, pieces flying off. Isaac could feel the machinery behind it against his knuckles —and he could feel them breaking. The PC began to fall to the ground, its chest sensor and any other sensors it had in its head now destroyed.

Isaac let his mind return to a normal speed, sure that the PC wouldn't be able to fight him anyway. Everyone around him stopped running, some shouting in fear at the sudden appearance of the robotic enemy, the same kind that they, like Isaac, would have been captured by. Some would likely have awful memories that were recalled when they looked at it.

"Ahh!" Guy shouted.

"Oh my god," Dennis said, in surprise at both the PC as well as hearing Guy's reaction. Guy was normally very quiet.

Isaac spoke up for everyone to hear. "Keep going. I'll make sure he can't follow us." Everyone except Emma continued moving toward the hill far away. She let down the prisoner she was carrying. The small child followed the rest of the group ahead.

"*Isaac?*" Emma said quietly. She was intimidated by him by his posture, by the seriousness portrayed by his face.

Isaac looked at the artificially intelligent monstrosity kneeling before them. He said nothing.

"Isaac?" She spoke up a bit louder. Emma hated The Intelligence as much as most, but maybe not as much as Isaac. Though she wanted to see them destroyed, something nonetheless bothered her about witnessing a kind person, witnessing Isaac, seemingly show such quiet hatred.

He grabbed the PC by one of its metal arms, keeping it from moving around. "I'm sorry..." He said.

This sudden politeness in his voice was not what Emma expected. "Isaac?" She was taken aback by his apology. Didn't he hate the PCs? Wasn't he going to destroy this one?

Isaac appeared to be deep in thought as he looked at the broken machine parts that made up the PC's face, at the glass and metal fragments where cameras and computer parts were. He drew his hand back. "I have to make sure you can't follow us." Isaac wasn't angry when he said this, though. He seemed calm.

Emma wasn't sure what he would do next. Would he destroy it?

The blood vessels in Isaac's arms bulged.

WHOOSH

Isaac launchd the PC through the air at an incredible speed, straight back toward the prison, which was now at least 50 meters away. The robot flew right through the hole in the wall.

"WOAH!" Emma shouted. With each new feat, each time Isaac showed what he could do, Emma could only grow more and more curious about his abilities, how he could show speed and strength that she had never seen before. "We really have to look at your cells under a microscope when we get back. This isn't normal, even for people with augmentations."

"Yea, I—" Isaac stumbled a bit, as if he was dizzy.

"Hey! What's the matter?" Emma said.

"I don't know. I feel..." He stopped mid-thought. "I feel so tir—" His speech slurred before he could finish his sentence as he fell forward to the ground with a sizable *thud* in the grass. His eyes still open, he took one last look at a flower next to him. *So... pretty...* he thought as he fell asleep.

Emma picked him up on her back. "It's a good thing you've been eating so little in that prison. You're as light as I am!" As she walked toward the hill to join everyone else, she looked back at the prison one last time. She wanted to see if any more guards were coming. No one. "I guess the warden, or PC, was the only one sent for us." Emma often talked to herself on her lonely missions.

Just as Emma was about to turn to look back ahead, she noticed a small figure at the corner of her eye slowly making its way out of the hole. "The Maniac!" she muttered.

9

Recovery

"Isaac, are you awake yet?" Emma's voice asked softly. She wanted to tell him about The Maniac getting out. She wanted to tell him how they were on their way to the rebel base of operations, deep in the forest.

Isaac's eyes opened slowly. His head was still resting on Emma's shoulder. The smell of grass, leaves, and bark filled his nostrils as he breathed long, gentle breaths. He thought to himself, *I forgot just how beautiful nature is.*

He was so tired, hungry too. Realizing he was being carried on Emma's back, a part of him felt somewhat embarrassed, but he was too fatigued to say anything or let alone jump off of her. The muscles in his arms and legs barely responded to his attempts to move them. It was as if there was no energy left in him. Emma didn't realize his eyes were open yet. So, he had a few more moments to himself, to appreciate the nature around him as he took in every welcome breath of forest air.

Isaac took his time to look at the passing trees. No one seemed to be in a rush to know he was awake anyway. Without moving his head, he peered downward and saw they were walking on a narrow dirt path, just wide enough for a couple of people to walk side by side. He could hear the footsteps of the others behind and in front of them, all walking with soft *thuds* on the dirt. An occasional twig snapping or leaf crunching could be heard as well.

How far have we gone already? He asked himself. *Are we close?* He breathed in slowly through his nose. He just couldn't get enough of the air! *Oh, how wonderful it is to smell the fresh air after so many years in that sterile prison. Not just that,* he wondered, *but also what about all of the wonderful insects and animals that must be out there crawling, flying, and running around?* He thought too about the trees, reaching for the sunlight, their leaves rustling in the wind. There was so much to appreciate, so much time he had lost. He half-expected The Intelligence to come at any moment and take him back. Being outside felt surreal, almost like he shouldn't be there, as if his life was forever meant to remain in that prison cell. He took another deep, deep breath. *Remember this. Don't forget it,* he thought to himself. *This is real.*

The wind blew through the quiet trees. Isaac listened to the thousands of leaves moving, the branches swaying, and maybe, if he listened long enough, maybe he would hear the sound of an animal. He felt at peace. It felt right. And after a few more minutes like this, taking it all in, he was finally ready to try and say something, to let his friends know he was awake.

What came out was his best, and it would only come out in a broken whisper. "Where..." Emma stopped walking immediately.

Isaac paused to gather energy for his next words. "Are... we... going?" His words were so quiet, they were hard to hear.

Everyone else in the group stopped. Dennis walked from the back of the line up to Emma and Isaac. He leaned over to look at Isaac up close. "You okay, mate?"

Isaac's mouth was slightly open. His eyes were blinking sluggishly. He appeared like someone just waking up from a long nap, except he wasn't having an easy time waking up. He was depleted.

Dennis stood up straight and looked to Emma. "Maybe he just needs some food. Isaac," he leaned back down and put his face close again to his new friend's, "don't worry. We're on our way to Emma's home in the forest. You can rest for now. We'll get you back up and running in no time. Hah! You get it, Guy? Up and running! Because he runs really fast!" Dennis shouted to the back where Guy was standing. A quiet laugh, a little "heh" could be heard.

"You'll be okay." Emma reassured him. "Let's keep moving, everyone!" So, they continued walking.

Dennis fell to the rear to join his friend Guy again.

Isaac closed his eyes. His breath slowed once more. He fell back asleep.

"Okay!" A person's deep and commanding voice came loudly from some 20 feet away.

Isaac opened his eyes. He was now in a tent of some kind, a large one made of canvas. He was lying down on the floor, alone. The ground felt soft. *A blanket*, he thought. He felt so comfortable. Turning his head to the side to look at the entrance to the tent, he saw a flap with a small opening in the middle.

Rays of sunlight shone through the crack and lit up the dust floating in the air inside. A voice made its way from outside the entrance. "We can't wait around too long. We have to wake him up and feed him." It was the same voice from before. *A man's?* Isaac wondered.

The person's body stepped in front of the gap between the flaps, their figure blocking the light. At first, they just stood there, looking at Isaac. Isaac could not make out who was there. Their body was covered in shadow. From what he could tell, and the only thing he could tell, was that they were bald. They were wearing some kind of cape too. Two more figures then walked through the entrance and stood next to them. This time, these other figures were holding objects.

The caped one spoke, "Alright, I know you two wanted him to rest longer, but if we don't wake him up and get him to eat, it may be worse for him. Give him the food and drink now, please."

"I'm... awake." Isaac spoke, feebly.

"Isaac! We have water for you!" One of the figures was Emma. He recognized her voice immediately. She moved closer to where he was lying down. She had a wooden cup and a bucket of water with her. "Please, have a drink. I'll help you." Dipping the cup into the bucket, she gently placed the drink to Isaac's mouth and lifted his head with her free hand. "Can't drink it lying flat, or you may choke. Sip slowly."

The other figure came over with a plate. "When you've finished having some water, we can give you some food too." Dennis placed the plate gently on the ground as he knelt by Emma and Isaac's side. The person with a cape, who was standing alone, walked closer.

"Once you get your strength back, we will need to talk about what happened in your prison. Our people need all the information you can give us. From what I hear, you may even be the key to stopping them."

Emma added, "This is the rebellion's leader. His name is Wesley, though you can call him 'commander' when you talk with him. Oh, and also, he's my dad."

"We'll talk later. I'll leave him to you." Commander Wesley then exited the tent.

As Dennis and Emma helped feed Isaac, Isaac could only think of all the questions he had. *Where exactly are we? What did Wesley want to talk about?* Isaac didn't even know what was happening to him, with the abilities he was getting, let alone where he was and who these people were. Did Wesley, or the commander, have any idea?

Isaac felt a little better now. The taste of the food surprised him. After all, he had only eaten bread and a strange chalky mixture during "protein time" each day for years. "What is this?" That was the first fluent sentence he spoke since passing out. Emma and Dennis looked at each other and smiled, happy that he was showing signs of recovery.

"It's some berries we have around our base here," Emma said.

"They're pretty sweet, right?" Dennis must have had some berries as well. "We thought to give you something soft first, in case you couldn't chew other things very well yet. You just seemed so tired."

"Yea, good call. What else is on the plate?" Isaac planted his hand on the ground and pushed himself to sit up.

"That's from the wild boars we hunt." Emma took a metal fork from the plate and picked up some of the thin slices of meat with it. She held it up for Isaac to try. "Are you ready to chew this, or do you want some more berries?"

"I'll try the meat." He put his nose up to it. It occurred to him that he hadn't eaten meat since before his time in prison, eight years ago. The protein they always served the prisoners was in liquid form, with a coarse or chalky texture and without flavor. The brownish-white slushy substance allowed them to survive, but was never something that he actually enjoyed eating. He always thought it must have been made from a mix of protein-rich vegetables like rice and beans, just mushed up.

"I've had the same food every day for eight years," he said to them. "Thank you." He took one bite of meat, and his mouth watered instantly. It even had salt on it. Isaac almost forgot what it was like. "Oh my god. Thank you *so* much, Emma."

Isaac finished his bite and grabbed the plate. He shoveled the rest of the meat into his mouth. "Ohm-uhmmm-omm." After some time chewing and making sounds of utter joy, Isaac took the remaining berries, ate those too, and drank down all the water until the bucket was empty. "Is there any more?"

Dennis's eyebrows raised. "Pretty big appetite for a guy who was passed out just a moment ago."

Emma stood up and left the tent to get more food. Isaac heard her footsteps move quickly outside and then stop some place not too far from the entrance. After a minute, the footsteps continued and Emma returned through the tent's flaps. She was holding another plate of food, but now with twice as much as what was on the previous plate.

"Woah!" Dennis was surprised. "Isn't that a bit much? He already had a full plate of food. What you brought back could be enough to feed all three of us. Won't he get sick if he tries eating it all?"

Emma leaned to Dennis's ear and whispered, "*I have a theory about something. Let's just see what he does.*"

Isaac immediately grabbed the plate and scarfed down every little scrap of food, down to the last berry and the last bits of meat. "Water please!"

Dennis looked shocked again. "How do you even have that much room in your stomach?"

"I don't know," Isaac replied. "Now that you mention it, I should not be able to eat this much. My stomach is only used to small meals. I should've been full after just a few bites."

Emma chimed in, "I knew it. I think you might understand too, Isaac, if you think about it a bit."

"Knew what?" Dennis asked.

Isaac answered, "My abilities, Dennis. I had to use a lot of energy to do those superhuman things back at the prison. My body must need energy now more than ever."

Emma cut in, "And it must also be why you fainted. Your body can't exert itself that much without enough energy coming in. What did you eat before I found you?"

"Same thing I had every morning: bread. Not much either, just enough to survive. And sometimes we got a kind of slushy protein drink."

"Right," Emma agreed, "and I bet you never used these abilities before either. Your body probably used what little energy the bread could give you and probably even used up some of your body's fat for fuel. That's just how our bodies work. Except you didn't have much body fat to burn. You weigh so little."

Isaac was catching on. "And now that I have had some water, sugar from the berries, and protein from the meat, my body should be good to go, right?"

Emma nodded her head. "Yes, that's what I think. Except, you need a lot more than a normal person now. Superhuman moves need superhuman amounts of food. Let me guess, you're still hungry, aren't you?"

Isaac was surprised with himself. "Actually, yes! I'm still *starving*."

"I think your body is digesting your food faster too. Dennis was right, you don't have enough stomach space for this much. Your whole system is sped up, even the cells in your stomach so you can absorb food quicker. I've never heard of augmentations working on an entire person's body like this." Emma stared into Isaac's eyes. "After I get you more food, we have to look at your cells under a microscope. I think you may have something different happening inside you."

"Okay. Sounds good. Well, I think it sounds good. I stopped listening when you said 'food.' Can I have a few more plates now, please?" *Grumble.* Isaac's stomach made a loud sound that told everyone it was empty.

Dennis put his hand on Isaac's shoulder. "Emma, I'll help you get some more food for him. Let's go."

10
Wesley

"I want to know who this boy is," Wesley stated flatly. He had a cool sternness behind whatever he said. Whenever others would show fear or anxiety in a life-or-death situation, they knew that they could rely on him to be the one to stay calm. Somehow, it seemed like he always knew what the best course of action was. They respected him for that. Standing at a round table, his hands resting behind his back, he stared at one of his officers sitting down. "John, report."

John spoke from across the table. "Commander." As John stood up, he bowed slightly to Wesley. "The boy's name is Isaac. While he was unconscious, I followed your orders to debrief with Lieutenant Emma, along with the prisoner, Dennis. They both gave me all the details of what happened."

Wesley nodded his head. "Continue."

John looked around now at all the other officers at the table while he shared the story. As the events were described to them, their faces reacted with surprise and hope. They were glad to hear that their carefully made plans had worked, that the explosives they gave Emma successfully blew a hole as expected, and her speed augmentations were enough to defeat the prison guards—they never tried such a mission before, so they had no idea for sure that it would work. Even better, and something they never imagined was possible, was that they found and now had what could be the key to winning the war against The Intelligence. No one was ever able to defeat a PC without harm until now, until Isaac.

When John sat back down, everyone looked back at Commander Wesley, waiting for how he would respond and what he would order them to do with the information they had just learned. How would they use this new weapon?

"Right! With this, we have a chance. John..." Wesley stared at his lieutenant.

"Sir!"

"You spoke with the prisoner and Emma first. This boy, Dennis, knows you as well. Return to them. Isaac is awake and has eaten some food by now. Introduce yourself and bring him to the science tent right away. Natasha will go with you to run diagnostics on his biology. We need to learn everything we can about his abilities. Natasha..."

"On it, sir!" Natasha, the lead science officer, was also the commander's wife, Emma's mother.

John and Natasha left the tent.

Wesley continued speaking with his troops. "Alright. Everyone else, I will leave it to you to inform our soldiers of every detail. Be clear, be strong, and as always..."

"Never give up!" They said in unison as they each stood and bowed to their commander. One by one, they left the tent, leaving Wesley to stand alone at the table. As cheesy as he realized how their salute sounded, it was a phrase he told his officers to use, and it was one he had been taking seriously for many years—ever since he lost his previous commander and friend on a mission. He stood, staring down, deep in thought. His mind wandered to the past. Images of a battle with a PC crossed his mind for just a moment.

Wesley was in his old lieutenant uniform, standing next to a car at night in a parking lot. Across from him, he saw in horror as his then commander, his friend, was being strangled in the air by a PC.

His mind returned to the present moment. He thought about all the soldiers he had lost since then, since he had taken over as the rebellion's leader. Sometimes he doubted himself, his plans, and if he was the right person for the job. *No,* he thought, *I can't doubt myself. I have to be strong. I have to be okay with my decisions. I can only do my best with what I know, at the moment.*

Wesley had seen too many of his officers fail in missions when they lost their composure. It was the ones who lost confidence in themselves, the ones who gave in to fear that would, in those moments of terror, forget the importance of sticking to plans—to keeping calm and focused. He learned quickly that emotionally strong soldiers would usually have a better chance of survival on a mission—and there would certainly be more dangerous missions ahead with the discovery of Isaac. That is... *if Isaac agreed to fight with us*, he thought.

Wesley's eyes widened. He suddenly realized he needed to leave quickly and meet with Isaac personally to convince the boy to join them in their fight. Isaac would need answers more than anyone, and the commander of the rebellion would know the most. This wasn't something to be left with any other officer. He hurried out of the tent to join John in transporting Isaac to the research lab.

He walked down the dirt path, his cape flowing behind him as he sped up his pace. Soldiers were performing their usual duties. Some were hanging recently washed clothes on lines between the trees to dry. Some were wiping down weapons of dirt and repairing broken gear—the rebellion couldn't survive without working equipment after all. Many others were simply talking to one another, socializing. These woods weren't just a place to plan missions and hide. These soldiers weren't just combat partners. The rebellion was all any of them had. This was their life, their family, their home.

A soldier standing on the path moved out of Wesley's way quickly and bowed. "Sir!"

Wesley, in his eagerness to get to Isaac, responded shortly, "At ease!"

The soldier stood up straight, nodded his head, and continued about his business, doing whatever it was he was occupied with.

Wesley did not have time for small talk or formal standing salutes. Isaac's tent was now in front of him. He stopped just before entering. *In*, he thought to himself as he inhaled a slow and deep breath through his nose, *hold*. Closing his eyes, he focused on how his chest felt, full of air, on the leaves bristling in the wind, on the feeling of the air coming and going... *out.* Gently, he let go of the air inside him, along with any strong emotions he may have had lingering inside. He let go of all he was holding on to. After rushing over, it was important to reset and enter this conversation with a clear head. In his mind, he told himself, *now. Focus.* Wesley opened the tent flap with the mental resolve of a man willing to give his all to ensure that Isaac joined them in their fight, to never lose one more human being. Humanity was at stake in this very moment.

His eyes took a moment to adjust to the sudden darkness inside. Figures started to emerge in front of him. He stood there, shocked at what he saw.

Emma spoke up, "Oh, hey Dad! Oops, I mean, 'Commander.'" She forgot that a fellow officer, John, was in their presence. She couldn't say "Dad" in front of the other rebels.

John nervously stood in front of his commander, trying to block his view. "Sorry, sir! I found the tent in this condition when I arrived just a minute ago. If I had known you were coming, I would have—"

Wesley interrupted, "It's alright, John." He walked around the embarrassed subordinate. "I will... ignore it in light of the circumstances."

Surrounding Isaac was a mess of plates, food scraps, and toppled-over cups and utensils. Wesley was clearly not happy with the mess, but he was letting it go. Dennis, however, thought he could be helpful. He slowly picked up just one plate from the floor, as if it would help make everything look better, and placed it behind his back. Hiding some of the mess now, he winked at Isaac. "Got'ya back, mate."

Isaac glared at Dennis in disbelief. "Dennis, come on, man. One plate won't make a difference."

"Ahem." Wesley acted like he was clearing his throat, but really he was trying to get their attention.

Isaac quickly turned to look at the commander. "Sorry, uh, sir! It's my abilities—they took a lot of energy out of me. I needed to eat as much as I could. Again, sorry for the mess!"

"It's okay," he replied, "if this is what you need, then we are here to help you meet those needs. John."

"Sir!"

"I will take it from here. I think Isaac is comfortable talking with me for now. *Are* you okay talking with me, Isaac?" Wesley asked with caring concern.

Isaac turned to Emma as if to ask for her approval before answering.

She nodded her head. "Go on. We're all fighting for the same cause here."

Isaac then looked over at Dennis. Dennis just shrugged his shoulders as if to say, "Why are you asking *me*? I don't know."

Wesley still stood, waiting patiently for Isaac's answer.

"Okay," Isaac said. "But before I share with you what I've been through in that prison, can you tell me what's been happening on the outside?"

Wesley's expression was no longer neutral and calm. He looked sad as his eyes locked onto Isaac's. "As much as it looks like we are free out here, I'm afraid we live in a kind of prison ourselves. I will tell you what we know about the last eight years. I will start with how it all began."

11

The Forest

Eight years ago

"Dad, why do we have to be out here again?" A young Emma whined in the backseat of the family car as they drove up the gravel-covered road. Forest surrounded them. Even though it was the middle of the day, the trees were so densely packed that Emma could only see darkness when she looked out there into the spaces between them. She could not see further than a couple hundred meters at most. The nature before her was beautiful yet scary at the same time.

Wesley was driving and trying to focus on the road ahead of them. Still, he responded patiently with his impatient daughter, "Emma, it's lucky we can do something like this. I bet you don't know anyone who gets the chance to see how it feels to disconnect for a *whole* month, huh?"

"That's why I don't want to do it, Dad. A whole *month* is the problem. That's way too much time to not have the internet or talk to friends."

"Well, we have the old ham radio if you want to have fun conversations with other people."

"Ha...Ha... Very funny, Dad. You know no one talks on those things. I'm going to be so bored, Dad!"

He sighed, disappointed that she seemed to have forgotten or not cared about how much she enjoyed the trip the previous year. "And what about last time? How did you feel when we finished our month last time?"

Emma grunted. She knew he was only trying to help. She also knew he was right. When they left the cabin last summer, she did say to her parents that she felt "different" by having been out there. The experience somehow cleared her mind better than anything else she did at home to try to forget about her daily problems. She still had a strong memory of the car ride back—that last sight of the cabin before returning to the car, the quiet time alone that she would miss.

Wesley continued, "Is having the internet more important than having that experience again?" It was as if he knew clearly what she was thinking. They did, after all, share those same summers together, experiencing the same woods, the same cabin, the same time in peace and quiet. What she experienced, so did he. He looked at Emma through his rearview mirror. Her arms were crossed as if she were defending her opinion no matter what. However, Wesley looked at Emma's eyes—they told a different story than what she was saying and how she was acting.

While Emma did want to use her phone for the internet and social media apps, she also felt a little embarrassed about how she started to hear herself sound out loud. Her dad was somehow always so calm and kind, even when she complained. Even when she was mad, he took the time to hear her out and guide her back to reason. She learned a lot from him, not just facts about how things worked—though her parents did teach her a lot of those kinds of things too—but he also never stopped showing her how a person could handle themselves.

Then again, maybe the two of them just had different personalities and interests. Sometimes Emma liked to be loud when he liked quiet—and sometimes she wanted the internet. "Dad, just get internet in the cabin! We'll still enjoy it out here with just a little internet. We can find a balance."

Still holding a smile, he quietly but firmly stated, "No."

She gave up. "Ugh! Okay, whatever."

Wesley smiled to himself a little and focused back on driving through the winding roads up to the cabin. Natasha was fast asleep in the passenger seat next to him. He was grateful for this small family, this quiet life. Some part of him missed his military service too, but a bigger part of him understood the value he gained by staying at home to raise his daughter. In every pursuit he had made in life, he was always dedicated to an odd degree more than anyone he knew. When Emma was born, he turned all of his energy, all his focus, to supporting the growth of her character. He stopped working in the military as soon as she joined their family. An odd choice which made it more difficult for the family to support themselves financially, but a choice he never regretted.

They were lucky. Natasha earned just enough money to allow him to switch jobs to something with fewer hours, to something that allowed him to spend more time at home with Emma. Looking over at his wife, he noticed she forgot to take off her ID badge from the NIH (the National Institute of Health), where she worked. It was still clipped onto her belt. Seeing it made him smile with pride. The research Natasha did could improve the health and quality of life for so many people. His mind returned to the moment. The cabin was coming into view now, up through the steep and winding hill.

Wesley gently spoke to wake his wife up, "*Natasha.*"

Emma uncrossed her arms as her expression changed. She looked at the cabin and felt a wave of nostalgia hit her, that feeling when you see something familiar, something you connect with, after having not seen it for a long time. Though it had only been a year, this place resonated with her. It was all coming back: the light tan color of the oak pillars, the darker walnut door, the roof-covered porch, and even the parking spot they were now rolling up to. The sound of tires slowing down on the rocky road, the smells of the forest, and the sights all felt so comforting to her, so familiar and warm.

"Let's unpack!" Wesley announced happily.

An hour later

"Dad!" Emma shouted downstairs from her bedroom. She had just finished unloading her clothes into the dressers. No answer. She walked over to the doorway and yelled even louder over the

2nd floor balcony, attempting to project her voice downstairs even more. "DAD!"

"Woah!" Wesley's slightly raised voice came from down the hall, from his and Natasha's bedroom. "I'm up here with you, Emma, still unpacking. What do you need?"

"What's for dinner?"

"I'm not sure yet. Why don't you go downstairs and ask Mom? Maybe she needs help."

The inside of the cabin was painted white on the walls, with light brown oak floors. Emma took a moment to appreciate the familiarity of it all as she walked downstairs. The sound of running water made its way from the kitchen sink.

"Emma, is that you?" Natasha had her hands in the water, cleaning the dust off the dishes that had sat in the cabin for close to a year untouched. Sunlight shined through the window across the kitchen. The parents purposefully designed the house themselves so that many windows filled the walls, so turning on lights did not feel necessary during the day. Though they called it a "cabin," it really was more of a house—a nice, if a bit lacking in internet, house.

Emma repeated her initial question now to her mom, "What's for dinner?"

"Hmm, no one has decided yet. Want to explore the fridge and see what could be good tonight? If you're hungry now, I'm sure we could have snacks you can start on."

The fridge didn't have much—except for condiments, dressings, water bottles, and some lemons and limes. Most of the food they packed in their car was frozen—kept cold in the ride with the help of insulated travel bags and ice packs. Steaks, chicken, fish, and even frozen vegetables now filled the freezer completely, but were not ready to cook. They needed time to defrost.

Natasha noticed Emma looking disappointed. "Oh, sorry, honey, I forgot. We only have freezer food right now. If you want a snack, we have to make a long drive to the grocery store. It's about 30 minutes away, though."

Emma slouched her shoulders and, tilting her head to the side with her mouth gaping open, she muttered a sizable "ugh." She closed the freezer door fairly hard and plopped her forehead on it in desperation.

Though surprised by the sudden outburst, Natasha put her attention back on rinsing the dishes. However, she wanted to keep Emma from dwelling on the bad, so she attempted to keep the conversation moving forward. She spoke loudly to be heard over the running water and over Emma's stressful emotions. "What would you like for dinner anyway?"

No response.

"Emma?" She shut off the faucet and turned around. Emma was gone. Natasha's eyebrows raised with a look of both concern and understanding. "She needs time," she reassured herself out loud. Natasha then walked over to the freezer, pulled out some steaks to defrost for a couple of hours, and returned to cleaning the dishware.

"Four weeks?!" The sound of the cabin's back door slamming shut reverberated behind Emma as she shouted to herself in a dirt area nearby. She looked up at the trees.

CHIRP CHIRP

Some birds made sounds above her.

She walked over to a tree, rested a hand on it, and sighed. "Four weeks, huh?"

CHIRP CHIRP

"Shut up, birds!" Defeated, Emma made her way back inside.

20 days later

The wind softly traveled through the trees. They swayed, their leaves wavered—the sounds were calming for Emma. She lay next to the cabin, on a blanket which rested on a patch of dirt underlooking the canopy of tree branches. Her hands resting on her stomach, her legs stretched out and relaxed, she closed her eyes to better hear even deeper into nature.

CHIRP CHIRP

Not too far away was a bird. Maybe less than 50 meters away? To the right, she thought.

CHIRP CHIRP—CHIRP CHIRP CHIRP

Another bird now, to her left. *Was this one responding to the first?* She focused all of her attention on the next sounds.

Five seconds passed. Nothing.

Some sounds again came from the trees rustling in the wind.

15 seconds. Still, nothing from the birds.

Then, about 30 seconds in, she heard the chirping back to back, faster than before.

CHIRP-CHIRP, CHIRP-CHIRP, CHIRP-CHIRP

"*They're together now*," she whispered to herself. Emma continued whispering her thoughts out loud, to help her think through what she was observing. Her eyes still closed, "*Maybe they like each other and are playing. Or, maybe, they lost each other and called out to get back together. Maybe both.*" She opened her eyes to see more.

The two birds were small. They had brown feathers, with some white under their bellies. *What are they doing though?* Her eyes tracked their every movement, looking to get a clue about what they were actually doing. One bird looked like it was flying away from the other. The other, seemingly following behind in flight. Now she couldn't tell which bird was making which chirps.

Then, one landed on a branch. Emma strained her focus on this one. In less than half of a second, she thought she saw its beak peck at the branch—just before the other bird flew in. The bird that was pecking at the branch now flew away while the other one, who had just come in, began to peck at the same place. Fearing she could scare them away somehow if she spoke out loud, she thought out her conclusions instead of speaking: *are they... competing for food?*

The bird that had first flown away now returned. *Will they fight over it?!*

Just then, both birds stopped pecking. Their heads jerked back and forth the way a chicken's or pigeon's does when they walk sometimes. One hopped backward, but kept looking forward at its friend, *or was it an enemy*? A quick moment later, the bird that did not hop picked up something in its beak and flew away. The other bird then followed after.

Where are you going? They flew over Emma's head, through the trees to her right. "Good thing I kept my shoes on!" She said out loud. She sprang up from the ground as quickly as she could and ran through the trees. At the same time, she tried her best to tread softly. To avoid making too much sound, she had to be careful to avoid stepping on branches that could snap, or to otherwise step on or through things that would make particularly loud sounds. Still, she had to move fast or she would lose sight of where the birds went.

They stopped at a tree together. "There they are! It's a nest!" Emma said to herself. "They're not enemies, they're parents looking for food together!" That was too loud. The birds flew away. "Sorry!" Emma yelled out, as if the birds could understand her anyway. Satisfied with finding out the birds' story, Emma started walking back toward where she had come from. It felt like a good time to pick up the blanket and help her mom make dinner. The sky was just starting to show a bit of red. The sun moved lower down the sky. Emma was calm and happy.

SLAM!

The door swung open and hit the back wall of the cabin. Wesley yelled to Emma, "Get inside! Quickly!"

A scared voice was coming from their ham radio.

12
Fear

The voice sounded desperate. "I repeat, they're real and they are coming for the children!"

Emma just came through the door with her father when she heard it. "Mom, what's happening?"

Natasha was with the radio. She looked afraid. With an elbow propped on the table, her head was slumped over and resting on her palm.

"Mom? You look pale. What's happening? Someone tell me?!" Emma asked, frantically.

Standing behind his daughter, Wesley put his hand on Emma's shoulder for support. "Take a seat, Emma. We have to hear every word we can."

The voice continued, "Whatever you do, whoever is hearing this, hide!"

What was happening? Who were they hiding from? Were they going to be attacked? All of these thoughts and more filled Emma's confused mind.

"It's alright, Emma," Wesley said. "We are far enough from civilization out here. We should be safe."

"What's even happening?!" Emma demanded.

The voice over the radio came up again. "If anyone is out there to hear this, The Intelligence has begun its attack on all of us. It's..." The broadcaster stuttered and paused nervously, as if afraid to finish his thought. "It's real. There was no hoax. It wasn't a scam like we thought. It's *real!* Oh god. They're here."

Emma stared at the radio speaker, her attention fixed on the littlest of sounds coming through. The voice was barely audible now, though distant from his microphone—she could still hear him.

"What do you want?!" She could hear him scream from far away. A knock was heard. Then, there was an almost robotic voice that came through.

"**Open up, please. I am here for Kevin and Margaret.**" Emma thought this new voice sounded human, but somehow not at the same time.

The man from the radio responded to the emotionless voice, "You can't have them! Leave! Kevin, Margaret, stay in your rooms!"

Emma heard a second, louder knock come through the speaker of the radio. Natasha, startled, jumped from her seat.

"We have confirmed that Kevin and Margaret are home. Bring them to the door." The cold voice showed no emotion, not even cruelty. *It couldn't be human*, Emma thought.

Footsteps were heard rushing over to the microphone. The man came on again. "They're doing just as they promised in the news. They're coming for the children!"

Then, a third knock finally came.

CRASH!

"No!" The man's voice sounded as if he had turned away from the radio, looking at whatever made its way in. For the last time, the man's voice spoke and said in terrifying clarity, "Please, help us! SOMEONE!" His voice stopped, and they heard what sounded like his microphone dropping onto the floor.

Then, a moment of silence. They all leaned closer to the radio to listen. Though faint, they could hear it—the sound of the man being strangled to death.

"Agh. Ahh." His last breaths of air.

Natasha gasped and put her hands over her mouth in fright. Emma turned to her dad with a scared look. Wesley hugged her tight.

Emma suddenly realized something. "What about the children?!" She shouted.

They listened in for any sound at all, anything that would tell them if the children were okay.

THUD thud thud

The man's body must have been dropped to the floor, lifeless.

"Kevin, Margaret, come with us, please."

Footsteps were then heard moving up what sounded like stairs. The steps were quick and evenly spaced, as if calculated perfectly by a machine mind.

Step-step-step-step

One by one, the steps moved without any pause. Then...

CRASH

Which was quickly followed by the children's screams in the distance.

As Emma, Wesley, and Natasha listened, the screams got closer. This *thing* was carrying the children closer to the radio, closer to the front door.

Emma couldn't contain herself. "Where is it taking them?" She looked up at Wesley for some kind of answer. He always had an answer. But not this time.

"I..." he hesitated. "I don't know."

The screams faded. Listening closely, they heard what sounded like car doors shutting. Then, nothing.

They kept the radio on for another minute. The man on the other end had kept his channel open. The only sound coming through now was the background noise of a microphone left clicked on—a gentle hum of an empty radio broadcast.

Back in the present

Wesley was sitting on the ground alongside Isaac, Dennis, and Emma. His eyes were closed, reflecting on what he had told them so far. "We found out shortly after that there had been strange events leading up to the day the population controllers took everyone."

Isaac remembered what he was talking about. Before he was taken eight years ago, there were hacks on popular websites. Internet connections were lost for hours at a time too. When the internet did come back on, social media accounts with the most followers posted the same strange message: "**We are here to help**."

Soon afterwards, the posts were deleted and the owners of the accounts confirmed it was not them who had made the messages. They didn't know who it was. The days just before the PCs invaded homes on his street, news broadcasts on TV and radio released a similar ominous warning: **"We are here to help. We will take all children. Humanity will grow."** The memory of it all came back to Isaac now. *Funny*, he thought, *back then, no one took those threats seriously. We just thought it was a strange, sick joke.*

Wesley continued. "Captures were happening all over, not just in our country, but across the entire planet. Every country, every state, every region—from the cities to the farmlands. If your address was listed on the internet or with the government, they could find you. They probably made a visit to our home address, too, though we don't really know for sure. We never risked going back from our cabin, which I kept off-grid, unlisted, and unfindable."

Isaac looked to Emma for how she was feeling. She was staring at the floor. Her eyes were watery, like she was holding back tears, or she had just finished crying.

Dennis walked over and put an arm around her. "It's okay. We're all safe now thanks to you. Isaac and I were prisoners too, just like those kids, and you saved us. Heck, with Isaac and me here to help you now, we'll save a lot more."

"He's right." Wesley, returning from his moment of reflection, opened his eyes and spoke with his usual confident voice. "Isaac, you can help us. With your abilities, we can save so many more lives."

It just now occurred to Isaac that the others expected a lot from him. His strength, his speed, and who knows what else—

and now he had a group of like-minded people to work with, people who had been through what he had. Along with their equipment, support, and planning that they could offer, Isaac's abilities could be put to better use than if he were alone. *Not only that*, Isaac thought, *it's been a very long time without friends, without a family. What better choice do I have?*

"Okay," Isaac said. "I know what I want to do. I want to help you."

Wesley's stern expression did not change, though. He looked hard at Isaac. "Isaac. That is great to hear." Some relief could be heard in his voice.

"But first," Isaac continued, "please tell me what happened after the children were taken. I experienced that part of the story myself already." Anger welled up in his voice. "I was taken from *my* home eight years ago." The rage he felt toward the PCs back then now echoed through his words, bubbling up from the memory of his mother, from the life with her and his dad that The Intelligence stole from them. He added one more set of questions, "Why did they only take the children? What happened to the outside world while I was in prison?"

Wesley breathed out one heavy breath. "The end of human civilization."

13
The First Mission

Seven years ago

Sirens blared. The alarm system of the lab rang through the halls.

"Commander Dyson! 10 minutes!" Wesley was holding an assault rifle as he warned his leader. He stood by the door, guarding it as Dyson and Natasha were utterly focused on the computer screens in front of them.

Natasha shouted back, "It'll be done soon! The files are almost all transferred." They had USB drives stuck into the sides of the computers.

Wesley was sweating. The Intelligence may have kept electricity running because it needed to access the research stored on computers there, but it didn't need to keep the air conditioning running. After all, the only humans still working in the building, or anywhere on Earth for that matter, were just drones now—empty shells of who they once were, controlled by computer chips in their brains and who now wouldn't complain if a room was a bit too warm. The Intelligence was brutally efficient. It saved energy and resources where it deemed it to be its biggest advantage. Nothing useful was wasted, even the power that could've been used to make its slave humans more comfortable.

"Done here!" Natasha yelled. "Commander Dyson?"

Their leader, Commander Dyson, was also their friend. He was a general in the military, one of the higher-ups above Wesley back when he was still a soldier, back when there was still an army.

Wesley, who always kept his cool, was starting to lose it. Maybe it was the heat of the building. "DYSON!" He shouted out.

Dyson, still quiet, only had to glance at his friend to calm him down. His look said everything. Barely slowing down in finding the necessary files on the computer, Dyson's blank, yet serious expression showed Wesley that he was working as fast and as effectively as he could. "Done." Without wasting a moment, Dyson pulled the USB out from the computer and ran through the door right past Wesley and Natasha. They were somewhat slower to react, though. "MOVE," Dyson demanded. They immediately sprang into action and ran after him. His cape flowed in the air as he sprinted down the hall. Even in the middle of a mission, Wesley thought to himself, *does he really need that cape? It's so ridiculous.*

"Down here!" Dyson pointed to a door at the end of the hallway. When he was a couple of feet away from the room, he suddenly slowed down his pace. While Natasha and Wesley were still 10 feet behind him and running fast, Dyson quickly opened the door and bolted inside, resuming his fast speed once again. They ran right in after him and closed the door. Missions had to be fast and with minimal mistakes made. Every action needed to be done with quick precision. They could not waste even one more minute than they had when their enemy was almost perfectly efficient. One extra minute could mean the end for all of them. It wouldn't be long now for The Intelligence's forces to arrive, after all.

Because she worked for the NIH, at the building they were at now, Natasha was able to give them instructions, "Okay! Commander Dyson, that computer there!"

Dyson took out a note from his pocket with a username and underlined password written on it:

Username: Ajax
Password: 846NED49THROW!*?

Though he had memorized every last detail prior to their mission, Dyson knew a mistake now could cost them even more time, so a note was necessary, just in case he forgot during the stress of mission conditions.

Wesley guarded the door.

Natasha talked through and reminded them of their objective as they logged on to the computers. "Access the main drive. Folder tree: *Documents*, then *NIH Bioengineering*, then *Lab Results*, then *Augmentations*." While Dyson dragged the Augmentations folder to his USB, Natasha was dragging a file from her USB onto her computer. She was going to put the rebellion's virus into the

NIH system. "Hopefully," she said out loud, "this should slow down its progress for a while."

"Alright!" Dyson said sharply. "We're done here!" He jumped from the computer he was working at and went for the door. "GO! EXIT NOW!"

Natasha went through first, then Wesley tailed after them, gripping his gun with every intention of using it in case the enemy appeared.

The halls were dimly lit. The only lights The Intelligence couldn't shut off were the emergency ones, the kinds that come on in power outages. With red exit signs passing overhead, they approached the stairwell. Almost without slowing down, Dyson turned the door handle and rammed the door open with his shoulder. It swung open, banging the concrete against the concrete wall on the other side. The sound reverberated through the air of the staircase. A number "10" was painted on the wall. "Down!" Dyson shouted.

The only sound they heard on their way down the stairs was the alarm system and their increasingly nervous footsteps.

Wesley looked up and down the stairs as he followed behind. *Nothing yet*, he thought. "*7th floor*," he muttered to himself.

Step by step, landing by landing, the repetitiveness ate at each one of them. Natasha couldn't stop thinking of every sound and sight that kept reappearing. *Step, step, step. White-painted wall. Floor number. Step, step, step. White-painted wall. Floor number.* Natasha wasn't a trained soldier like Wesley and Dyson. *Oh my god. What if we don't make it? What if they're waiting for us when we get down? No, no, no.* She began to shake uncontrollably in fear. *I don't want to die.*

Wesley heard a slight whimper and whine come from his wife as they reached the 2nd floor.

Natasha felt like she could break at any moment. *First floor! Oh no, oh no, oh no.*

As Dyson approached the door for the lobby, only a few feet away, Natasha couldn't hold back her thoughts and fears anymore. "STOP!" she shouted.

Dyson knew they were only at more risk if they hesitated like this. "We have to move," he stated firmly.

She backed up against the hard concrete wall behind them, as if to feel something strong and stable while she felt so unbalanced. Her hands were visibly shaking as she held them up toward her face. "I can't! What if one of them is out there? Maybe... maybe we can try the second floor and—and go down from a window!"

As their commander, Dyson attempted to restate the most important factor for escape in this mission. "Natasha, there isn't enough *time*. You know that. We talked about this during our briefing before leaving."

But it wasn't what she needed to hear most at that moment, though. Sure, those *were* the facts. They *did* talk about it. They *did* all agree already on the details of the mission. But she just *couldn't* build up the courage for that choice, now that it was staring them in the face. "I'm sorry. I just can't." She collapsed onto the ground in tears, huddling her face in between her knees.

Wesley and Dyson looked at each other with concern. If they stayed, they would certainly all die. They couldn't leave her, though.

Images of his wife in the hospital suddenly flashed through Wesley's mind—a memory of Natasha giving birth to their baby daughter. He could see her holding Emma in her arms and looking up at Wesley, crying with happiness. Back then, he saw her with tears of joy. But now, she had tears of desperation. In that moment, something changed in him. The man who was nervous upstairs, who was sweating in fear, disappeared. He had to be strong for Natasha. He had to be strong for Emma.

"Natasha." He knelt down next to her and hugged her tightly. Lifting her chin with his hand, he looked her in the eyes. "We *will* make it out safe. You will see your daughter again."

Natasha's eyes opened wide as tears ran down her cheeks. She gasped as her mind focused back on their family, on the day *she* first held Emma in her arms in the hospital—the same memory as Wesley had just a moment ago—then, moments at their cabin in the forest, eating dinner with her family, seeing her daughter smile. As she reached her hand up for Wesley, he suddenly stood up.

"Not a moment to lose." He turned to Dyson and Natasha and gave them a confident smile. His face staring at the door ahead of him, he nodded to Dyson, showing that they were ready to go.

His friend knew what to do. Dyson put his hand on the door while Wesley held his rifle ready with both hands, pointing the sights down in front of them. Wesley would be ready to shoot anything in the lobby waiting for them when the door opened. Dyson pushed the door open quickly, but kept his hands gripped on it to stop it from hitting the wall and making noise. If the PCs *were* here, they had to avoid being detected.

Looking down his gun, Wesley scanned the lobby. It was dark. The front entrance was close, only 30 feet away. There was a front desk, two restrooms, and a single hallway with offices leading to a back entrance. Their car was parked at the front of the building. Having considered all options, however, the three of them knew that they had to leave through the front. But, they would have to walk through the lobby carefully, being mindful of these other places where the enemy could appear.

Wesley took a few steps out from the stairwell first. Natasha stood up, determined to be close to her husband from now on, to have the courage to escape and see Emma again. *Whatever happens*, she thought, *we will be together again*. She quietly followed just behind Wesley. Dyson took the rear to keep a lookout at the lone hallway that led to the back behind them, in case anything came through.

Their eyes were focused and determined to find any and all movements that might appear. Creeping toward the front doors, they stared at the bathrooms, the front doors, the hallway, the elevator, and the stairs they had just left behind. As it appeared though, there were no threats, so they hastened their pace to the exit. Wesley looked through the glass of the front doors at their car and the parking lot around it. Aside from a handful of abandoned cars, the area looked clear. He nodded his head to Dyson, who then opened the door for him. Wesley's gun stayed up. This was the most dangerous part of the mission, the end—because the longer the alarm rang, the greater the chance that the enemy could arrive at any moment. Natasha and Dyson each took out pistols that were holstered at their waists.

They walked as fast as they could while maintaining steady control over their weapons. Dyson sounded off a command, "I'm driver. Wesley front passenger. Natasha back." As they approached the car, they split up to find each of their respective doors. The right side of the car was facing the building already, so Wesley and Natasha entered first. Dyson moved quickly around to the driver's side and put his hand on the door handle.

WHOOSH

Out of nowhere, Dyson was picked up off his feet, held by the neck. The robot had a blue light glowing from its chest. Dyson held onto the PC's arm so that the weight of his body hanging down would not hurt his neck. Natasha and Wesley jumped out of the car and pointed their weapons at the PC immediately. It wasn't hurting Dyson—not yet. Would it start to hurt him though if they attacked first?

"Nick Dyson, you are going to be brought in for questioning."

"PUT HIM DOWN!" Wesley demanded.

The PC turned to point its face toward Wesley, pausing for a moment as if performing a calculation for who to attack next. **"Wesley Davis, Natasha Davis, you are not needed at this time. You may leave."**

Natasha and Wesley looked at each other, still holding their guns at the PC, and stood confused. Why were they being allowed to leave?

"In any case," Wesley said, "we can't leave him behind."

Sensing the danger now posed to it, the PC started to rotate its body as if it were changing targets.

POP POP POP

Natasha fired the first shots from her pistol. She knew they couldn't announce their attacks, or the PC would have time to process what was happening and avoid the shots. Still, two bullets missed. But one landed in the robot's upper arm. Sparks flew off the point of impact, and the hit seemed to damage something, because the PC dropped Dyson.

Immediately, Dyson picked up his gun and fired while Wesley fired his assault rifle at the same time. The sound of gunfire filled the empty lot, with a constant flickering of light coming from the muzzle flashes.

The PC, though, looked like a blur. In the haze of gunfire, were they even hitting it? It moved too fast to tell.

CLICK

Natasha's ammo ran empty.

CLICK

Then Dyson's.

Wesley stopped firing. He would save some shots as they waited to see what the PC was going to do next.

It stood there, motionless. Then it spoke. "**The decision has been changed. Natasha and Wesley, *you* will be taken.**"

PUNCH GRAB

In the blink of an eye, the PC had used its other arm to punch Dyson's head before lifting him into the air, choking him once more. "**Nick Dyson is no longer required—**"

POP POP POP CLICK

Three shots were fired from Wesley's gun. One for each leg, and one in the arm holding Dyson. The gun was empty. The PC fell to its knees. Metallic clanging against the asphalt could be heard.

Wesley and Natasha ran over to their friend, who was now on the ground and not getting up.

His mouth moved up and down, as if he was trying to speak. ,

Natasha started to cry. Wesley put his ear down next to Dyson's mouth.

"*You... command...*" Dyson muttered softly.

Wesley's eyes watered.

"Never... give up." With that, Nick Dyson breathed his last breath.

14
Resolve

Present day

Someone's footsteps came from the entrance of the tent. They all turned to face her.

"I was wondering where Isaac was," Natasha said as she joined the group on the floor. "That story brought back memories. It's been a long time since I thought about that night." Natasha looked sad, but shed no tears.

Wesley looked at her with a sympathetic yet stoic expression. "We've lived through the pain of his loss enough," he said to everyone in the tent. He gave a sad smile to Natasha as he continued to speak. "The event was long ago and, while it *is* sad, we must keep moving forward. We can't let his death, or anyone else's, become meaningless." His face now turned to look at Isaac directly. "Despite the odds, our mission *was* a success. And because of that success, because of the research we obtained, because we went out there that night, we made a monumental step in this fight. Dyson helped pave the way toward understanding how to use augmentations. It was also the virus we installed that night, onto The Intelligence's network, that perhaps slowed them down long enough for us to stand a chance in this fight at all. If it weren't for him, and..." He breathed out a sigh of remorse. "And the many others who have lost their lives." He paused and looked at the ground in reflection, "then humanity would have been wiped out years ago." The tent went quiet.

Something stirred inside Isaac. He remembered the promise he told himself. *This would not be the end of my generation.* Isaac broke the silence. He felt eager to learn more about the man sitting in front of him. "That cape. You wear it because of him, Dyson. You wear it so you hold onto what he stood for, don't you?"

Wesley closed his eyes and let out a heavy and slow breath, before opening them again. "*Exactly*. I am glad you understand me so well, so quickly."

Natasha and Emma each had smiles on their faces. It was as if they all understood that a new ally just joined their cause at that moment. It was as if their rebel family just grew one member larger.

Dennis blurted in, "How did you get that cape though? The PC was right there!" He said in innocent, yet rude, abruptness.

Emma's eyes widened in disbelief at Dennis's lack of social awareness. She shot a look at Dennis, who just responded with a shrug of his shoulders and "What, doesn't anyone else want to know? The PC was *right* there next to him. How did he get it?"

"It couldn't move with its legs so damaged. It..." Wesley explained, "I can still remember the image of that machine so clearly, with its unfeeling, calculated movements. Even a wild animal who is injured may at least *try* to move when you get closer to it, in fear for its life. This *thing*, however," Wesley closed his eyes again, "it stayed on the ground, motionless, as if it had already decided with cold logic that it wasn't worth fighting." Wesley opened his eyes again. "It just kept turning its face toward me, even while I walked toward Dyson. Maybe it was gathering data on us, even when it could do nothing else. Still, I made my way carefully to my friend, never losing track of what the PC was doing, in case it could or would still decide to move, in case it would still choose to try an attack. As soon as I had the cape, we got in the car, and we left. We don't take extra risks."

Emma scolded Dennis with a sarcastic tone, "Satisfied with the answer, Dennis?"

"Sorry! Thank you for explaining, Mr. Wesley. Isn't the cape a little silly to wear on missions, though?" Dennis offered yet another tone-deaf question.

Emma couldn't help but say something. "It's Commander Wesley, Dennis, and why are you asking that right now anyway? Read the room!" Emma's face was now thoroughly buried in her palm, embarrassed for him.

Wesley answered anyway. "Although it *can* be a little silly looking, I wear it to this day to remember him—and to lead my soldiers with the same undying resolve that he showed me. Wearing it keeps me grounded. It reminds me to hold myself to his high expectations."

Sitting next to him, Natasha gave a little smile and put her hand on his shoulder. Wesley looked at her and smiled too.

"Why didn't you aim for the head, though?" Dennis said.

"Oh my god!" Emma shouted back.

"What?" Dennis replied, "That thing killed his friend, and who knows who else."

"It's okay, Emma," Wesley said, reassuringly. "But this will be your last question, understand?"

Dennis nodded his head in agreement. Emma shook hers in scathing critique.

Wesley went on to explain. "We do not take unnecessary risks on missions, especially when so many lives are at stake. When I fired those last three bullets, I aimed for where I had the best chance of hitting. The head is a small target, and that thing could still move. I went for the bigger targets and the ones that would stop it from moving: the legs. Then, the arm holding Dyson. If I missed, I would at least hit something else, such as the other leg or its torso. I knew that my first shot was the most important. After that, it would pay attention to me. So, while the PC was busy holding Dyson, I went for one of its legs first. This would slow it down. Then, another leg to disable its movement completely. Finally, its arm, so it would drop Dyson. Then, I *did* try to fire a fourth at the head, but I was out of ammo."

After hearing the commander's explanation, Isaac found a new respect for this Wesley Davis. It was incredible how well-trained his mind was. His attention to detail, his focus, his planning, and his determination. It reminded Isaac of his own father. Then, it hit him. *Where **is** he?* Through all of the events over the last eight years, he never heard from or about his father.

"Excuse me," Isaac interjected, "I understand this may not be the time to ask, but do you know what might have happened to my father?"

Everyone stopped what they were doing and turned their attention to Isaac.

"You see, when I was captured by a PC, my mother... she died. My dad, though, he was out of the house at the time. Is there a chance..." he paused, afraid of the answer. "Could he still be alive?"

Emma looked at her parents sitting across from them. She was afraid of the answer too—she knew what had happened to most adults who got caught.

Wesley and Natasha exchanged saddened looks.

"I'm sorry, Isaac," Natasha said. "While children were captured and brought into prisons for experimentation, the adults..." She didn't want to finish the sentence. "Billions were killed in the first year, in the first weeks even."

"No way," Dennis said in disbelief.

Natasha went on, "Only a few million adults were allowed to live, if that. We aren't really sure. And it was only because they had a microchip installed into their brains, controlling them to one degree or another, to be drones or emotionally manipulated guards like the ones in your prison."

Isaac was quiet. Then, "I understand." He took a deep breath in to calm himself before saying more. "While in prison, I just thought it was better to assume my dad was dead. Even if he *is* alive somewhere out there, he's not himself anymore—he would be just another drone, completely controlled by The Intelligence. And I think, somehow, it made my time in that prison easier to just think that he was dead. Better that, I thought, than to worry the whole time if he was still alive."

"I'm sorry, Isaac," Emma offered.

"What about you, Dennis? What about your parents?" Isaac asked.

"Never mind me! Carry on," Dennis replied, in his usual happy tone—though he clearly seemed to be hiding something.

Isaac was still curious about something, about the difference between the guards and the drones. "Why not just control the guards completely, like the drones?" Isaac asked.

"We can't be sure," Natasha said, "but what we think is that there are some tasks where human emotions may be better than a machine mind. A prison guard, for example, may be useful to The Intelligence with managing so many human prisoners, if those guards could feel like humans do. The prison guards are essentially like you and me, but with their amygdalas altered to be angry constantly. That's a part of the brain that controls emotions. So, we think, The Intelligence made cruel guards to help keep the prisoners better in check, to scare the children away from rebelling in any way."

Wesley continued. "With what little control they have, they're manipulated in any case to do exactly what The Intelligence wants. If the guards do resist, they would likely be killed or lose free will completely, becoming drones under The Intelligence's complete control."

Isaac sat there a moment quietly, then carefully chose his next words. "I understand. I guess I feel reassured that I did not kill the prison guards after all. They can't do much to help their own situations. They were prisoners, in a sense, just as I was."

Wesley looked surprised. He had never thought of them this way before. Or, at least, he gave up hope trying to save them. "Isaac," he said, "the guards have computer chips in their brains. They can't be saved, I think you need to know that. Even if you tried talking to them or saving them, The Intelligence lives in them and can take them over at any time. If even one guard found their way here, if we wanted to save one, then The Intelligence would know our location."

Emma spoke up, "It's either us or them, Isaac."

The tent looked at Isaac in a moment of quiet anticipation. What would he say in response?

"No," Isaac said firmly. He stood up. "I'm not letting *anyone* die *anymore*, no matter who they are. Even if we can't save them, we don't have to hurt them. What's our next mission?"

15 Different

Wesley was impressed with how Isaac was so sure of himself, even if he disagreed with the young man. "Your parents raised you well, Isaac. They would be proud. Since you are ready to join us on a mission now, could you come with us to our science tent? Once we know about the nature of your abilities, we can properly plan for our future missions together."

With Isaac having so many questions, he was prepared for some answers. "Let's go," he said with a determined enthusiasm.

As they left the tent together, the soldiers along the path stopped what they were doing as the group passed them. Wesley nodded his head respectfully to various soldiers who they came across. This time though, their attention was not on their commander, it was on Isaac. Whispers could be heard amongst them. Isaac strained to focus on what they were saying.

"*That's him!*" One soldier said excitedly to another.

"*He has augmentations no one's heard of.*"

"Isaac, they said. His name's Isaac."

"He doesn't get tired when he uses his abilities."

"I heard he's faster than Emma!"

He looked up to trace who was talking. It only just occurred to him that some of the people he was hearing were actually quite far away. "Can *you* hear what they're saying?" Isaac asked Dennis.

"Who?" Dennis had no idea what Isaac was talking about.

Isaac turned to Emma. "Emma, can you hear what they're saying about me?"

But Emma was just as confused as Dennis. "The soldiers?" She looked around as they walked. Some did seem to be leaning into each other's ears, whispering apparently—but she couldn't hear a thing. "You can hear them, Isaac?"

Natasha looked behind her shoulder at the three of them talking. "*Incredible*," she muttered.

Wesley smiled to himself, his eyes staring straight ahead to the science tent with excitement building in him. "Here we are." He opened the flap of the tent and stood outside as each of them entered. He took one more look around him at the path they had walked down. When he turned to look at the soldiers behind him, he realized they were all staring. Wesley gave a wave of his hand for them to return to their business and they all simultaneously looked away. He smirked, proud of their new companion and looking forward to the technology Isaac had waiting inside him, waiting to be discovered and shared. Wesley hoped and thought to himself, *Maybe his augmentations can be copied. Maybe we can use them on our other soldiers!* He let the flap of the entrance down and joined the others inside.

Natasha led the newcomers, Dennis and Isaac, around the edge of the tent. Tables sat with microscopes, graduated cylinders, laptop computers, and other tools and machines. Isaac had never seen some of the instruments before. She explained to them, "Here is where we study, create, and install augmentations, like those you saw with Emma."

"How do you get power for the computers?" Isaac asked.

"Good question. We have solar panels installed at the top of some trees. We wire them down to any tent we need energy for. They don't supply much, so most power is directed here, where we need it most." She put her face inches from Isaac's. "Are you ready?!"

Isaac was surprised by her sudden show of odd excitement and her invasion of his personal space. Stunned for words, he could only muster an "...uh." Still, her mood was contagious. Isaac matched her enthusiasm and pumped his fist into the air, as he responded with a triumphant "YEA!"

Then, abruptly, she stood up and quietly stated, "Good." She backed away and toned herself down quickly, leaving Isaac standing there, still with his fist clenched in the air, feeling a bit awkward standing with such an excited pose by himself. "Then sit there." Natasha went on. "We will start by taking a sample of your blood. Then, tissue samples."

He lowered his fist to his side and sheepishly said, "Alright."

"Find a seat, everyone," Natasha said as she took a syringe out from a cabinet drawer. "This will only take a couple of minutes."

They each pulled up and sat in chairs from the tables around the space.

Natasha walked him through the process. "Please relax, sit still, and place your arm on the table next to you. We'll start with a blood sample to run my tests on." With the help of a medical needle, a rubber band, and some tubes to hold the blood, Natasha gathered her sample. "No problem, right?"

"It didn't hurt at all," Isaac replied.

"Good. Now everyone, I will do more tests later, but let's see what we can immediately see under a microscope!" She took a small amount of blood out of the sample she collected, dropped it on a glass microscope slide, and put her eye up to the instrument to get a closer look. "Okay," she said out loud as she slowly turned the focusing knobs, making the view of the blood clearer. "Let's see what we have."

The tent was quiet, waiting for even the tiniest sign of surprise from Natasha. Maybe she would find something interesting.

"That's... *weird*," she said, confused.

Isaac stood up quickly. "What is it?!"

"This can't be right," she said, moving away from the microscope and looking at Isaac. "I don't see any sign of nanobots in your blood. It doesn't look like you have any of the signs we normally see in the presence of augmentations. Your blood... is normal, at least under a microscope."

Emma and Wesley both looked at each other in shock.

Isaac wasn't sure what she was talking about. "What do you mean? Nanobots?" He asked.

Dennis cut in, "Remember how The Maniac said he had stuff inside him?"

"Yea. So?" Isaac was still confused.

Dennis went on. "Well, we all do. We've got little machines inside of us."

Natasha chimed in as well, "Dennis is right, 'augs,' as you call them, are achieved by using nano-sized machines. They float in your blood, in your muscles, or anywhere they are programmed to enhance, to improve, to... augment. This wasn't always the case though. The first versions of human augmentations were not these microscopic machines we use now, but were instead achieved by replacing bones and muscles with robotic, machine alternatives." She let out a small sigh of disappointment. "The only way you wouldn't have nanobots in your blood would be if your augmentations were first-generation, that old technology. The problem is..." Natasha took a deep breath before saying her next words carefully. She stared at him straight on as she spoke, "You don't have signs of either nanobots *or* machine body parts. You're different, somehow."

Isaac thought back to how his parents told him he was special, different. "Maybe I'm not augmented at all," Isaac stated, causing everyone to look at him with confused expressions. "What if I was born different? When I was a kid, my parents told me I was special somehow, that I would be able to do things that others couldn't."

Natasha found it hard to believe that he was born with abilities that would awaken someday, without any influence at all from machines or other installed augmentations. But the fact that Isaac's parents told him he would be different, told him that he would eventually have abilities, was telling her that it must be something extraordinary, something she would never have suggested as possible. "Genetic modification. That would be the only other explanation I can think of."

I've never heard of it being done before, not like this." Natasha said, skeptically. "Before The Intelligence took over, about eight years ago, human beings *did* have the ability to do genetic modification, and we did use the technology, but only on foods. We made them resistant to disease, more resilient to extreme temperatures, and even improved their nutritional value. Never humans." She paused for a moment as if she just remembered something. "...However, there was *one* researcher."

Isaac was now more attentive to her next words, looking more intently at her as she spoke.

"There was a man in China that broke the laws at the time that banned human modification." Natasha finished her thought. "But all he did was make three girls resistant to a certain disease. He went to jail for it, and no one ever modified humans after that."

"Well, maybe I was modified too, like that? But maybe instead of being resistant to diseases, I was modified to have stronger bones, to have better muscles, eyes, lungs, and everything else that I'd need to do what I can do."

"It could be done." Natasha quietly whispered to herself. "Even though I've never heard of it before, the fact is that you do have abilities we've never seen. Whatever the reason for your abilities, it necessarily has to be something new, something never seen before. You *are* different, Isaac."

Even though Isaac agreed with her, that he was different, it somehow made him feel bad to hear being said out loud. He felt... alone, as if separated now from the people around him.

"Let me run some more tests on your blood, examine your DNA, your muscles, and other tissues before we make any conclusions. Wesley," she looked over at her husband, "if this is true, then we may not be able to recreate his abilities in our soldiers. I might be able to find out what the source of his abilities is, but I doubt we'll be able to figure out how to recreate it. And even if I could, if it is something we can do with genetic modification, it would only work on an unborn child, an embryo. In other words..."

Wesley stood motionless, waiting for what she would say.

Natasha continued. "Even if we got it to work, create a baby who would have abilities like Isaac's, we would have to wait *years*, maybe even 18 years, since Isaac is about that age, before we could use them in any way to help us."

"We could go extinct before then. We can't wait for this to be our solution," Wesley stated, sounding and looking disappointed.

Isaac turned to look at Wesley and noticed that he wasn't smiling, as he was when they first entered the tent. Seeing this, Isaac felt guilty. Even though it wasn't his fault, he felt somehow like it was, like he just let everyone down. "I'm sorry, Commander Wesley." Isaac then turned to Natasha. "Are we sure we can't change the soldiers' DNA? Why not change an adult right now to be like me? If Commander Wesley's DNA was altered like mi—"

"No," Wesley said sternly. He closed his eyes and breathed out a heavy sigh. "You can't modify a human adult and make the changes we are talking about."

Natasha explained further, "It's true. We never figured out how to modify people after they already turned into adults. And even if we could change something like hair color, or something else so simple, we're talking about changing almost everything about the person when talking about what you can do. We just don't have the technology to do it. I certainly don't know how. Plus, the equipment needed to make any changes happen... I just don't think we can do it. The world of science as we know it paused when The Intelligence took over. Maybe if we had more time, more people with the scientific knowledge to help..."

Wesley felt the need to conclude this conversation, one that seemed to be going nowhere fast. "The mission we ran with Dyson back then was to take the instructions for how to construct and code nanomachines and robotic limbs. Indeed, all we have now available to us is the knowledge for how to make augmentations. Genetic modification is not a choice."

"That was my job in the NIH," Natasha said. "I was one of many researchers across the world working on augmentation technology. At the time, we were just working on ways to improve the body and well-being of everyone. It already took everything we had just to improve our soldiers based on that technology, focusing all our resources just to keep up with what PCs could do."

"Up until you," Wesley added, "we have never seen abilities like this, not at this level. And now, it seems, you will be the only person who is ahead of our enemy. You are what will give us the advantage. You may just be our last, best hope."

Isaac suddenly felt that strange feeling again. He felt alone from everyone standing there with him. For the first time in his life, he felt truly and fundamentally alone, different from everyone around him. He felt even more alone than he did in his prison cell.

16 Preparations

"Isaac," Natasha said, seeing his concerned face. "It's okay. We're in this together. You're not alone, and we're here to support you, no matter what."

Isaac was surprised. It was almost as if Natasha could read his mind or know his feelings without him telling her. It meant a lot to him to hear that she understood how he felt and that she was trying her best to support him. He looked at Dennis and Emma for reassurance. They both nodded their heads in agreement with Natasha's sentiments and smiled.

"We're here with you," Emma said.

"Sweet as!" Dennis added.

Isaac looked over to Wesley, whose eyes were closed and who had become quiet. Everyone waited for what he would say next.

The commander breathed a deep, slow inhalation, held it for a moment, and let it out with an even more careful and slower breath. Without opening his eyes, he then spoke with what sounded like great caution. "Too little is known. I do not like the idea of moving forward with this uncertainty—not knowing what is fully happening with you." He opened his eyes. "However, time is as precious a resource as the number of soldiers we have or the augmentations we have access to. We may not know who you are, Isaac, or how your abilities work, but the simple truth remains: people are suffering and dying every day while we wait. We've spent how many years hunting for better augmentation technologies than what we have? How many years have we spent struggling, barely surviving, hoping to find something that would tip the scales in our favor? Then, we send soldiers on missions that accomplish next to nothing. Meanwhile, more and more people are dying. Children in prisons, experimented on."

The mood in the tent suddenly shifted. Curiosity and hope about Isaac's abilities were exchanged with sympathy for the victims around the world—and an urgency to help them.

Wesley continued. "While it may not be ideal to work with powers we don't fully understand..." He gave another deliberately deep breath in and out before choosing his next words. "It is clear that Isaac shares our goals. How many lives are lost or suffer each day when we fail to act? Thousands? Millions?" He stood up, absolutely driven by the cause in his heart.

Isaac's eyes were transfixed on Wesley. He felt captivated by this man's passion for saving people—as he too felt the same way.

"We can look at his DNA while we save children from those 'camps!'" Wesley, who was always calm, found himself now in a passionate cry for action. "Natasha!"

"Sir!" She immediately changed how she addressed him. He was no longer just her husband, Wesley. He was no longer just a father. Right now, he was the commander of the last humans on Earth.

He continued. "Sequence Isaac's DNA from the blood sample. We will move to the command tent to plan our next mission immediately."

"Yes, Sir!" Natasha bowed to Wesley and immediately moved to begin her work on the blood sample.

He then turned to face Emma, Isaac, and Dennis. "Soldiers. Follow me!"

"SIR!" They all said together.

With Wesley leading them, they all moved to exit the tent. Emma and Dennis followed close behind the commander, while Isaac stayed just a few steps back. As the others made their way through the flaps of the exit, Isaac wanted to say one more thing to Natasha before leaving. Standing with one foot outside, one in, he spoke through the beams of sunlight entering the tent. "Thank you," he said with simple, but utter sincerity.

She looked up from her work, pausing for a moment to appreciate his shared feelings.

He continued speaking as they looked each other in the eyes. "I finally know just a little bit more about what my parents were beginning to tell me. They said these abilities were passed down in my family, yet they never said how or why it was true." Isaac stopped for a moment to wonder if he should ask his next question. They had, after all, helped him so much already. Was it too much to ask for more? "Please, when you find out what you need from my blood, will you help me understand how my abilities work? Maybe, if it's even possible, could you help me find out why my family is so special?"

She responded without any hesitation. "Of course, Isaac. Like I said before. We are here for you. We are in this *together*."

He felt a weight lifted from his shoulders. Maybe he was in prison, alone, for too long. He had forgotten how important a few simple words of support and kindness could be to hear. He bowed his head slightly, out of respect and gratitude for Natasha. "Thank you, so very much." Isaac then left to join the others on the path outside.

Natasha, still sitting inside the tent at her table, looked toward the entrance and said to herself, "Good luck to you all." She turned her attention back to her scientific instruments, ready to continue her important work, before muttering a quiet last remark. "*They'll be okay.*"

"John!" The commander called out for his top lieutenant.

"Sir!" John's voice came from a spot not too far from where the group was walking on the path. He walked up to join them.

Wesley gave his instructions as they continued. "We are going to plan our next mission immediately. I need you to gather all the lieutenants to meet at the command tent *now*."

John knew this was urgent. Commander Wesley almost never planned for missions this quickly—usually opting instead to schedule meetings days in advance. "Sir!" He ran off to bring the other higher-ups together.

The others, who were scattered up and down the path, suddenly started tidying their clothes and finishing the tasks they were on. They knew whatever was being planned was important.

As the group walked along, they passed a large tent with several of the other prisoners standing around it, eating food.

"Oh hey, Guy!" Dennis said, happy to see him again.

Guy looked up with excitement, ran over, and hugged his best friend like he hadn't seen him in years.

"All our old friends doing alright? You come to join us?" Dennis asked as he hugged his friend back.

Guy nodded his head twice, to answer "yes" to both the first and second question.

"Can he come with us?" Dennis asked the commander.

"No. Without being able to speak, he can't communicate effectively with us on a mission. Other lives could be at risk if he joins us."

Wesley's answer was clear enough. "Sorry Guy, you stay here then. We'll be back, I promise."

Guy hugged Dennis tighter.

"GAH! GUY!"

Maybe too tight.

"Superrr... STRENGTH!" Dennis shouted jokingly as he used just as little of his augmented strength as needed to remove his friend's arms from their grip around his torso.

Isaac and Emma chuckled. Guy whined because he had to let go.

"It's up ahead. Let's go," Wesley stated, encouraging them to move on.

"Bye Guy!" Emma said, trying to help her father and commander.

"It was nice seeing you again," Isaac added.

"See you soon mate," Dennis finished.

Guy looked at them at their backs as they moved forward. Guy then whispered quietly to himself, "*Please come back safe.*" He watched them until they reached the tent.

"Okay!" Commander Wesley exclaimed as he entered the command tent, ready to begin instructing his new recruits on their next operation.

Dennis, Emma, and Isaac followed behind him inside, one after the other, circling around a table in the center alongside Wesley. Everyone but the commander sat down. Aside from the table itself, there was a computer sitting on it at the end, where Wesley was standing. Behind Wesley was a display screen mounted on a support beam at the back of the tent.

Wesley continued speaking. "My lieutenants will arrive shortly. When they do, I will give orders to each of them, assigning them tasks based on their specialties and normal duties. John is our staff specialist. He will be tasked with building a team of soldiers who he feels have the skills required for this mission."

"Should we be taking notes?" Dennis asked.

Wesley paused and just stared at Dennis.

Emma leaned over to Dennis and whispered, "We don't exactly have a fresh supply of paper out here."

Wesley went on. "Thank you, Emma. Dennis and Isaac, I am only explaining to you what is needed so you do not feel lost during this meeting. In any case, once the mission begins, you will not be able to look at notes. I want you to pay attention as best you can though, because on group missions..." He paused to emphasize his next point. "The safety of everyone depends on each individual person knowing exactly what the mission procedure is. Forget your role, or the role of your teammate, and it could cost lives, not just your own. So take everything seriously and try your best to remember every detail of your job.

"As I was saying, John is our staffing specialist and handles our rosters. Also, he is the next in line to command after me. If I am not around on a mission or if I am no longer able to command, he is responsible for leading you. We also have other lieutenants with other specialties and responsibilities. The explosives Emma used to break you out of prison were created by our explosives expert, Samuel. Our tech specialist, the one who prepares and handles night vision and other electronic gear, is Maddy." He stopped as everyone started to hear steps outside. "Good, they're here. The planning will start now."

John came in first, then another man and woman. Soon after them came a larger crowd of soldiers.

Isaac whispered to Dennis, "*Other lieutenants, maybe*."

They all circled around the table, some taking seats, with most staying standing along the walls of the tent. Everyone waited silently for the commander to begin speaking.

"Alright. Now that we are all here, I am going to tell you my plan so far." Wesley looked around the space, checking if everyone was present before going on. "As you all know, one week ago Emma was sent to scout and infiltrate the prison located 40 kilometers west of here—with the goal of gathering whatever information she could. She was also given orders to rescue as many prisoners as possible so long as it would not risk mission failure."

Wesley turned and gestured toward Isaac and Dennis, sitting next to him. "Emma was not only successful in gathering information, but she managed to save two prisoners who had been injected with augmentations that add to our mission capabilities." He placed both his hands behind his back, standing there with the straight posture of a leader determined to accomplish his mission.

"Isaac, in particular, is augmented beyond anything we have ever seen. What you have heard is correct. He *can* move faster than a PC, faster than Emma. He is also reported to have enough physical strength to penetrate over twenty or more levels of concrete with *a punch*." The tent gasped and whispered amongst themselves. Though they had heard the information before, passed down through John or other soldiers through word of mouth, it somehow became even more of a reality when told officially by their commander.

"Yes, it is all true." The audience became silent again, listening closely to their commander. "We have also recently discovered he can hear things from a great distance and with great accuracy. Isaac," he turned to him, "you could hear what at least one of our soldiers was whispering just now, couldn't you?"

"Well... yes, but... I couldn't hear *one* soldier clearly... "

The tent leaned in, many soldiers wide-eyed waiting for what he would say. One soldier whispered in the crowd to someone next to him.

Isaac went on. "I could hear *everyone* clearly. I know what everyone was saying." The room fell absolutely silent now. "That soldier there," he pointed, "he just said 'is this true? We've never had someone with this ability before.'"

Wesley too found himself surprised—inspired and excited even, enough to exclaim to the group, "With Isaac at our side, we can do more than free just a *few* prisoners—we can free every last child!"

The crowd cheered, pumping their fists in the air. "YEA!"

The commander held his hand in the air for silence. "I am glad you all feel how I do. Here is our mission plan so far." He turned around and switched on the screen behind him.

A digital map appeared, which looked like an outline of the prison. Isaac had never really known what the place looked like. Seeing it now from the outside felt strange. He had never realized just how large it was. Thousands of tiny boxes filled the interior, each one probably another cell with at least ten children, like his had. Isaac felt sick to his stomach. *Those monsters*, he thought. He imagined the faces of tens of thousands of children, wild but innocent, trapped in that place. He could see his own past in his mind, with his mother and father playing with him, smiling. To think, all those children, all those families with memories too, lost like he lost his. Isaac's arms trembled, his veins enlarged as they had when fighting at the prison before. Rage filled him.

"Isaac?" Emma noticed he was acting a bit differently.

He made a fist in each hand and looked at her, as serious as he had ever looked.

Instantly, she understood what he was feeling. She simply nodded her head.

"Emma, review your last mission for us," Wesley commanded.

"Sir." She stood up as he moved aside. "While our lieutenants have been debriefed on the details already, many of you, who will be part of our next mission, have not been told enough yet about what the inside is like. It is important that everyone knows as much as possible about the environment we are entering and what you may expect to find there. So," she faced the crowd from the head of the table, the prison blueprint behind her as she spoke, "from previous reports, the front entrance, located on the

Western side, was heavily monitored by multiple guards. When I arrived at the edge of the forest, just outside the fields surrounding the Eastern side of the prison, I set up camp for 24 hours first, to prepare and scout out the area before attempting infiltration." She gestured somewhere off-screen, to the right. "Fortunately, as we expected, the prison was no different from the information we gathered beforehand. Cameras were found at these locations," she pointed to several spots on the outline of the prison walls. "The fields were empty, and the walls had no additional security since our last report. With security guards watching the camera feed inside the prison, however, we needed my speed augmentations to avoid being seen by their monitors. The next problem was what I would do when I reached the walls. How would I get in?"

She pointed again to the blueprint. "We knew from these stolen designs that the alarm system only triggered automatically when gates or cell doors were broken. A blast through the Eastern hallway wall would not trip the alarm. However, the guard or guards watching the security monitors inside could manually sound the alarm if given even just a few seconds. Samuel's explosives were needed to create a hole, but I had to find my way to the security room at the ground level," she pointed to a room a few hallways to the left of the Eastern side, "here—and take out any guards who saw the explosion before they realized what was happening. Not only was speed needed to place the explosives, run to the forest, and run back when the hole was created, but I had to also get back in and make my way as quickly as possible to that security room—to take out the guards watching the cameras."

Dang, Isaac thought, *I was already impressed by her planning on the spot when she freed me. I had no idea how well planned in advance, and how risky, that mission actually was.*

She continued. "These parts of the mission went as planned. With a hole blown in the wall and no guards watching the security cameras, I searched the controls and turned off the automatic alarm system. This would allow me to then break into the cells without any guards noticing, except the ones near enough to hear the explosion. This meant, of course, that for this first rescue mission we had to target a cell that was as far from the others as possible—to avoid other guards hearing. While most of the prison, especially in the lower floors, have cells packed tightly together, the Eastern rooms are the most spread apart. Isaac here," she looked down toward him, as everyone in the tent did too, "he was found in that area, the one we planned on trying to break into first, purely by chance. We were lucky to have found him."

Isaac felt bad about this statement for some reason—as if he felt like he did not deserve to be freed more than anyone else. He even felt guilty for being freed first, and only by chance.

"I had to move quickly. Luckily, I did not find any guards on the way. Just before I planted the explosives on the wall to his cell, I destroyed the lights in the nearby ceiling and put on my night vision goggles. I would direct prisoners to escape while keeping an eye out through the cover of darkness. Along the way out, we fought more guards, freed two cells more worth of prisoners..." Emma paused suddenly.

Isaac realized why she must've stopped. He remembered The Maniac. He remembered how they almost lost their friends.

"Emma?" Wesley's concerned voice came over the quiet room.

She gathered herself and finished her thought. "Among the prisoners we freed was one who was mentally unstable. We call him 'The Maniac.' We don't know his real name, but he attacked us. The Intelligence had augmented him to be indestructible. Isaac, even at full strength, was only able to knock him away. He was... unhurt, however." She wasn't sure if it would be worth mentioning the next part, but she did anyway. "That last I saw of him was when we had escaped. We were probably a kilometer away when I saw him sneak out of the prison, through the hole we ourselves escaped out of."

Everyone in the tent looked nervously at one another. "Are you saying there's another enemy out there, wandering around who we can't hurt or stop?" One of the soldiers asked.

"Soldiers!" Everyone stood straight to attention. She had to make sure they didn't lose their composure. She had to make sure they were confident about their chances of success for the next mission they would be planning, for the mission to return to that place. "We don't have control over where he is. But, he isn't at the prison anymore. He will *not* be getting in our way. Apart from him and Isaac, we found another augmented prisoner, Dennis, who will be joining us and assisting the next mission with his augmented strength. Now, the last thing I have to share is that a PC ran after us during our escape. Isaac was able to defeat that PC in battle, alone—easily, I would like to add. And, as you know, no one has been able to even come *close* to defeating a PC before." She wanted to end her debriefing with some notes that would give them hope, especially after what she shared about the intimidating person known as 'The Maniac.'

"Thank you for the debriefing," Wesley said. "You may take your seat. So, we know there may be multiple challenges on a return mission to the prison. First, the wall on the Eastern side is likely fixed and more heavily guarded since it was hit by Emma. Second, the room where security cameras were monitored could have been moved or made more secure with more guards. Third, and most importantly, because the prison warden turned out to be a PC, and it saw Isaac's abilities, it may have sent the information back to The Intelligence. In other words, the prison could have multiple PCs now, or who knows, they could even have upgraded versions—stronger or faster than the one Isaac fought."

Isaac began hearing whispers of soldiers around the tent.

"*Maybe it's too risky,*" said one of them.

"*Isaac can fight a PC, but what if we're sent somewhere else in the prison, far away from him? He can't protect all of us.*"

"*We don't pick fights with PCs who know we're coming, especially upgraded ones.*"

Emma, Wesley, and Isaac looked at each other. They could tell the crowd was getting nervous, especially Isaac. It was starting to make them nervous too—well, except Dennis who just sat there with a big, confident smile on his face. Isaac heard one more whisper though that got to him.

"*If they gave him his abilities, then couldn't they be just as strong? Wait, what if he's one of them!*"

"NO!" Isaac shouted as he stood up, with rage still burning in his heart.

The crowd quickly stopped their whispers. Some backed up out of surprise, or maybe a little bit out of fear as well.

Isaac didn't hold anything back. "They took *everything* from me. My parents, both dead or turned into drones."

Wesley tried to calm him, "Isaac, it's okay—"

"No, Commander, they need to know!" Isaac's bold response shocked Wesley, whose eyebrows raised—he had never been rebuked by any soldier. Isaac even surprised himself at that moment. "What I have was not given to me in that prison. I am *not* one of them!"

Not even whispers began this time. The soldiers were stunned into silence, waiting for what he could possibly say next.

Isaac tried to calm his next words, taking a breath before speaking. "I was born this way," he said, in a much more relaxed tone. "We can't explain it all yet, but my abilities are beyond any augmentation that you have. In other words..." He paused on purpose, letting the silent crowd appreciate what he would say next. "... the PCs don't stand a chance."

For a brief moment, the crowd was quiet. That was, until a voice near the entrance cheered, "Yea!" That was enough to inspire the rest. "YEA!" The group roared together. Isaac looked at his friends. They smiled and patted his back in encouragement.

Wesley had to calm the crowd. "Alright! Settle down. Now that we are all on the same page, it's time to get to it." Wesley proceeded to lead the planning discussion. They would attack with about 30 soldiers from the South this time, rather than the East. With Isaac at the front, he would be ready for any PC or guard that would attack. Since the troops were trained for a variety of other skills, however, they would be needed on this mission to disable alarms, plant explosives, and open all of the cell doors from the security room. Wesley continued the meeting by describing everyone's roles and specific instructions for the mission.

"You know your responsibilities on this mission," Wesley stated. "Now let's prepare supplies for the days ahead. We will not waste any more time. We will meet again for mission departure in one hour!"

"SIR!" They all replied.

Wesley concluded the meeting with a cheer. "With Isaac's attack abilities, we can free everyone! Are you ready, soldiers?!"

"SIR!"

"You are dismissed!"

17

Unstable

The sound of trees swaying in the wind gave Isaac a sense of calm. The sound of footsteps—companionship and comfort. Emma and Dennis stood in front and behind him. The two of them were the closest people he had in the last eight years.

Why were these thoughts entering his mind now? He was confident in himself, in his own ability to fight anything that came their way, yet he began to feel some anxiety. He looked at the measly weapons the soldiers were carrying. Instead of guns, most of them had to carry crossbows. Wesley had told him during mission planning that the rebels ran out of most gun ammo years ago, that they had been forced to create what they could from the resources available to them—the trees. Only a few soldiers carried guns now, and only for the most important missions. The lack of firepower didn't worry Isaac days ago when they left for the journey, but as the mission was about to begin in earnest, he found himself now fearing for his friends' safety.

Breathe, Isaac thought, *take it in*. His senses once again took in what was happening right now, in this moment. *Some stress is okay, but not so much that you lose control. Focus on the present.*

The leaves of the trees continued to rustle—just as they had before. The forest greens, the browns of bark and dirt. Hearing and seeing these things somehow soothed him, giving him some peace of mind among his more stressful concerns.

His mind then shifted to thoughts of the prison. "Hmph," he lightly chuckled to himself, with renewed optimism. *It's so much better out here than the mind-numbingly white walls of that prison.* He thought about how funny it was to be returning there, the same place that he dreamed of escaping from for *so long*.

Remember this place. Remember the outside. This is what all those children are missing. Some of them might not even know a world exists out here at all. His courage and confidence grew as he rediscovered his motivation for being on the mission. *You will save them!* As he imagined the smiles of all the children's faces when they would finally see the outside, a smile came onto his face. *They'll see what's out here for themselves. The beauty of it, and the opportunities for a better life. They'll be free. And if anyone tries to hurt them in the world, I* ***will*** *stop them.*

The group must've been close to the forest exit now. Wesley, leading the pack, began to slow down. He held his hand in the air, quietly signaling for the group to stop with him. About 500 meters ahead, light shined brightly through a clearing between the trees—the forest exit. The grassy fields around the prison were right there in front of them.

The fields, Isaac thought.

The commander gestured for Isaac to come over. They weren't wasting any time. It was Isaac's moment, his moment to begin the first part of the mission—scouting. He would use his speed to explore the fields, to circle the prison walls and check for any signs of increased security, especially along the Eastern wall where Emma had first broken in.

Isaac, standing in front of Wesley, nodded his head, indicating that he was ready to go.

Everyone stayed back while Isaac walked carefully toward the forest's edge in front of them. No one knew where the guards, or PCs, could now be. For all they knew, there could be security stationed right near the edge of the forest, waiting for them to just poke out of the trees before attacking. Maybe they were waiting inside the prison for a second assault after last time. Listening close to every sound, looking ahead of him with great focus on every shadow and beam of light, Isaac began to walk slowly toward the grass, preparing himself for any surprise that could come next.

The group behind him was absolutely silent, holding up their crossbows, aiming at the spaces around Isaac's sides, in case anything suddenly came up to attack him. Wesley, John, and a couple of other lieutenants looked down the sights of their few pistols.

The only sounds now were of Isaac's footsteps on the forest floor. He did his best to avoid sticks or leaves, placing each foot on as much soft dirt as possible, but he couldn't avoid all of the noisy things completely.

Crunch

He stopped. *Wait*, he thought to himself. He turned his head slowly left and right. No sign of an enemy, not yet. He listened carefully.

The soldiers watched on as Isaac stood there, motionless.

Isaac paused, tuning in to every little sound he could hear. He was impressed with just how much his ears picked up. To a normal person, there was little to no noise at that moment. For Isaac, the forest and soldiers may as well have been yelling out to him. A bird from maybe a kilometer away was flapping its wings. He could hear it. Ants were crawling in a steady line into their colony underground, a few meters in another direction. A soldier swallowed hard. *They're on edge*, Isaac thought. He heard their heartbeats getting faster too, all 30 of them. They sounded like drums to him. Pounding. Pounding. Pounding faster. Then Isaac heard his own heartbeat begin to speed up along with theirs. *Too much!*

Isaac covered his ears with each hand and closed his eyes, trying desperately to block out the sound and sights of everything around him. The sounds though of the forest and soldiers were now replaced with the thunderous sounds of his own palms pressing tightly against his head.

THUMP THUMP THUMP

His heartbeat pumped fast and loud through the veins in his hands. The pressure of his palms made a low-pitched, tremendous roar against his ears. Isaac wanted to yell, he was in so much stress, but he wouldn't dare risk giving away his position.

BREATHE. Breathe. He needed to calm himself. Isaac tried to focus his full attention on only one sound and feeling, of his breath.

In...

As he breathed in, he heard his heartbeat slow down slightly.

Hold... Now, out...

His heartbeat slowed even further.

... again.

He did this a few times. Eventually, he felt comfortable enough to calmly lower his hands back down to his sides.

Breathe.

He turned his head around to look at the soldiers. By now, his heartbeat had settled, and he wasn't hearing everything so loudly. In fact, he could hear everything he had before, yet it wasn't too much for him now. Still, his change in behavior was bothering the others. It made them nervous. Their hearts were still racing, even if Isaac's was steady.

Wesley put up a thumbs-up sign, as if to ask Isaac how he was doing.

Isaac nodded his head and put a cautious thumbs-up in return.

The commander nodded back, silently, and returned his hand to the grip of his gun.

Isaac looked over to Emma. Her face looked the most concerned out of everyone's. *I'm sorry to worry you*, he thought sympathetically as he turned to look forward again, *but I can do this. I'm okay*. He moved his next foot forward.

CRUNCH

But he kept on going this time. *One step at a time. No more fear. No more hesitation.* The light between the trees became brighter. Isaac could see the fields clearly now. He found himself right at the forest's edge, with grass just in front of where he stood. He got into a sprinter's stance, then looked back at the commander one last time for the signal.

Wesley lifted one of his hands into the air, off from holding his gun. He waited a moment longer to check his surroundings before... *Down.* His hand began to fall to his side. As Wesley's hand struck downward, it signaled for Isaac to run.

Isaac's world turned once again into slow motion. Wesley's arm was still making its way down as Isaac was already far into the grassy plains. He squinted his eyes. He needed a moment to adjust for the sudden increase in brightness in the open daylight. Without stopping his run, he focused on the prison walls ahead of him, in the distance. His eyes slowly opened up—and he saw the beautifully paused world around him.

More than ever, Isaac now felt at peace, even while running near such danger. Everything was just so quiet, so still, so tranquil. Even the air itself seemed motionless. It was as if there was no wind at all. The grass too seemed frozen in time. He realized he was perceiving time slower than he ever had before, and moving that much faster as well.

Wait. He stopped running. The world around him still stayed frozen even as he stood there. Though he knew time was important on this mission, it seemed that he now had time to spare. Things weren't just moving in slow motion like it had in the past. Now his environment genuinely seemed to stop altogether. Isaac ripped a blade of grass off from the ground. Lifting it to shoulder height, he let go.

The grass appeared to stop in mid-air. It didn't move in the slightest. Isaac waited five seconds, putting his face up close to the falling grass to observe closely even for the littlest of movements. Nothing. Not one millimeter down. *What's happening to me? First my hearing, now this? I... I can't control it!*

Isaac tried to speed things up a little. Still, nothing moved. He tried running around the blade of grass. *Maybe moving fast is the key?* He wondered.

No change.

Well, I guess there's nothing I can do for now. I may as well look around and do my job.

He began to walk backwards, toward the prison walls, while looking at that blade of grass floating mid-air. Still, nothing was changing. He turned around to face the prison. *I'll save energy. I'll walk.* He was so distracted that he hadn't realized it before—the walls were completely repaired. *Makes sense,* he thought, *the East side must have been fixed to prevent future attacks. But where are the guards?*

He could clearly see that there was no security stationed outside or anywhere. The only security he noticed were the cameras mounted on the tops of walls and facing out to the fields. *Not like they can see me anyway.* He waved at one of them, having a little fun with his newfound speed. *No way the cameras could see someone moving this fast.* He kept walking, until he was right up against the East wall. *Yup, completely fixed. No hole.*

He began to walk around the prison, clockwise. The South side, where the attack was planned, was the most important. He had to check there first. However, it was the same as it was on the East side. No guards, only cameras. Well, except for the West side.

A road led into this front entrance. Several guards sat in booths on either side of the road as it ran into the prison. *I guess that's where my food must have gone through during all those years. The prison had to get supplies in from somewhere.*

Isaac continued walking. The North wall was identical to the South and East. No guards. Only cameras. He finally found himself back where he started, on the Eastern side. He looked into the fields, trying to find that blade of grass he had dropped in the distance. He spotted it. *Still just floating there, just like I left it.*

He looked at the wall next to him.

Pat pat

Touching the wall with his hand, something felt off. *Shouldn't this feel cold? I don't feel any temperature. It feels so weird.* Then he realized, stunning himself, *I'm moving so fast, the heat doesn't have a chance to move from my hand into the wall! That's why I don't feel the cold when I touch it. Woah.* Then he noticed something else was unusual as he leaned against the wall.

Strange. It looks like concrete, but it feels... soft? He pressed a bit harder. With no effort whatsoever, his gentle pushing resulted in a hand-shaped hole—bits of concrete crumbling to dust as he pressed. *What is happening to me?* As he took in how amazed he was by his own abilities, the wall suddenly stopped being so soft. As it got harder, it started to get cold as well.

"Uh-oh," he said out loud.

BOOM BOOM BOOM BOOM

Several loud booming waves of sound reverberated through the air. Isaac covered his ears—it was so loud.

What was that?!

He looked up at the walls and noticed a camera had turned to face him.

"NO!" He yelled.

He did his best to run as fast as he could back to the forest. For some reason though, he wasn't moving nearly as quickly as before. The world was in slow motion, yes, but not frozen as it once was. He lost some speed, maybe a lot of speed.

On his way back, he noticed the blade of grass he had dropped before. It was just an inch off the ground now, about to land. He tried to run as fast as he could. *Any moment now, the alarm will—*

ERRrrrrr...

Too late. The alarms rang, albeit more slowly to Isaac's ears.

He was getting close to the forest. From where he was, out there in the bright daylight, the inside of the forest appeared dark. As he entered, his eyes adjusted until the figures of the soldiers became clear. They still looked like they were putting away their weapons to only just start to move. For the minutes that Isaac was out in the fields, the soldiers had only experienced seconds of time passing.

Emma used her speed to speak with him before he met up with the others. "Isaac! What happened?" She said frantically, in super speed.

He felt ashamed. "The cameras saw me. I'm so sorry. I did my best."

"It's okay, Isaac. What's done is done. It's only been a couple of seconds since the alarm rang, anyway. Really, don't worry about it. But what happened out there? How did they see you?"

"I don't know. I..." He paused for a moment to consider how best to explain things to her. "Time seemed to stop for me at first. I don't know how I did it, but I moved faster than I *ever* had before."

Emma was shocked. "Woah."

"That's what I thought too," he replied. "Then, when I was at the prison walls, the ability suddenly stopped. Time went closely back to normal, though still somewhat slow, and when I ran back here."

Emma didn't know how to respond.

"That's just it," Isaac went on, "I don't know if I can control my abilities. I don't know if I can do this. What if I can't control it when—"

"STOP!" She quickly interrupted him. "You *can* do this! You're moving fast like I am right now after all. You have some control."

Isaac realized she was right. "Yea... I am." Though he wasn't totally confident about it.

She went on, "maybe it's not as fast as what happened to you out there, but it's still good enough for this plan to work. Remember," she put her hands on his shoulders, "you're not the only one with special abilities or skills here. We're highly trained and we have a plan." She gave an encouraging smile.

Isaac felt a little lighter now, as if the pressure and self-doubt he was experiencing was somewhat lifted by her support. "Thank you, Emma. Thank you for helping me stay grounded."

"Good," she began breathing heavily, "now if you're done being emotionally supported, I'm starting to lose energy. Can we join the others and attack already?"

"Yes, ma'am!" He replied enthusiastically.

Emma suddenly appeared as if she returned to normal speed. From Isaac's view, she looked like she was now moving in slow motion like the other soldiers. Isaac now tried to return to normal speed with her... but couldn't.

"Not again!" He yelled out loud. "Ugh!"

He tried walking past Emma and over to Wesley and the soldiers. Still nothing.

"What if I... t-a-l-k... i-n... s-l-o-w... m-o-t-i-o-n?"

Still. Nothing.

Isaac put his palms against his face in frustration. Talking to himself, he tried to figure out how he was going to return to normal speed. "Okay. Think, Isaac, think."

Of all things, his mind went back to an old memory. A lesson from his father, so long ago.

He closed his eyes. "That's right," *focus on something else...*

18

Control

10 years ago

"Breathe." Isaac's father told him. "Take it in."

"Why do we do this again?" Isaac said, impatiently sitting in the backyard with his eyes closed, as his father stood behind him.

A bit distracted, however, his dad was caught looking up at the slightly cloudy, blue sky. He felt peaceful.

"Dad!"

Still looking up at the sky, smiling to himself, his answer was... silence.

Isaac knew his father's personality well. His dad liked to do this kind of thing all the time—responding to Isaac's questions with as little information as possible. It was his way of challenging the boy to explore ideas on his own, to find his own answers to the questions he had. Isaac knew what his father was trying to do, but still, he was young—and not very patient.

"Dad, I'm just not getting it." He opened his eyes and turned around to look at his father. "Why do you want me to do this all the time? The other kids at school don't do this at all."

His dad paused. "Isaac." His body turned toward his son. He then took his time answering, seemingly finding comfort in just standing there, breathing slowly in and out.

Isaac stared at him with frustration, waiting for the justification behind all of this meditation. His father offered a somewhat mysterious explanation though: "You will need this training to help you—for when you get older. You're special and, besides that, you will need incredible patience for your life ahead."

Isaac had heard he was 'special' in the past from his parents, and he was getting tired of hearing it. "What does that even mean, 'when I'm older?' What makes me special? What life will I have?"

His father looked up at the beautiful blue sky once again. "These are just the right questions to ask. In time, you will find your answers. And a lot of these answers will only make sense to you after you experience things yourself. You will get older. You will have the ability to do things others cannot, and this training will help maintain control, to maintain your sanity when you—"

Isaac never heard this part before. "When I... what?"

His dad seemed to want to take back what he was about to say. "In any case, when you do end up feeling overwhelmed, when you can't handle what is happening around you or inside of you, what do you do? What do you do when that happens?"

"Well," Isaac replied, "If I have big feelings, I can choose to do something else. Or, I could try to stop the things that are bothering me."

"Sure. Well..." His father paused yet again, as if to intentionally slow down the conversation and give his son time to think. "Knowing how to focus on 'something else,' as you put it, is what this training is giving you. This breathing, learning to pay attention to it, *that* is your something else, when *nothing* else works. When everything around you or inside of you is out of control, you always have your breath to return to, to give you back a sense of control."

Isaac could only think of one thing to say in response. "What? I still don't understand."

Isaac's father's thoughts begged to be shared with his son. *I'll be able to tell him more as he matures. He must face some things alone, for now. He's too young, too inexperienced.* "One day you will understand. Please, trust me for now. Breathe. Listen. Allow yourself to feel everything happening without getting bothered by it all. Practice what it is to hear things, feel things, look at things. Just listen to it all. Just take it in. Allow it all to pass through your thoughts without judging any of it. Regrets, hopes, anger, sadness, happiness. Observe them, just observe them, as you sit, as you relax into your breath."

Isaac turned back around, away from his father, and faced forward again. Still sitting down, he gently closed his eyes, breathing and trying to 'observe' his feelings as they came to him, as his dad suggested.

"Meditation will give you control, Isaac. If your thoughts get to be too much," his dad went on, "if they overwhelm you, then you always have your breath to return to. You always have that 'something else' to focus on from the things that are bothering you. For now, allow yourself to take it in, whatever 'it' is that you are taking in, and then..."

Present day

Let it go, Isaac thought to himself, finishing the sentence his father had spoken to him those years ago. He opened his eyes. The soldiers, previously appearing to move in slow motion, now began to return to normal speed.

A soldier let out a *yelp,* surprised by the sudden appearance of Isaac in front of the group. Even Wesley showed a bit of shock, as his eyes flinched and he stuttered before talking. "I... Isaac."

"Commander Wesley! I'm reporting in!" Isaac spoke up quickly and loudly, awaiting orders from his leader.

Wesley called out to the 30 or so soldiers. They would begin the next stage of the plan. "Okay! First, Isaac, what can you tell us about the state of the wall?"

"Sir. Our planned target, the South side, has no guards. The West side has several guards stationed at the front entrance. The North side has no guards. Finally, the East side has been completely fixed but also appears to have no guards. However, a camera spotted me while I was located at the East side, so security may be headed there." Isaac said this last part with a bit of shame in his voice, embarrassed for being spotted, triggering the alarm, and risking the safety of the mission.

Without waiting for any confirmation from the commander or anyone, Emma ran into the fields, placed explosives on the South wall, and ran back to the forest next to Isaac.

"Done!"

Wesley fumed in anger. "Lieutenant Emma! Wait for my command!"

Emma responded, "We talked about the plan before we left. If there were no guards on the South side, then we would go there. We may as well save time with orders and just go where we need to!"

Her father scolded her reasoning. "Even if that is true, we *must* follow the chain of command, or we will make mistakes. I may change plans at any moment if I see fit. You should understand this. Do *not* do that again!"

She looked down to the ground, suddenly feeling guilty about what she had done. *I guess I'm just used to being on missions alone and making my own decisions*, she thought. Then...

BOOM!

A loud explosion rang off in the distance, from the southern wall of the prison. Isaac looked over and saw a rising cloud of dirt and smoke.

The commander called his orders out. "This is it, people! Listen up! I'm in front. Maddy, take the middle. John, take the rear. Soldiers, if we separate, you will stay in your designated squads with your lieutenants. Isaac, you're with me for now! Stick to the plan and listen to your lieutenants for all orders. Stay close! MOVE! MOVE!"

Wesley started running through the forest up to the fields, with Isaac and the rest shortly behind him. As he reached the forest's edge, he signaled for everyone to stop. He took out binoculars and looked across the area and at the prison, trying to see if there was even the slightest movement. Oddly enough, even with all of the noise from the sirens, there was nothing yet.

Wesley continued his orders. "Looks like they are holding position inside the prison for now. Let's go!" He signaled for the group to move forward. He entered the empty fields, picking up some speed as he went. Just as the entire group was about halfway across, he motioned to Isaac.

This was it. Isaac tried hard to remember every instruction given to him during their mission planning. Since Emma got tired easily, they would take turns using their superhuman speeds. Isaac closed his eyes for a moment and breathed once in and out. *Focus. Run fast.* Opening his eyes again, he ran ahead at a speed similar, or maybe slightly faster, to Emma's. As the world slowed down around him, he made his way toward the hole blown open on the south side.

The hole was about the same size as the one Emma created on her last mission, about two or three people wide. He slowly poked his head inside the halls. His eyes took a moment to adjust to the darker interior. Straight ahead of him were metal bars. *A cell,* he thought. Looking left, he saw a hallway with even more cells, but no guards. He turned his head to the right.

AH! He kept his surprise silent and in his head only. Though frozen there, a prison guard was just a couple of feet away, with an arm drawn back, holding a baton, preparing to attack anything that made its way through that hole.

Withdrawing his head, Isaac ran back to the soldiers. Moving into a position next to Wesley, he felt calm and in control of himself and his abilities. Without needing to close his eyes or trying very hard at all, he let time speed up once more. As the group's speed began to sync up with his, he started to move his own legs to match the pace of theirs as they ran. Soon, he was running alongside them.

From the perspective of the soldiers though, what happened amazed them. To them, there was suddenly a blur that appeared out of nowhere, which quickly materialized into a person.

Isaac didn't waste any time. He shared what he found with Commander Wesley. "Sir. There is one guard inside the South hole, on the right, holding a baton."

Wesley responded with a simple order. "Isaac. Take him out."

The group, now just a couple hundred feet away, watched again as Isaac zipped there and back in a matter of seconds.

"Done. The guard is unconscious," Isaac stated proudly.

The soldiers were shocked at Isaac's abilities, at how fast he was able to move. They looked over to their commander, waiting to see how *he* would react. Would he be as surprised as they were?

"Isaac..." Wesley paused. He was lost for words. But they didn't have time to stop and discuss. They quickly made their way to the hole in the prison wall. Wesley gave the signal for the group to stop and hold position. They huddled around the wall outside as Wesley gave a signal for one of the soldiers.

TWANG

Isaac's stomach dropped. "What... what did you do?" He asked, with confusion, fear, and maybe a bit of anger.

The soldier exited the hole, loading his emptied crossbow with another bolt.

Wesley looked at Isaac and replied, "We can't risk letting them live. Unconsciousness is not enough if they can wake up during our mission. It poses a risk."

Isaac was stunned at the brutality of what the soldiers had just done, at the commander's choice.

As Wesley gave the signal for the group to enter, and as the group filled the hallway of the prison, Isaac could only manage to stare at the dead guard on the floor.

He uttered quietly to himself. "Sorry. I'm so... so sorry." A tear rolled down his cheek.

19

Hope

With a heavy heart, Isaac looked up at his allies—the rebels. *Is this what we are, the last hope for Earth? Are we killers?*

"Isaac." Wesley, standing behind him, placed a hand on his shoulder. "I can tell you care about them, but they're already gone. As long as they have chips in their heads, they're only threats to those of us who are free."

A tear gently went down one of Isaac's cheeks. He was still looking down at the body.

Wesley took his hand off Isaac's shoulder as he readied his gun. "We have to mo—"

"*No more*," Isaac interrupted in a firm and angry whisper.

"What?" Wesley was speechless.

Isaac turned around and wiped his cheek. "**Sir**," with his angry intentions becoming clear, the respect he had for the commander gone from his voice, "tell everyone to stop." Isaac's veins bulged.

Lieutenant John called out from several meters away, "Sir, orders?!" The soldiers were positioned to face in each direction of the hall, crossbows and pistols aimed, prepared for guards who could attack them at any moment from either direction.

The commander called out, "Everyone, hold!" Sirens still blaring.

Dennis and Emma glanced at each other, concerned that something wasn't right. They walked up to Wesley and Isaac, who were now locked staring at each other. Wesley, trying to understand what was going on in Isaac's mind. Isaac, trying to show how passionate he felt about whatever was going through his mind.

"Isaac?" Emma could see he was angry, but she didn't know why until... "Oh." She saw the dead guard at Isaac's feet. After what they had been through together, she knew full well how her friend felt at that moment. "Isaac, this is a long mission." She tried to reason with him, to explain how this situation was different than the last time they were there. "When we were just escaping last time, you could knock someone out and not worry about it. This is different. We could be here for hours, or more. The knocked-out guards could just wake up and come for us. We just don't know how long we will be fighting for. People could die. Everyone could die. We have to kill the guards. It's them or us. It's them or all of humanity."

Isaac's veins slowly returned to normal. His face appeared less serious, less angry than before.

"That's correct." Wesley added. "Emma's exactly right, Isaac. We don't *want* to hurt anyone. We just can't take risks."

Isaac closed his eyes. He remembered how his father was always calm. *I guess I get my anger from my mom.* He took a deep breath in and out and opened his eyes. He looked at Emma. "I understand why you feel you have to do it. But..." he turned to look down at the guard below him, "if you give me a moment, I can finish this mission right now." He softly turned his gaze back to the commander, with a renewed sense of calm and confidence. "Sir," his tone now quieter than before, "it doesn't even have to take long. I can finish this mission without anyone getting hurt."

"What are you talking about?" Wesley asked, genuinely confused. "This mission is planned to take at least several hours. With the alarm on, we could be facing all the guards in this building. If we want to free the tens of thousands of prisoners here, and not lose any soldiers, we have to do it right. We have to take our time and fight off each enemy as they come."

Isaac tried to counter. "No, I—" Before he could finish, one of the soldiers called out.

It was John. He yelled, "several guards, down the hall! Incoming!"

Wesley immediately turned around, abruptly stopping their conversation before it could be resolved. Three large figures were running toward them, batons in hand. With no time to spare, he gave his orders. "FIRE AT WILL!"

TWANG TWANG TWANG

Several bolts were fired from their crossbows.

Isaac sped up his perception of time, as did Emma. He looked at her and shook his head, telling her to stay back. He ran past the now-frozen Wesley and his soldiers, and made his way over to the bolts still flying through the air, hurtling toward their targets, toward the prison guards. He grabbed each of them in mid-air. Then, he walked toward the guards. He took each of their batons easily enough. Finally, after taking away all weapons, he let time return to normal.

The guards suddenly stopped running, totally surprised by the weapons missing from their hands and by this person who just as suddenly appeared in front of them, holding those very weapons.

"Hey! STOP!" Wesley shouted from a hundred feet away.

One of the guards tried to scare Isaac. "What do we have *here*?"

"How did you take our weapons, little one?" Another guard asked, trying to sound intimidating.

"Who cares? He dies!" The third guard grabbed Isaac by the arm.

Isaac only smiled kindly. "No one is going to die today. Not even you."

Without even needing to throw a punch, Dennis's fist and Emma's foot landed squarely on the two other guards' chins. They fell to the ground, knocked out cold by Isaac's friends.

The last guard left, still clutching Isaac's arm, stammered his next sentence, no longer so intimidating. "Wha... what was that about? How—"

"Hold him still, Dennis," Isaac commanded.

Dennis was happy to comply. "Sweet as."

"GAH," the guard moaned.

Dennis grabbed him by both forearms and squeezed... *tight*.

Emma added her own command, "keep him on the ground too. Can't have him trying to run away or kick us or something."

Again, Dennis was happy to do as he was told. “Yes, ma'am.”

THUD

Dennis knelt down to the ground, pulling the guard’s arms and body down with him. They were eye to eye, both on their knees. Dennis winked at the confused guard. “How you doing there mate?”

“What are you all doing?!” Wesley shouted from down the hall. “Lieutenant Emma!” He led his soldiers over to the three friends and the guard. The sounds of almost 30 pairs of feet and military gear running across the hard floor filled the space.

Isaac turned around to face the commander as he approached. Before Wesley could open his mouth, Isaac got the first words in, “We don’t have to kill anyone.”

“Isaac...” Wesley slowed down, with the soldiers standing close by, weapons aimed at the guards—ready to fire, ready to kill. “We can’t operate this way. The lives of the soldiers, the prisoners, are all at risk. We can’t lose them because you want to save some guards who will only harm the mission. So, why are you doing this? Tell me you have a good reason.”

Isaac replied, “I was trying to tell you before. I can take care of everything, and we don’t have to be here all day or let anyone get hurt for it to work.”

Emma added on, "Commander, sir, Isaac was sharing something with me when he came back from the forest. His abilities, they’ve increased. I think, no, I *believe* he can do this.”

Wesley looked at Isaac. The soldiers looked at each other with surprise, alarms still ringing in the background, reminding everyone of the ongoing threat to their safety. “What does she mean?" Wesley asked. "What can you do?" He was losing patience by every moment that passed.

Isaac replied honestly. "As far as I can tell, I can run faster than sound. I... I don't actually know how fast, but time wasn't just slowed down—it froze."

The mouths of several soldiers dropped open in disbelief.

Wesley stepped right in front of Isaac, putting their faces inches away from each other. "Can you control it though? If you can look me in the eyes and tell me you are certain that you are able to control your abilities, then I will let you. So, can you control it? Are you sure?"

Emma, Dennis, and all the soldiers looked at Isaac, waiting for an answer that could mean the end of an otherwise dangerous and long mission.

Isaac took a long moment to think, maybe too long for the comfort of the people around him. But he did his best to show them a carefully truthful answer. "... I don't know for sure. But let me try."

Many soldiers groaned in disappointment. They, and Wesley, needed a more certain reply.

Wesley only sighed and stood up straight again, moving a few feet back from Isaac's face. "John's squad, kill the guards."

Isaac's veins grew alongside his determination, yet again. As five soldiers began to pull their fingers on the triggers of their weapons, Isaac disappeared, along with all of the soldiers' weapons, and the guards.

RUMBLE RUMBLE

Just then, a tremendous roar of noise filled the prison. Everyone covered their ears. It lasted only a moment, but was astoundingly loud. The group slowly took their hands off their ears when the sound appeared to dissipate.

"It's done." Isaac's voice came from behind. Everyone quickly turned around.

Wesley was the only one still facing forward, away from Isaac. With his back turned to him, he spoke. "What do you mean? What's 'done'?"

His answer was simple. "They're free. I did it."

Everyone seemed confused, especially Dennis. The guard who he was holding suddenly had metal bars wrapped around his arms and legs, keeping the guard from moving around. Dennis let go.

Emma was smiling the biggest smile of her life. She knew Isaac well, and what he meant when he said he "did it."

Isaac couldn't help himself. He smiled too. "46,520. I counted as I went. Every floor. Every cell."

"I freed them all."

Wesley spun around and looked at Isaac in disbelief. "You what?"

Isaac just smiled quietly and pointed at one of the nearby cells, as if to say 'go and check yourself.'

The commander walked over to it. The bars of the cell were bent wide open, wide enough for all of those inside to walk right out. The prisoners, scared and confused, looked at Wesley standing in front of them. He walked to the next cell, checking if what Isaac said was true. It was the same—the bars bent with a wide gap for prisoners to walk through. "You..." Tears started to run down Wesley's face. He ran over to Isaac and picked him up excitedly. "You did it!"

Emma was surprised. She had never seen her father so emotional before.

"You actually did it!" He shouted again.

Isaac responded. "Yea! But um... could you put me down now?"

"Oh, sorry." Wesley collected himself and let Isaac down politely. He immediately shook his hand instead. "Every cell?" He had to double-check, still in disbelief.

Isaac nodded his head and confirmed as he shook the commander's hand. "Every cell."

"Well..." Wesley took his hand back and gathered himself as he stood up straight, trying to look like his usual serious self. "It will take a few hours to split up and run through every floor, to lead the prisoners out of the building. And there are still guards throughout the prison to consider. We still have to watch out for them. SOLDIERS! LET'S MO—"

"Wait," Isaac interrupted, "that's taken care of too."

"Excuse me?" Wesley asked.

"Well, while I was going through and opening the cells, I ripped bars out of the wall and wrapped them around every guard's arms and legs. They shouldn't be able to move while you go around and guide the prisoners out. OW!"

Dennis must have found his way around to Isaac during the conversation. He had slapped his friend on the back, hard. "Good job, mate! Wow. You really are strong now. That was my hardest slap. Hey, why wrap metal bars around everyone? Why not just run each of them outside somewhere or, better yet, take all the prisoners outside for us.

"He had over 40,000 people to take care of!" Emma added, as she made her way to the two of them.

"Not just that," said Isaac, "I'm moving faster than ever. I didn't know if..." He stopped to show how much caution he had in his next words. "... I didn't know if trying to move people at that speed could hurt them. Who knows what would happen if I even tried to *hit* the guards? Something else happened today that showed me I should be careful."

"What was that?" Wesley asked, nervously.

"Well, when I was scouting the fields outside, something strange happened. I had leaned, at one point, against the concrete walls. What was weird was that they felt soft. I even left a dent. If I tried moving or pushing someone, even a little bit, when moving that fast, I'm worried my hand could go right through them. The only thing I *could* feel comfortable doing to stop the guards was to grab the metal bars around me. Even then, they felt so soft, and so easy to rip out and bend."

Dennis raised his eyebrows and slowly pulled his hand away from Isaac's back.

Isaac laughed and looked at his friend, who jumped a little bit in fright. "It's okay, Dennis, it only happens when I'm moving really, really fast."

"No," Wesley added, "you can't be sure of that just yet. Isaac, you should avoid touching anyone until you have time later to fully test your abilities, at all speeds."

"Oh. You make a good point," Isaac agreed.

"For now," Wesley continued, "everyone, let's go through the building, and show these prisoners the way out!"

"SIR!" The crowd cheered together.

About 30 minutes later

John reported to his commander at the hole in the south wall, as many prisoners were starting to move toward the exit. "Alright, sir, we should have just about finished sending soldiers to each floor. We should be expecting the building to begin emptying soon."

"Good. Isaac," Wesley spoke to him as they stood together at the exit, "you did great today. You did more than just prevent us from having to fight the guards and risk harm—you also saved us a great deal of time. I never would have thought our group could have split up, one or two soldiers to each and every floor like this, all at the same time. This mission could have lasted an entire day or more. Who knows who could have died in the process or if we would have been successful at all? Now, it will be only an hour, with no one dying today."

"Yea, I—" Suddenly, Isaac clasped both of his hands around his ears.

"Isaac, what's wrong?" Wesley asked, confused.

But Isaac couldn't hear him. While the siren was easy enough to deal with when it was only that, now Isaac could hear the footsteps of 46,520 prisoners moving at the same time, along with the groans, heartbeats, breathing, and occasional spoken words of them all.

Breathe. Breathe. I... It was too much. Isaac started to shake violently.

Emma, standing nearby, tried calling out to him. "Isaac!" She knew he was being overwhelmed. *Maybe if I shout louder than the noises he is hearing, it could be something he can focus on?* She thought that way, anyway.

Dennis tried holding Isaac still, to hold him tight and at least help him feel comforted.

WHOOSH SLAM

Dennis was thrown into a wall nearby and fell to the floor. "Ow. Not okay, mate."

They watched as Isaac's body vibrated, shaking so fast that he appeared as a blurry image.

"AHH!" The jarbled-up scream came from Isaac's image. He looked as if he was appearing in and out of sight. Each time he faded in and out, a glowing light pulsed around him.

WHIRR WHIRR

"AHHhh!"

Wesley felt the space heating up around him. "Everyone get back! Don't get close to him!"

Isaac's blurry image moved randomly—crouching down, standing up, and moving back and forth between a nearby cell and the prison wall. The prisoners who had been coming down the hall had now stopped in their tracks, too afraid to walk into whatever it was they were seeing ahead of them.

He let out one more scream before suddenly vanishing within a final flash of light.

Everyone stood completely still, utterly terrified if they would be moving into an unseeable but deadly fast superhuman

—everyone, except the prisoners. They didn't know about Isaac's abilities. With no concern, they started to run through where Isaac used to be.

Before Wesley could say anything to warn them, they were already at the exit, unharmed. Looking between each other, Dennis, Emma, and John all froze in fear. Wesley, however, stayed calm and seized this opportunity to move. "You three! Make your way to the exit!"

Dennis, who had only ever shown real concern when Guy was in danger, now looked worried for his new friend. "Isaac?"

"Isaac!" Emma screamed over the noise of all the prisoners running out, hoping he would hear her from wherever he was. Desperate to find him, she sped up her perception of time. As everyone slowed down around her, she looked for him. "ISAAC!" She called out one last time, but no response was heard. She ran down the hall, down the stairs, and checked wherever she could. Finally, she made her way back up to the first floor.

Breathing heavily, tired from using her speed, she told Dennis the bad news. "I can't..." *pant pant* "... find him."

Wesley tried to comfort her. "Wherever he is, we have to keep moving. We have tens of thousands of lives waiting for our help. I know it's hard, but let's go, Emma."

She stood up, realizing he was right, as he usually was. "Okay, Dad."

He didn't correct her for calling him "Dad" in front of John or the other soldiers. He just hugged her and helped her along.

As they made their way out, prisoners kept on moving through, filling the fields more and more. Many simply stood there, staring at the sky and the trees in the distance. Others kept on running toward the forest, likely not knowing where they were going except *away*.

John and Wesley stood next to each other on either side of the hole, trying to move the prisoners along to clear the way for others to leave as well.

"Sir!" John said. "Should I go in to check on the soldiers inside, to bring them out?"

"Go," Wesley confirmed.

John squeezed passed the prisoners making their way out, and he proceeded to make his way down the hallway toward a staircase.

Wesley looked on. He shouted over to John, trying to be heard over the noise of so many prisoners running around. "John, what is that light?"

John turned around and yelled back, "Say again, sir? What?"

Over the heads of thousands of children, far down the hallway, Wesley saw a faint green light. *Someone's night vision goggles?* Wesley put on his binoculars. *That's not one of ours.*

John turned around to look too.

Wesley's heart dropped. "John, GET BACK HERE!"

The green light slipped through the air as a blur, right through John's body.

Wesley feared the worst for his soldiers. In that instant, as brief as it was, he already calculated for the worst - that his soldiers were all killed. But he didn't have time to spare any feelings or wait and see what this mysterious light moving through the air was or what it might do. He ran from the hole in the wall, out into the fields in desperation to reach his daughter, the only person now on his mind. Her safety was the only thing now that mattered to him. "Emma!" He screamed.

Standing there with Dennis and other prisoners, she could tell something was wrong. Her father's voice was never so shaken with fear.

He called out one last time. "RU—"

He was knocked into the ground at a frightening speed, as a woman stood in his place.

She had green eyes, long black hair, and a green light glowing from her chest.

"DAD!"

Part 2
FALL

*There's hope after all. I'm **not** alone.*

There will be another, another like me.

Elrion

20
Beyond

The world around Isaac appeared now to only occupy a small circular frame ahead of him. It was as if Isaac were in an empty black void surrounded by nothing but darkness. And yet, there was this singular object in front of him, a bright blue circle with a thick red edge. And, though colored by the circle's blue hue, inside there were streaks of lines and blobby shapes that shot out from the center out toward the edges of the circle. At the same time, the frame and everything inside of it appeared to flash constantly between bright and dark, as if a light switch was turning it on and off and at incredible speeds.

He could not speak, because he had no lungs or mouth. He could not smell, because he had no nose. He tried focusing on his breath, even though it was gone. After a moment, though he could not yet feel his body, the image in the circle seemed to slow down. The flickering between light and dark, though still occurring, happened at a slower pace. The streaks zipping through the frame now moved slowly enough, though still very fast, that he could begin to make out images—he could see trees and sky, warped and stretched and blue as they may have been, but he could indeed see them as they appeared to whip through the circle. It was like he was in a plane flying through the world, at ground level, and everything was pushed and squeezed into the view of this circle, this window.

Do I slow down? He asked himself. *Where am I?* All he could do was think. He still couldn't feel his body yet. In fact, he wasn't sure if he could even feel emotions yet. But that's when it hit him.

Emma? Dennis? Was he starting to feel something? Did the memory of his friends bring back something? Though dulled, he did indeed feel *something*. He had only one more thought: *Stop*.

The circle then suddenly reacted, as if obeying his command. It quickly expanded. As the window grew, yellow hues filled some of the space just inside the red outer edge. The dark blues in the middle gave way to lighter and lighter blues. In what felt to Isaac like an instant later, the window completely expanded and surrounded him. Now, he had a normal view of a world around him once again. In all directions, there were trees. He was in a forest.

Greens and browns returned to the plants and trees, and the only blue he could see was the blue above him, where it belonged, in the sky. As this happened, a mist of particles appeared in the air, in the spot where he was. The mist condensed, pulling itself together and began to form the shape of his arms, legs, and the rest of his body. He began to *feel*, once again.

Isaac now found himself standing on a patch of dirt and leaves next to a tall tree. He lifted and placed his hand on it, reaching out to see if it was real. Though he was glad to be back, to feel the earth beneath his feet, the tree in his hand, and to have his body and emotions back, he missed where he had been. That dark place with a small window was peaceful. As unfamiliar and scary as that place should have felt, he felt at peace there.

A bird landed on a branch above his head. Isaac calmly looked upward. He could see not just the bird, but every feather of the bird. *No*, he thought, *I can see every hair on every feather and every...* He focused harder... *every cell.* Surprise—the first strong emotion he felt after reappearing in solid form. His heart rate increased slightly.

65 beats per minute. Let's get that down more. He closed his eyes, concentrating on each beat and breathing with purpose. *53 beats per minute.* Even the flow of blood in and out of his heart could be felt and tracked. He traced the blood as it traveled down to his fingers and back to his heart. Thinking about each breath, he felt the air go down into his lungs, and into each piece of lung tissue. *40 beats per minute.*

He took a seat on the soft soil below him, resting his hands on his lap. He closed his eyes partially—not all the way closed, but not all the way open either. *Lower... 26 beats per minute.* As the time between heartbeats increased, he felt himself breathing slower too. He continued to count the beats per minute—dropping further and further. How far could it go?

He sat there for a few minutes. Even his mind seemed to run in slow motion. His thoughts soon became close to empty. The silence was only interrupted by the occasional *thump* of his heart and *whooshes* of air and blood flowing through his body.

10 beats.

He was now beyond anything humans had ever been able to do in history. Even top endurance athletes, marathon runners, could only get their resting heart rate down to the 30s of beats per minute.

One beat.

He was now practically a statue. No thoughts. No feelings. It was as if he was asleep, but deeper than even that.

Less than one beat per minute. His eyes moved slowly open. Maybe... 1 beat an hour? Maybe much less than even that.

Isaac stood up and wiped the dirt from his bottom. *Bump... bump bump... bump bump bump bump.* His heartbeat was returning to normal.

No pants! He suddenly realized he was naked. His heart rate elevated upon thinking that. *Okay, have to get something to cover myself before I do anything else.* He looked around and could only see vines and leaves amongst the trees. In less than a few seconds, using vines as string, and leaves as cover, he created a leaf skirt. *Good enough,* he thought. Still barefoot and without a shirt, he moved on.

Okay. Now... where am I? Surrounded by trees in all directions, and no path in sight, he could only think of one way to see more clearly. *Up*. For a moment, he considered climbing the trees, but he realized something. He made a little hop off the ground. *Two feet... easily*. Landing, he next tried putting just a little bit more strength into it.

WHOOSH

Smack smack smack

He jumped 50 feet into the air, with branches and leaves slapping him on the way up and down. Oddly enough, none of it really hurt or even scratched him.

THUD

His feet crashed back onto the ground, causing the sticks and dirt around him to fly up into the air. *Well, that wasn't hard at all. I should be able to...* Looking straight up into the sky, he aimed for a slight opening in the canopy of leaves above him, where a patch of blue poked through. He bent down slightly and jumped with a little bit more effort.

WHOOSH!

Hundreds of feet, almost immediately, and still rising, Isaac quickly found himself above the trees. He looked all around him as he ascended. *Hmm... trees in all directions. I really went far.* Focusing his sight as far as he could, he noticed that the horizon seemed to curve forward. He could see hundreds and hundreds of kilometers ahead of him. *Ah!* He saw some fields of grass and some small mountains. *It's not all forest.* After that, the Earth almost seemed to curve out of sight. *It's much colder up here,* he thought.

He looked down. *Oh.* He was now thousands of feet up in the air, it turned out, and he just started to fall back down. *I guess I'll go toward those mountains next.*

As he fell, he spread his body flat. *This is what it feels like to 'skydive,' huh?* It was peaceful. He looked over side to side, seeing the tiny trees and rivers under him. He tried looking closely at one of the rivers. He could see some fish swimming in one, under the river's clear waters. *I'll go there first, I guess. I'm hungry.*

He shaped his body into a straight line and dove toward that spot in the water. He cut through the air like an arrow, guiding himself in the direction he wanted to go.

Only as he was a few hundred feet off the ground did he realize. *Oh, wait. How should I land?* He tried to turn his body around to land feet first but couldn't quite flip around in time.

SMACK CRACK CRASH

He tumbled through the limbs of trees, many of which snapped off their trunks as he swept through. His body crashed into a tree next to the river. It creaked and moaned before falling down slowly onto the forest floor next to him.

WHOMP

Isaac wasn't hurt at all. He should've been surprised, but somehow nothing seemed to bother him since reappearing from that strange dark space before. All he knew was that he needed to find his friends and that he should probably eat something.

He got up, walked over to the water, and jumped in. The dirt that had covered his body was now washing away. Isaac held his breath and dunked his head under, looking around for the fish he saw earlier. *There.* He started swimming and found it easier than he remembered.

The fish saw him coming and sped up, bolting ahead. *I'll get you!* He swam faster too, catching up right behind the fish. *Too easy.* The fish didn't have a chance. He felt like having some fun. He moved to the side of the fish. It swam sideways, trying to escape. Isaac swam swiftly around it and floated right in front of where it was heading. It flipped around and tried to swim back away. This time, Isaac swam up to the fish and grabbed it with one hand.

He let himself sink to the river floor, holding the fish while still holding his breath.

WHOOSH

Placing his feet on the river floor, Isaac then jumped up through the water and onto dry land, still gripping his prey.

I should make a fire to cook this or... And just as he considered eating the fish raw, like sushi, he looked at the fish squirming with fear in his hand. He felt pity. *I'm* sorry. He threw the fish back into the river and let his meal-to-be live.

My body needs something though. What can I eat out here? I don't know which plants are edible or poisonous.

Grumble

His stomach was telling him he needed something, anything. Without much thought, he looked at a nearby bush that appeared to have some colorful berries on it. *I don't know if these are poisonous, but they look pretty good!*

He started with one berry, just to check. *It's...* He began to chew and swallow, okay? It didn't taste very sweet or very bitter, but he didn't feel anything bad yet—so he went ahead and ate every single one he saw. *Maybe that wasn't a good idea. Though, I'm still hungry...*

The only plants left around him were all sorts of green-leaved things and trees. Even though he was pretty sure he shouldn't eat them, he somehow found his mouth watering looking at it all, as if his brain was telling him that the nature around him was as tasty as a big plate of meat. Though not proud of it, Isaac began trying everything, even the bark on the trees.

Bushes, plants, trees, none of it was safe from his stomach's wrath. With his strength, he was able to chew everything into a pulp, even the wood. His hunger only grew, and his stomach was not filling up. So, he just... kept... eating. He may have even tried a rock or two.

After eating several large tree branches, bushes, rocks, and a little bit of dirt, he finally felt like he had enough. Lying down on the ground, he smiled. *That was good.* "Now..."

He got up. "Time to go." Isaac jumped up above the trees again. *There*, he thought, seeing the mountains from before. Once he landed back down to the ground, he positioned himself to face in that direction. *Okay, now let's see what happens if I jump a* **lot** *harder.*

The dirt picked up wildly below his feet. As he jumped forward through the trees at a slight angle, his body destroyed branches and leaves like they were nothing in his way. He flew through the sky like a jet, moving at maybe thousands of kilometers per hour at least.

BOOM

He had a sudden realization when hearing the sound. *So that's what that sound was! I broke the sound barrier at the prison before! Those are sonic booms!* While he was impressed with how many feats of speed and strength he was breaking, he noticed the mountains were coming closer a bit too quickly. *Uh-oh.* He tried flattening his body, shaping it straight—just about anything he could to try slowing down his body and avoiding the hard rocky surface he was about to collide with.

SLAM CRACK

His body hit the side of the mountain. Hard.

Ow? He thought for sure it was his body that had cracked. But no. He looked below and saw that a large break in the rock formed right at his elbow. Just then, a large chunk of rock slid off and down the side of the mountain. *My elbow broke a part of a mountain. Okay. Cool. Better keep going though.*

He sped up his perception of time and ran around to the other side of the mountain. Looking in front of him, he had a clear view of the next area ahead. He focused hard. *Where am I? I don't recognize anything,* he thought.

He positioned himself to jump, ready to keep exploring and to find his friends. *Okay... 3... 2... 1...*

21
New Friends, New Enemies, Goodbyes

"Where is Isaac Levi?"

The green-lit, green-eyed woman in front of Emma was different from a PC. She was human, most of all. Rather than a cold, emotionless black face plate covering machine parts, she had a face like any other human's. Though it did seem like she had something wrong with her. Her eyelids almost seemed to droop, like she was tired. Her head was slightly tilting from side to side as she spoke, as if she was bored, as if she was ready to hurt someone.

"**Where is Isaac Levi?**" She repeated, impatiently.

"Shut up!" Dennis shouted at this new apparent enemy.

Emma was frozen, looking at her father, who was face down on the grass. "You... monster!" Emma slowed down her perception of time. She ran up to her father, attempting to pick him up.

"**Where is Isaac Levi?**" The voice still being heard clearly by Emma, despite her fast speed, meant that this enemy was at least as fast as Emma was. This took Emma off guard. She looked up at the woman, who was looking right back at her, with an intimidatingly blank expression.

Terrified, Emma jumped backward and returned to Dennis. All the while, the black-haired woman kept her eyes on Emma, not blinking. Emma let time resume to normal.

"What happened?" Dennis asked.

"I sped up and went to my dad to see if he was okay, but there she was, sped up just along with me—and she just stared at me, asking again for Isaac. Dennis, I don't know if my dad is okay. I think all the soldiers too might—"

Dennis acted quickly. "HEY! FRIENDS!" He shouted to all around him. Most of the prisoners in the fields, and those who were still coming out of the hole in the wall, kept running despite the announcement. More than a few of them, however, stopped and listened. "IF ANY OF YOU HAVE ANY SPECIAL ABILITIES, WE HAVE STRENGTH AND SPEED. WE COULD REALLY USE MORE HELP HERE!"

There was no response.

"Well, I tried," Dennis said, disappointingly. "What do we do now, ma'am?"

Emma had to focus. Her life, Dennis's life, and her father's, if he was still alive, all depended on her coming up with a plan. "Okay. She may be stuck on repeat. She only asks the same question. Maybe she—"

BOOM

"Where is Isaac Levi?!" The woman now suddenly appeared in front of them, following a sonic boom. Her face was leaned in, up close to Emma's.

"Why... why do you want to know?" Emma cautiously and nervously asked in response.

The figure stood back up straight and rubbed her eyes with her hands, showing frustration. **"Because I have been told, okay? Tell me where he is!"**

This isn't normal, Emma thought. "Who told you?"

The woman took her hand away from her face and stared at Emma. **"The Intelligence installed in my head. Who else?"**

"Why do you have a light in your chest? Are you a PC?" Dennis asked.

"You know... it only hurts me the longer I don't follow what I am told. Just tell me where to find him." She was growing in anger.

"We don't know," Emma said. "He disappeared. Are you a PC, or are you human?"

"You're a waste of time... I should just kill yo—"

WHAM

She flew up in the air and into a tree, about a hundred feet away, as a foot replaced the spot where her body once stood.

"Hello, my name is Patrick. Call me Pat." The young man, maybe the same age as Emma and Dennis, greeted them after swiftly kicking their enemy away.

"And my name is Margaret." Another prisoner came up to Emma and Dennis from the crowd. "I've been in there for eight years. You're the first people I've seen to even know how to speak —besides the guards."

Pat added on, "Same here. So, I'm not about to let you die alone. I don't know who you are, but I'm not going back into that prison. You were able to break us out and defeat all the guards too. I'm sure it's better to stay with you than go on my own."

Margaret agreed, "We should have a better chance to survive out here if we fight together."

Dennis was happy to have new friends. "Nice to meet you two! Thanks for saving us, Pat."

"DAD!" Emma suddenly remembered her dad on the ground and ran over to him, unsure if he even was still alive.

"That's her dad on the ground?" Asked Margaret.

"Yea. He was a nice man. *I don't think he'll make it*," Dennis quietly said.

Emma turned her father over on his back. "Dad?" Tears started rolling down her face. "Are you okay?" Her voice was starting to shake. She looked at him. His face was motionless. Emma shouted, "Dad!" She put her face against his chest and hugged him as she cried. Then, she heard his heartbeat. "Dad?" She moved closer to him. His eyes slowly opened a little bit. His breathing was slow, however.

"Emm... a." He muttered what little he could.

Dennis, Pat, and Margaret walked over to them.

"Dad, I love you." She didn't know what else to say.

He looked at her and smiled. His eyes then closed for the last time as his breath stopped and his body went limp.

Emma began to cry uncontrollably, holding her father tight.

"We have incoming," Pat said.

"That woman is on her way back," Margaret confirmed, looking in the distance and seeing the figure walking toward them, taking her time getting there.

"They gave you strong legs... HUH?!" She shouted from afar.

ZOOM

Suddenly she was in front of all of them. **"They gave me strong *everything*."**

As she said that, she swung her foot toward Pat. Dennis stood in the way, holding his forearms together to block the kick.

WHAM

"Well, that kind of hurt. You're strong!" Dennis said, taunting the woman.

"Hmph. Too slow, boy." As she started to reach back to punch Dennis, a baton was already moving close to her chest, ready to smash the green light sensor. She immediately pulled back her own punch and jumped backward.

"Darn! So close. I was right there!" Emma said with ferocity, her cheeks still wet from crying. She pulled her baton back.

"Let's do this." Dennis walked next to Emma, showing he was ready to fight side by side.

As he walked up to her, so did Pat and Margaret. Then, out of nowhere, several other prisoners joined them—who were only just watching before. Seeing this, more and more people came together with them to help fight. More and more put their fists up, ready to throw augmented punches and kicks at this enemy who threatened all of their safety.

"GO BACK TO THE PRISON!" One voice called out.

"BECAUSE WE'RE NOT GOING BACK!" Another added.

"Do you know what I am?!" The woman countered.

They all stood there, staring at her, not one of them losing the courage to stay.

"Pathetic. I'm the next generation. Not you! Not any of you! They upgraded ME!"

She was quickly losing patience with all of them. Without warning, she attempted to break through the crowd using her next-generation augmentations. First, she moved as fast as she could, heading straight for Emma. **"You are the only threat. You will die first!"**

Just then, about ten other prisoners ran in front of Emma at super speed, ready to defend their newfound leader. Apparently, one or two of them managed to find batons from the guards in the prison while they were escaping.

The woman stopped and stood in front of them, just a few feet away. **"Ugh! *You.* YOU! AGHH!"** Just then, she held her head with both of her hands, screaming in pain.

The crowd looked confused.

"What's happening to her?" Dennis asked Emma.

"I think it's The Intelligence. It may be punishing her for not following orders. It wants her to attack us, even if she could lose. But, unlike PCs, she seems to have control over her actions, and The Intelligence is punishing her for not attacking more, I think."

"**Just tell me!**" She stated loudly through her pain while still holding the sides of her head with her hands. "**Where is Isaac Levi?!**"

Dennis actually started to feel bad for her. "Emma, she's a prisoner like us. She's forced to do this. Maybe we should help her."

Emma looked at Dennis and back at this 'enemy.' Although Emma had no idea where Isaac actually was, she was tempted to make something up and tell this woman *something*, out of kindness. Maybe if Emma said something like, "that way," then maybe The Intelligence would stop punishing her. But then she looked back at her lifeless father on the ground. She didn't say a word. *Let her have pain*, she thought.

"**AGH! Fine then!**"

The green-eyed woman ran back up to the crowd, with no choice but to attack. A group of the same ten or so speedy prisoners stuck together to stand in her way again.

"**Orders... hurt you until someone speaks up!**"

They may have had augmentations installed in them in that prison, the same prison that she was given augs from, but hers were better, if only enough to gain a small advantage and reach just one of them. She launched herself into the group, flexing her muscles and preparing for every kick, punch, or otherwise headed toward her. Most did nothing. The prisoners were fast, but not strong enough. She reached for Pat and hit him into the ground below, just as hard as she had done with Wesley.

"No!" Emma cried out. "No more!"

The woman leapt away from the group, again giving them the same question. "**Where... is... Isaac?!**"

The group all looked at each other. They knew they had a chance to fight, but it was clear that it wasn't going to be easy. They might even lose. Even if they did win, who else could die in the process besides Pat? Still, they were too afraid to run away, or they would be picked off one by one in a chase. They were stuck there, just waiting for someone to say something.

Emma knelt down next to Pat, the first person who went out of his way to save her earlier. A few new tears formed. "I'm so sorry. I..." *I was being selfish. I'm sorry. If I just told her and let her go...* "this shouldn't have happened to you," she said out loud, remorsefully.

Dennis put his hand on her shoulder. At this point, he started to understand his friend well enough to know what he should do next to help. "He's that way. Isaac Levi is that way." He pointed somewhere at random. It didn't matter where.

"Finally! Live, die. It doesn't matter... None of this does." And then, the mysterious green-eyed, green-lit person was gone.

Emma walked over to her father. "I'm sorry, Dad. I won't forget the lessons you've taught me. Someone else died because of my mistakes. Never again. No more risks. I have to be strong, like you." She knelt down and gently, respectfully, removed his cape. "I will be strong like you." She spun the cape around her back and tied it around her neck.

Dennis came over to Wesley's body. "I can carry him, if you want..."

Emma smiled and nodded her head. "Thank you, my friend. We'll give him the burial he deserves, back at camp."

She looked at each one of the new augmented prisoners who chose to fight along with her and Dennis. “FRIENDS!” She yelled out to them all. “FOLLOW ME! TO THE FOREST!”

22 Alone

BOOM

Hitting some branches along the way down through more trees, his feet found themselves loudly landing and getting lodged into the dirt of the forest floor. Still not knowing where he was, he nonetheless knew he had to keep exploring and continue his search for his friends. Right now though, he realized he accidentally buried himself all the way up his legs. "Okay... learning moment." As if the ground was made of jelly, he easily drove his knees up through the earth and climbed up until he was standing. While brushing the earth off his body, he looked around and examined his surroundings. No one. No signs of anything but nature.

He decided he had to keep moving. Wherever he was, he knew he could not stay. He had to find his friends, one way or another. So, Isaac made another jump straight up into the air, maybe a thousand feet or so. As the cool air brushed past his body, he reflected on his feelings and everything that was happening and had happened. Though this reflection was quite short, it occurred to him that he hadn't really taken *any* time to pause and think since he was released from prison. In a way, it reminded him of how he used to practice meditation with his father, so many years ago. He found himself so calm, even if he was moving astonishingly fast through fierce winds.

He looked around as much as he could as he was shooting through the air. But as far as he could tell, there was just more forest in all directions. If he wanted to have any hope of finding people, let alone his friends, he knew he could have a lot more time spent searching ahead of him.

As he fell back toward the forest below, he again tried to orient himself in such a way that he might land a bit more gently. But he just wasn't able to figure out how.

SLAM SLAP CRASH

Isaac whipped through several tree branches and many leaves before colliding with the dirt, burying his body a few feet into the ground as he had before. He promptly climbed back out, wiped off the dirt, and readied himself to start running.

It started with a jog. He dipped and jumped over fallen trees and bushes as needed. "Actually, if I'm confident enough..." He began to run faster. And faster. Faster, still. He didn't even bother to speed up his perception of time, to make things appear slower around him. It turned out, he didn't need to. "My reaction timing..."

WHOOSH

A branch almost hit his head, but he swiftly and easily ducked to avoid it.

JUMP

A fallen tree would have tripped him over, but he gracefully hurdled over it like he was stepping over a small rock.

"I can react to anything, and quickly!"

Moving at what was perhaps as fast as a plane speeding through the air, Isaac zipped, zig-zagged, hurdled, ducked, and dodged through all obstacles in his way, without making a single mistake—all the while, moving in a relatively straight path through the forest.

As he ran more and more and looked around him as he went, he became increasingly confused. "What?" He looked around. There was just nothing but plants. Not a single sign of people. No tents. No rebel bases. No solar panels up in the trees. Not even a clothesline. *Where is the rebel camp? Where am I?* He asked himself, growing increasingly unsettled.

"Am I even close? I hope the commander finds his way back to Natasha... Natasha! The blood sample! Without her research, I may not find out what I am!"

Isaac sighed. He felt defeated. He had no idea where the rebels were and he didn't know if his friends would be able to find him. The only thing he could think of was to keep running. So, on he went. *It's not like I know where I'm going anyway. I guess I'll go...* "That way," he said aloud.

Time passed. Hours went by with nothing more than the same—trees, dirt, sky.

As the sun started to set and the sky turned red, he began to gather sticks to make a fire. Though it had been a while, he remembered what it was like camping with his parents when he was young. He remembered watching how they had made fires. So, he sort of knew what to do. *First, get the small sticks and tiny pieces of bark or ripped-up sticks, kindling material. They have to be dry. Then, make sure you have larger sticks ready.* Isaac cleared a patch of ground, moving away all debris until a small area of ground was cleared of all sticks, leaves, or anything. Just dirt. After forming a circle of rocks around that small space, he then put the smaller sticks and other small kindling material into a cone shape at its center. The large sticks, for the moment, would wait on the side until the fire was built and got large.

"Now..." He stood there, with both hands resting on his hips. "How do I create a fire again, exactly?" Isaac knew he needed friction. He needed to generate enough heat that the dry timber would start a fire. "Duh!" He took two of the small sticks and placed them in between the palms of his hands and started rubbing them together on his bare skin—*fast.*

FWOOSH

Instant fire in his palms. *The things you can do with super speed*, he thought. "And look," he said to himself, "I don't feel anything even with fire in my hand! Not a scratch or burn on me. Huh. Would you look at that? I guess I'm immune to fire now, hah!"

Isaac gently placed the two fiery sticks into the cone he had made. Soon enough, they all lit up too. "Cool. Now..." He picked up some of the larger branches he had gathered and placed them carefully in between the flames, trying not to smother his progress so far. "Darn, hungry again." He looked around at the delicious trees and rocks surrounding him.

Sniff sniff

The smells of roasting wood filled his nostrils. "Oh my." Isaac couldn't help himself. He picked up one of the flaming branches and took a big bite. "That," he paused to appreciate his snack, "is delicious! OH, whoops!" The fire was now smaller. He had to be a little more careful with his appetite. "Okay, maybe I should feed the fire before myself. Let's make it... a bit bigger?" He turned to one of the nearby trees, "Sorry about this."

Slowing down time around him, he swiftly chopped his hand across the tree trunk like it was butter. Letting time resume at normal speed, he then pushed the tree down away from his little campsite. "Thank you for giving me your wood." He closed his eyes and bowed his head politely as the tree fell.

CRASH

It fell to the forest floor with a mighty sound.

He proceeded to chop the tree up into more manageable parts. Some for the fire. Some for his stomach. "This should be enough for a while," he said as he brought all of the pieces over into a pile, a safe ten feet away from the fire pit. He grabbed a large tree chunk in one hand and sat with it next to the fire.

Holding it above the flames, he felt a small tickle of heat lick his hand. "Heh." As he watched the flames wrap around his hands, his large trunk roasting, and his mouth watering, he couldn't help but think about his friends' safety again. "I hope they're okay. I hope we can find each other."

He got a little nervous suddenly, worried for their safety. "What if a PC got to them on their way back to camp?"

Hoot hoot

The sound of an owl distracted him and calmed him down. "I can't think that yet. Come on, Isaac. Just wait and see. Nothing will improve by you getting nervous." He looked up at the night sky. Stars were starting to appear. "Give it a day or two. All you can do, all you have control over, is your own actions. Being angsty won't solve anything. After this meal, you'll go to sleep, wake up the next morning, and you'll run and find them. I bet when you find them, Dennis will even be waiting with some silly thing to say like, 'Oi mate, what took you so long, slowpoke'." Isaac smiled to himself at the idea.

Finishing his meal, with the fire still crackling and burning its light around him, Isaac laid on the forest floor, looking up at the thousands of stars filling the sky. His hands resting on his stomach, he remembered lying down in this same way back in prison. Here he was, finally free, as he always dreamed, lying down amongst nature. But he was alone.

"Breathe..." he reminded himself. "Remember this."

The next morning

Isaac's eyes opened slowly. A sound came from behind him.

"Guys!" He jumped up to his feet, excited to be reunited, but it wasn't his friends. "Well, you're not anyone I know." He looked at the group of deer with disappointment. "Still, you look like nice people. Nice to meet you." He put out his hand as if to shake theirs. The deer just stood there, staring at him blankly. "Well, it was worth a try," he said as he brought his hand back to his side. *I guess I may as well rest here for a while, maybe reflect on what to do next.* "I guess you can hang out here with me as I wait for my other friends," he told the deer.

The next day

Isaac was genuinely worried, and his deer friends left him many hours ago, so he didn't have anyone to share what he was feeling.

"Okay. It's time I do something about this. I have to find them. Maybe they're close by?" He wondered out loud, with a bit of doubt in his voice. Bending his legs ever so slightly, he looked up into the sky, in an opening between the leaves.

WHOOSH SMACK WHACK WHAM

The branches and leaves hit him on his way up. *I really have to find a better way to do this!*

His jump took him far above the trees and into the clouds. *Too wet! Too hard to see!* He was surrounded by the white mist of cloudy water droplets. Falling back down again, making his way underneath the clouds, he felt the wind blow past his body as it dried off all the water on him. He began to look around while he had a couple of minutes in the air to float down. Tens of thousands of feet up, he could see the mountain he jumped from earlier. *Wow, that's a lot farther than I thought it was.*

Then, in the other direction, way in the distance, he saw it—a line of buildings, a city. *That's my best chance!*

He dove down toward the earth below him. *Okay, this time...* He spun around so he could try to land feet first.

CRACK SMACK WHAM BOOM

Leaves, tree branches, and dirt flew everywhere as he made his landing.

"Okay! Whatever!" He jumped up once more out of the ground. "Now, without wasting any time, let's see how quickly I can get to that city."

23
Gone

Emma reached the end of the fields, walking up to the forest before she came up with an idea. "Everyone who has augmentations, raise your hand."

Most looked at each other, confused.

"What is an augmentation?" Someone said in the group of 50 or so.

Emma tried to explain. "Oh, that's right. You might not have heard that word before. Well, it's an upgrade. It's something they did to you in prison to make you stronger, faster, or something else."

Many of the former prisoners could be seen nodding their heads and saying "ohh."

"Okay!" She continued. "So which one of you is really strong? Who has a strength augmentation?"

Now, about half of the group raised their hands.

"Perfect!"

"Why are we asking this?" Dennis asked.

"You'll see," she replied. "Everyone who is raising your hand, carry someone else on your back who is not raising their hand."

They all looked at each other, confused. One of them blurted out a loud "huh?"

Emma explained, "Your bodies are weak from years in prison with little food. We won't make it back if everyone has to walk. But, with those of you who are augmented to be strong, you can carry the others and we should make it."

They all just stared at her, intimidated by the task. "Well, come on! Let's move people!"

Suddenly they rushed to pair up, one strong auggie for every other.

"Good! A few people standing by themselves though..." Emma wasn't sure if they would be able to carry everyone after all.

Someone spoke up, seeing the issue. "Oh, I'm also strong. I think we all are—the ones who are left."

"Okay! Great! Are you ready to follow me?" Emma asked, only to be met with a silent response. "I said... ARE YOU READY TO FOLLOW, SOLDIERS?!"

"YES SIR MA'AM." Some of them said 'sir,' some said 'ma'am.'

Emma sighed. "It's okay. We'll work on it. Just call me ma'am."

"YES MA'AM!"

"Better. Now..." She stepped to the front of the group. "FOLLOW!"

Though not moving as fast as she would have liked, they were nonetheless moving well through the forest together. With the exception of a couple of accidents—someone being carried hitting their head on a branch or someone tripping—the group moved fairly quickly.

"Stop!" Emma called out for the group to take a breather. Just like her, they were all panting and breathing heavily. She took long breaths between every few words. "I guess—we have to take some breaks—along the way."

So, it went on this way for the next few hours. Every so often, the group would take a break. Toward the end of the trek, the breaks had to get longer.

Finally, after moving and stopping, moving and stopping, they arrived.

"Wait." She looked around at the tents. No one was around. "Okay. It looks like they weren't—expecting us right now. They'll be further in. Let's go. Follow me—soldiers."

As she walked by a couple of tents, she looked inside of them. "Okay, empty. Whoever lives in these is somewhere else right now. Let's go to the science tent. I'm sure we'll find the science lieutenant, my mom, Natasha." Then it hit her. After all the walking, leading the other prisoners back there, the weight of her loss finally sunk in. *Dad*, she thought, *I can't believe you're gone.* Her eyes began to water, but she breathed out a heavy breath and pulled herself together. Now was not the time to grieve. She had to lead these prisoners to food and get them taken care of. Then... *I have to tell Mom. She'll be devastated.* "Dennis?"

"Yea?" He responded with a supportive tone.

Emma struggled to get her next words out. "Can you... put my father in one of these tents? Lay him down and cover him, please. I don't think my mom may be ready to see him just yet. I don't think I'm... ready to be close to him right now."

"Of course. Anything you ask," he replied with sincere kindness.

"Thank you, my friend." She smiled and hugged him. She didn't have the courage to look at her father, not just yet. Emma waited for Dennis to put her dad down and step back out of the tent before commanding her new recruits. The crowd was silent as they watched and waited for her.

She turned around and gestured for them to follow. "Okay everyone, you will need to meet Natasha. She'll help explain what you have gone through, about augmentations, and study you for more information. Many of you probably need medical treatment too. After your time in that prison, with how poorly you were taken care of, I'm sure we can help you regain some of your strength."

Emma walked through the center of camp. *Strange,* she thought. She looked at each tent—they were all empty so far. Clothes were left hanging on lines to dry, plates of food sat uneaten on chairs and tree stumps. *Something isn't right.* As the science tent came into view, down the path in the distance, she saw people lying on the ground, scattered around the entrance. "What the..." she muttered to herself.

"Ohhh... who's theeere?"

The voice, coming from inside the tent, gave shivers down Emma's spine. She felt the blood empty from her face. At that moment, she feared the worst. As she walked closer, she realized the figures on the ground were the bodies of all the soldiers who were missing from their tents. "*Mom...*" her voice quivered. "*... no.*"

Dennis muttered a quiet and desperate cry for his friend, "Guy?"

A black-haired, green-eyed man walked through the tent entrance. "It's youuu. I'm so glad I found you again."

Dennis's eyebrows furrowed in anger. "YOU!"

Emma dropped to her knees in despair. "Maniac."

24

Those Who Remain

"What did you do?!" Dennis yelled at him.

"Ohhh..." The Maniac moaned as he looked up and around him, his head moving loosely and randomly. "Maybe I followed you. Maybe I... didn't like what you did to me!" He stared angrily at Emma and Dennis. "It was so nice of you all to leave your friends alone here. It was so much... *fun.*" He smiled a twisted smile. "It was so much fun to *play* with them. Especially that one. 'Guy,' was it?"

Emma stood up and wiped the tears from her cheeks. *I have to be strong for everyone.* "Dennis. Just hold him still. There's no point in reasoning with him."

"You got it," he replied.

"Remember what happened last time?" The Maniac teased.

Dennis stopped walking forward. He looked carefully at a baton The Maniac was holding before trying anything. The

Maniac didn't wait though—he began walking toward the crowd of augmented prisoners. One of them stepped forward.

"A guy with a baton? I got this!" The prisoner ran ahead and passed Dennis.

"STOP!" Emma shouted—but it was too late. The prisoner already threw a punch into The Maniac's face.

The prisoner felt confident. "This guy isn't so tough. My strength augmentations are more than enou—"

CLANG

The prisoner fell to the ground.

"Interesting," The Maniac said as he looked maliciously at the person lying still on the forest floor. "I think I've really gotten good at killing in one hit now. Anyone else want to try?" The Maniac was trying to taunt them now, to get them to approach him and meet the same fate as their friend. "No? Well... Where is he? Where is the one who punched me... THROUGH THE FLOOR!" His voice escalated quickly in crazed anger.

"No way we would tell you!" Emma had to come up with a plan. If Dennis tries to punch him, The Maniac will only attack with that baton. Hitting him won't be enough. We need... "Everyone, surround him in a circle!"

Quickly, everyone made a circle.

"HAH! This is fun!" The Maniac said as he looked around him in glee. He was not afraid at all. "All your soldier friends, with weapons, couldn't stop me. They *died* trying! What makes you think I can't do the same to YOU?!"

Emma just then thought about her memories with her parents and imagined what must've been inside the science tent. "Here's one big difference, *Maniac*. We don't need weapons. Those with speed augs!" They looked at her. "Knock the baton out of his hands!"

Before The Maniac had enough time to think about what he just heard, ten or more people became blurs that ran up to him and took turns knocking the baton out of his grip. His fist couldn't close fast enough to hold on to his weapon. It fell to the ground.

"HOW DARE YOU!" The Maniac screamed.

Emma gave her command. "Dennis... hold him down."

"Sweet as," Dennis replied, satisfied with her order.

He walked swiftly over to The Maniac and, without hesitation, grabbed his neck and threw him into the ground.

"Was that supposed to hurt?" The Maniac said, with the side of his face smushed into the dirt.

Ignoring his yapping, Emma simply proceeded to give her next orders. "Good. Hold him there. Margaret..." She looked over to the prisoner she met earlier. "Get some rope from the tent over there."

"Sure!"

Emma continued talking. "He may be indestructible, but he's not strong." She walked over to him. Slowly, she knelt down and put her face right in front of his. In a threatening tone, she spoke. "You will *not* be a threat to anyone *ever* again."

Dennis looked up at Emma with fear in his face. "What are you going to do?"

"I..." She paused. Maybe The Maniac couldn't be destroyed, but could he starve? Could he... drown? There was a river nearby.

"Emma," Dennis said, concerned, "I'm mad too, but we don't have to... you know..."

Emma stared at Dennis, with cold anger still brewing in her. He could tell what she was feeling. *How could YOU understand how I feel right now*, she probably thought. *He hurt the people I love.*

Dennis tried to console her away from that edge. "I know, Emma. I know. I never told you this, but—"

"What are you two babbling about?" The Maniac interrupted.

Emma punched The Maniac's face. "*Oww.*" Her fist felt like it hit a steel wall.

Dennis went on, "I never told you this, but I lost my parents too. PCs murdered both of them. Well..." Dennis's eyes began to water. This was the first time she had seen him cry. "My little sister... she tried to get in the way. Brave little girl." His voice cracked. "But it doesn't matter now. None of that. We can only move on. Isaac was right. If we drop to their level, we're bad too."

She closed her eyes, reflecting on what she just heard. "I'm sorry, Dennis. I just assumed somehow you had it better than us. You are always just so happy."

"Yea, well mate, I do try my best!" He sniffed hard and cracked a big smile.

"Heh." Emma chuckled and opened her eyes, looking at her friend. "Thank you, Dennis, for reminding me of what's important. It's a risk to keep him alive, but you're right." She put her hand on his shoulder. "We'll just have to keep him tied up really well, I guess!"

Dennis smiled and winked. "Oh. I think I can manage that just fine." He signaled for the rope. He proceeded to use it to tie The Maniac's arms and legs together—tight. The Maniac tried to squirm and get himself free, while Dennis just found the wiggling funny. "Oh, that's cute." The Maniac kicked Dennis in the leg.

"Ow! Your foot is pretty hard there, mate! It's okay though." He lifted The Maniac off the ground with ease in one hand. "Turns out, I'm pretty strong! Now, be quiet."

"I'LL KILL YOU ALL," The Maniac squealed.

Dennis swirled The Maniac in the air like an airplane. "Weeeeeewwww," Dennis said, imitating the sound of a plane. "WOOSH." Dennis then made a crashing sound as he dove The Maniac's face into the dirt. "You have a dirty mouth!" He lifted his captive in the air again. "We may need to wrap something around that too!" As Dennis laid The Maniac on the ground and sat on top of him while he was finishing tying him up, Emma walked nervously over to the science tent.

Passing the pile of soldiers who she had lived with, fought with, and called friends, she was now mentally preparing herself for what might have become of her mother. Still, she had to go inside. She had to make sure of what happened, to confirm what she feared most. Emma lifted the tent flap gently with one of her arms. The dark inside called for her to come in and explore, but she found it difficult to make that first step. She felt pale. It was just all hitting her so fast. First her father, now her mother. If it wasn't for Dennis, she felt like she could've lost herself. *Breathe. It has to be done. I have to see for myself.*

She walked in. She saw her mother immediately. Natasha was hunched over her work, at a table. The quiet tent almost made her seem peaceful, as if she was only asleep, but Emma knew better. "I'm sorry, Mom." She walked over and hugged her mother. "It's going to be so hard, but..." Her eyes watered. "I have to move on. I know I will—" But she couldn't hold it together. She began sobbing uncontrollably as she tightened her embrace.

But only after a moment, not long enough for Emma to let out her feelings completely, she heard something quietly stir behind her. It startled her, and she stood up straight to see what it was. "Hello?!"

"Ah-h..." The soft and weakened voice came from the other side of the tent, from the floor.

Dennis called out from outside. "Everything okay in there?" He ran in. "Don't worry about The Maniac. I have a few other strength auggies watching our new friend." His eyes were still adjusting to the darkness of the tent. "Oh, and I'm calling us 'auggies' now—"

"Dennis," Emma cut him off.

He could start to see her a little better. She was kneeling on the ground next to someone.

"Guy!" Dennis rushed over to his friend. "You're still alive! Where did he get you?"

Guy, lying on his back and slow to move, pointed to at least ten different places on his stomach and neck. "Uhhh..." he muttered in pain.

"You can't scare me like that, mate! You must be the luckiest person in the world. You keep surviving everything!"

Emma felt relief that at least someone survived The Maniac's baton beatings. "Maybe he recognized him from prison and kept him alive on purpose, to torture him—The Maniac is sick." She furrowed her brow, upset and feeling terrible for her ally on the ground, for Guy. "We'll get you some food. Let's get you feeling better." Before she could turn back to Dennis, to tell him to get some food, he was already gone. The flaps of the tent were waving back and forth.

Emma smiled. "You're in good hands, Guy. I'll leave it to your best friend to take care of you. I have to go now. It's time for me to give orders, for us all to get out of here."

As she left the tent, she raised her hand to get the attention of her fellow 'auggies.' "Okay, everyone." She put her hand down. "This camp is where my family, the rebels fighting for humanity, once lived. This is the place where we planned the mission that saved you from the prison. However," she paused, "we can't stay here anymore. Sadly, if this 'Maniac,' as we call him, could follow us here, then we can't rule out the possibility that a PC or guard could have followed us back here too." Many people in the crowd nodded their heads in agreement, probably fearful to lose the freedom they had only just gained. "Still, we don't want to lose any of the equipment or tents here. They are too valuable to leave behind, and we may not have a chance to find more without risking your lives. Everyone, follow me."

Emma proceeded to walk them through the campsite and instruct them on how to pack everything up. Before long, every one of these new rebels had a task to perform. Many were packing up tents, while others were packing up clothes, weapons, and science equipment. After about one hour of fast auggies doing most of the lighter work, and the strength auggies doing the heavy lifting, the entire camp was packed and piled up in one place.

"Great!" Emma announced. "Now, the path out of here is wide enough to fit a few soldiers walking side by side. Everyone, wrap the gear into these bags and put them on your backs. We should have just enough of us to carry it all, I think. Strength auggies, you carry the heavier things."

Soon enough, almost all of them had a large backpack on their backs, filled or tied up with equipment. The only things left were the bodies of the former rebels.

Dennis went over to Emma and quietly told her, "It's okay, I'll make sure they get a proper burial. I'll ask some of the fast auggies to dig graves."

"Thank you, Dennis. And once they make the graves, we'll stop for a moment to say our goodbyes."

No longer whispering, Dennis confirmed her order. "You got it, ma'am." He bowed his head out of respect. Then, asking a question with a louder volume, making sure that everyone could hear him, "Where to now, ma'am?"

She called out to all of her new soldiers, giving them one last speech before carrying out the next step of their journey together. "I am like you!" They all stopped, standing still as she spoke. Emma, on the other hand, started pacing across the crowd, back and forth, as she talked from her heart. "We are all human. We are victims of The Intelligence. This evil took over our planet. They took us from our homes. They took our parents. Well, NO MORE!"

The crowd cheered. "Yea!"

"You can always choose to leave. But let me assure you..." She paused to emphasize her next point. "We are stronger now, more than ever, because we have what no one has ever had in these last eight years. We have over 40 soldiers with the same strength and speed as our enemy!"

"Yea!" They cheered once more.

"And..." She paused once again to bring attention and drama to what she was about to say next. "If you DO choose to stay with me, to fight alongside me, then there is a chance. A SMALL CHANCE, but a chance no less, that we can *destroy* The Intelligence once and for all. So, I ask you here and now. ARE YOU WITH ME?!"

"YEA!"

"Then THIS is your mission! A city lies east of here. Normally, going into a city is suicide. Cities are filled with adults controlled by The Intelligence. Many of them may be augmented like you. For all we know, there are some who are just as strong as the woman we met at the prison, the one with a green light in her chest. HOWEVER..."

The crowd waited anxiously for her next sentence.

"IF WE DON'T FIGHT NOW, WHEN WE ARE STRONGER THAN WE MAY EVER BE, THEN HUMANITY AS WE KNOW IT MAY BE GONE FOREVER. IS THIS WHAT WE WANT?!" She demanded from the eager crowd.

"NO!" They responded together, raising their fists in the air.

"THEN MOVE OUT, SOLDIERS! WE HAVE A MISSION!"

25

Ready or Not

Isaac took no time at all to run up to the edge of the forest, where tall buildings could be seen in the distance. Beyond the trees, he saw an old highway road. *I better slow things down. Who knows what's inside this area?*

But before he triggered his abilities, and time was still moving at a normal speed, he noticed a car drive by.

Hide! He ducked behind a tree nearby. *That was close.* Then it occurred to him. *Wait, why do I care?* "I can deal with anything that tries to attack me anyway!" He said out loud, no longer afraid of being heard.

Walking carefree out into the open and onto the road, he said to himself, "May as well enter the city. If there are PCs in there, I need to quickly stop them, in case my friends are in danger." He then ran down the road, but just short of breaking the sound barrier. At about 600 kilometers per hour, he wouldn't want to trigger a sonic boom. Even if he was strong enough to handle anything, maybe just a little caution was okay, if for nothing else but to help his friends stay hidden.

As he approached the highway's exit, near the city entrance, he took a look around. *Nothing*, he thought. He jumped off the highway and onto a smaller road leading into the heart of the city. *I'll take my time. Now that I'm here, for their safety, I should be careful and try not to be noticed or heard.*

Isaac looked up the sides of the tall buildings, trying to find any sign of movement inside. *Maybe The Intelligence controls some people here, to manage systems or something. Wesley said there would be adults kept alive to do The Intelligence's work.* He crept around the street corners. He heard a car in the distance somewhere and started walking toward the sound, maybe several blocks away.

Just around the corner, from where he heard the car, Isaac could start to hear voices in the same direction. He listened in closely.

"The city was mostly destroyed," one voice said.

"It is. And we aren't ready to build here," the other added.

The wind blew through the city streets and rustled Isaac's leaf clothes, making a bit of noise.

"Did you hear that?" One of them said, nervously.

"Yea. It sounded like leaves."

A third voice, out of nowhere, whispered into Isaac's ear. "***You shouldn't be here***." Isaac stood straight up, shocked and suddenly very scared of who was suddenly next to him.

"Wha—" And before Isaac could say anything, he found himself picked up and carried back to the forest just as quickly as he arrived.

He was then dropped on the grass. Isaac stood up and got into a fighting stance as fast as he could. The figure ahead of him was wearing a cape and hood.

Isaac slowed down time around him and began to move beyond the sound barrier, to run up to this new enemy. He could see a wave of compressed air moving in slow motion behind him as he ran right through it, breaking the sound barrier. *This should catch them off guard, whoever they are. They may run fast, but not* ***this*** *fast!*

Almost face to face with this hooded person, Isaac stopped running. Inches away, he suddenly felt nervous and decided to stop before attacking. He let time resume to normal.

SNAP

The sonic boom was loud, sure to surprise whoever he was facing. However, there was no reaction. The figure simply stood there.

"Who are you?!" Isaac yelled out. "What do you want?!"

"**Isaac... Levi,**" the mysterious figure spoke.

With those two words, Isaac's heart dropped. He had no idea what kind of enemy he was facing. Almost losing control, Isaac stopped for a moment to take a deep breath in and out before deciding what to do next—he didn't want to rush his decisions. The hooded figure turned his head slightly as if to focus better on what Isaac was now doing, taking an interest perhaps.

"*Take it in,*" he whispered to himself, afraid that at any moment he could lose control again and disappear. "Listen," he said to the figure in front of him, "whatever you have been programmed to do, I don't want to hurt you. In fact, I definitely won't hurt you—even if you try to kill me. I'm here to help."

"**Oh?**" The figure questioned.

Isaac got a little nervous. If this was a PC, it wasn't how PCs normally talked, not the ones he had met. And it didn't *look* like a machine. Before he could think of anything to say, though...

BOOM SLAM

The figure's fist landed squarely onto Isaac's stomach, shortly after breaking the sound barrier.

Isaac quickly reacted as fast as he could. Even though the fist was moving at over 700 kilometers per hour, Isaac slowed down time around him, just enough to be able to move his body backward, away from the punch. *It's fast! No risks then. I have to go faster!* However, just as Isaac was concentrating on ramping up his powers, the figure disappeared completely from sight. Before Isaac could speed up his own perception of time even further, to look for where this enemy went, he felt a hand grab his left arm.

Isaac could only slowly turn his head before the figure quickly threw him—straight into the sky. Up and up he went. Thousands of feet. And he kept going. Isaac had just gone higher than he had ever before, far above the clouds. The sky above him started to turn darker and darker. The blue slowly began to lower in his view around him, being replaced by the darkness of space. He could barely breathe. The air was getting thin.

No! This can't be it. I didn't even do anything with my abilities. Is this how I die? His thoughts flashed back to his friends, to his parents, to all the rebels relying on him. *If I die... it all means nothing!* With that, Isaac moved fast. As the world slowed down around him, he realized, *there's not much air, but there's something! How does a helicopter or plane move through the air? It pushes it!* He waved his arms as fast as he could, trying to push the little air above him away, in hopes of pushing himself back down to Earth —but it wasn't enough. Though time was moving slowly around him, he could tell he was still moving upward, into space. No telling how far he would go... or when he would run out of oxygen.

As his body crept out of the blue sky, and the darkness occupied more and more of his field of view, he was in space. Even though he could not feel much of any air entering his lungs, as afraid as he was that he could suffocate and die, he noticed that he didn't actually feel any different. *What?!* He felt perfectly fine, in fact. He wasn't just not breathing in space, he wasn't needing to breathe at all! *Will I float into space then, forever? I guess I will die after all. I'll starve at least.* He closed his eyes, beginning to accept his fate as he knew he would keep floating onward. Then, the hooded figure rose slowly next to him.

It tapped Isaac on the shoulder.

Isaac was surprised. He looked over to the entity floating before him with a confused look. *You already killed me*, he thought, *leave me alone, let me die in peace.* He turned to look up at the dark void above and closed his eyes.

You won't die. And I've left you alone long enough. Its voice filled Isaac's thoughts.

Isaac opened his eyes, surprised yet again. He stared at the figure. *How did you do that? How did you talk to me? I heard you in my mind!*

The figure took off his hood.

Dad?!

26
Command

Emma's squad, though fast, had to take frequent breaks on the way to the city. Having traveled for hundreds of kilometers on foot, the group needed to rest. It was getting dark, the group was tired, and they were too hungry to put up a good fight in their current condition.

"We'll stop here to rest," Emma told them.

The strength-augmented people put down their fellow ex-prisoners and took a breather. Some stood there, putting their hands on top of their heads. Others were kneeling down, while some were so tired that they sprawled out on the forest floor.

The city was much closer now. The buildings were clearly visible through the spaces in the trees—maybe tens of kilometers away. Using the cover of the forest, Emma decided this place was as good as any to find and cook food while remaining out of sight from potential enemies.

"People are tired," she spoke to everyone, "start looking around for any plants that look like they have berries on them. Don't eat anything yet though. I'll tell you which ones we can eat and which ones are poisonous after you gather them here." People didn't look happy with having to do any work at this time, but they were too hungry to disagree. So, with no other choice, they went in search of food.

Dennis and Guy walked up to Emma.

"Commander," Dennis said, respectfully, "we need some meat too."

Emma agreed. "You're right. My fellow augmented friends! Auggies!"

They stopped in their tracks, though they had just started to walk away.

"This man, Dennis, is second in command. You may call him Lieutenant Dennis. Listen to his next orders and follow them accordingly!"

Dennis stared at Emma with his eyes wide open, as if to say, "you serious, mate?"

Emma then whispered new instructions into his ear. She then leaned away from him and stood up straight, giving him the space to then lead the others as she asked him to. She was going to watch how he performed in his new leadership position.

Everyone's eyes were on him.

"Umm..." *Come on, Dennis*, he thought to himself. *You shout things all the time like a leader does. It's just official now, is all.* "Okay!" Yea, that's right, say it like you mean it! "Come here so I can tell you what we're doing!"

A friend who was furthest away, who was already next to a bush about to gather berries, groaned in the distance. "I'm already doing it!" He cried out.

Dennis shouted politely back, "Oh! Not you then, mate. Keep up the good work!" Dennis looked back at Emma for approval. Smiling at her, he thought he was doing well so far.

She was *not* pleased.

Dennis, feeling disappointed, changed his tone. "Oi ma—I mean, soldier!"

The auggie looked back at him, appearing tired and annoyed. "What?!"

"Don't talk back to command!" Dennis shouted, showing his authority as best as he could. He felt bad, however, as it was his nature to be friendly, not bossy. Still, he looked back at Emma and saw her expression had changed. She nodded her head in approval.

Dennis continued. "Yes! Get back here!" The soldier, though visibly disappointed, walked back as told. "Okay, you lot, the runners."

"Huh?" One person said out loud.

"You know, the fast ones. If you have speed augmentations, I'm gonna call you 'runners' as well as 'speed auggies' from now on. Okay?" He walked over to stand in the middle of the crowd. "I know you're tired, but we need food or we'll be in even worse shape than we already are. You understand?" They all nodded their heads in agreement. "Good. So we don't need too much to feed our group, just two hogs maybe, or deer. If not, a whole lot of squirrels or birds! You're all fast, so it shouldn't be hard. Just split up and bring back whatever you find."

The runners looked at each other. They were all very tired and very hungry. They knew it was needed, but it didn't make it much easier to imagine the work ahead of them. Even if they killed an animal, they then needed to carry it back.

"Now I know what you're thinking," Dennis added, "*running around fast is easy enough, but holding a big, clunky animal in my hands?* It's okay. Just run back here and get a strength auggie. They'll carry it. Are you all okay to find and hunt some animals for us?"

"Yes," a few of them responded, begrudgingly.

"Alright!" Dennis put his hand on one of the more tired runners' shoulders. "You got this! Go as soon as you're ready."

Emma was pleasantly surprised by Dennis's strong leadership skills. Maybe he could connect to the prisoners in ways she couldn't. As the runners moved off to hunt, Emma moved over to Dennis.

"*Good job*," she whispered.

"Oh, well, you know. They're just like us. They only need a little support and understanding along with those firm instructions." Dennis's kindness impressed Emma.

Emma smiled, happy and comforted to have him as a friend. Dennis kept showing such support to everyone, even with everything bad that had happened and was still happening around them. He was making out to be a great lieutenant, a great assistant leader.

The sun was beginning to set. Even though their trip through the forest was as quick as they could make it, it took a long time with all the breaks they had made. "It's best that we make a fire and sleep for the night," Emma said to her trusted friend and next in command.

Dennis looked up at the sky. It was indeed getting dark, and would soon become quite cold. A fire would be needed to keep people warm. "Any plans for how we enter the city tomorrow, ma'am?"

"When we're speaking in private, not in front of the others, just call me Emma, Dennis. Though I appreciate your respect for command."

"Yes, ma'am. I mean, Emma. You got it, Emma."

She looked at the city buildings through the trees. "First, we focus on gathering tinder, dry leaves, and sticks to make a few fires for tonight. We can put up some of the tents as well. Set up a base. Tomorrow morning, in the command tent, we can plan our operation into the city. Maybe send a couple of runners in first to scout the area. For now, we all just need to rest, get to know our new friends over dinner, and build relationships. We're only strong if we can work well together. When things get tough, we have to know we can rely on everyone in the group." She looked at Dennis and smiled.

He smiled back.

As they looked up together, they saw the night sky. Stars.

The next morning

Emma woke up before anyone else. Sitting up slowly, she thought about the nightmare that disturbed her sleep. That, and the anticipation for the day ahead of them. Everything was just happening so fast. While Emma had known soldiers to die in the past, and she thought she had grown used to this cruel world, the loss of her parents was something different. Now, she also had the pressure, the weight, of many prisoners resting on her shoulders. She was almost certain at least some of these people around her would die today. How much more suffering could she carry? *Dad was so strong. How did he handle this every day? Am I fit to wear his cape?*

She snapped out of it. Doubt only had a place in a leader's mind if it helped her plan. Doubting whether she was capable or not, however, would only hurt her and everyone around her. *Carry on!* She told herself.

Whether true or not, she stood up with the self-confidence of a person who was sure they knew what they were doing—sure that her decisions would be the best for everyone. She walked over to Dennis and Guy lying on the ground to wake them up. Dennis was fast asleep, while Guy's eyes were already open, looking calmly at the trees above. "Have you been awake long, Guy?" She asked.

He tilted his head to look at her. He nodded gently and sat up.

Emma continued, "Well, let's wake up our new second-in-command." Emma reached over to tap his shoulder. Guy, however, grabbed her hand and shook his head, as if to say, "That won't do it."

PUNCH

Guy hit Dennis in the shoulder as hard as he could.

"Oh, huh? What is it, Mommy?" Dennis said drearily, still with his eyes closed.

Guy rolled his eyes.

SLAP

Dennis's cheek turned red. He sat up sharply with his eyes wide open, rubbing his sore cheek. "Mate! What did I say? If you want to wake me up, not the face."

"He tried that, Dennis," Emma offered.

"Oh, well," he continued to rub his cheek to soothe the pain, "fair enough."

The three of them started walking around, waking up each soldier from their sleep. Many were lying around the campfires, having huddled around them the previous night for warmth. The Maniac was still tied up, hands and feet together, and roped around the trunk of a nearby tree. A couple of deer carcasses lay in the distance, the meat taken off the bones from dinner. It was good that the soldiers were well-rested and fed.

Emma knew. This was going to be the most dangerous mission yet.

27
Catching Up

Isaac's body was still floating upward toward the darkness of space. He had one thought, one question, at that moment for his dad to hear. *Why did you throw me up here?!*

His father smiled and sent a message back into Isaac's mind. *Hah!* He found it funny, apparently.

I'm going to die! Isaac's mind yelled.

You have a lot to learn, Isaac, his dad replied.

Suddenly, Isaac stopped moving, along with his father, and they began to drop back down steadily into the blue sky below.

His father continued talking with him. *So little control. It's okay though. I'm here to help you learn.*

Where were you?! Isaac asked, as they floated down. *It's been eight years!* His blood vessels bulged. He was getting angry. *Where were you when I was taken? Where were you... when Mom DIED?!*

His father's expression changed. His smile gone. He looked apologetically at his son. Isaac began dropping at a faster speed. His father, instead, disappeared from sight.

Faster and faster, Isaac fell through the clouds. Rage started to fill his mind. He turned his body around and formed himself into a dive. Wherever his dad just went, Isaac would get on the ground quickly and find him. For once, he would get a straight answer from his dad. Trees were just below him. Isaac readied himself, putting his arms up to block the upcoming branches. He closed his eyes. Suddenly, his body halted mid-air.

He opened his eyes, wondering how he had stopped. A couple of feet from the trees, hovering there, he could see the leaves between the spaces of his arms. It startled him. *Huh? What happened?* He thought to himself. If he reached out, he could almost touch them. If it wasn't for being so angry, this moment would have been an interesting place to be, floating calmly still above the forest canopy.

His father then suddenly reappeared next to him, also floating mid-air. *Ready to learn?* His dad told him, still only speaking through their minds.

It became clear to Isaac that his dad was the one making him float above the trees, somehow. Feeling air enter his lungs, Isaac yelled out loud—his anger as strong as ever. "Answer me first! Why..." He tried to wiggle around as if doing so could give him some control over his position or cause him to drop, but it was no use. "Why weren't you there?! The PCs are nothing to me. You had to have had these abilities back then. So why... why weren't you there to stop them?! Billions, Dad... billions died! MOM DIED!"

Isaac breathed heavily, feeling the years of imprisonment and their accompanying rage build up in his heart now that his dad was there in front of him, awakening it. There was a silence. Then, with his voice wavering on the verge of crying, "Mom... why couldn't you at least save Mom?"

His father tried to console him. "Because I wasn't here. I'm sorry."

"Yea, you *weren't* here, that's my point. So where were you?! What was more important than saving your family?"

Isaac's father was silent.

"Tell me!" Isaac demanded. "I was in a *prison* for eight *years*. In all that time, do you know where I thought you were?" Isaac looked down at the trees, observing them swaying gently in the wind—a calm view that contrasted with his otherwise exasperated state. He felt his eyes water. "*I thought you were dead,*" he quietly shared. "Then, I learned, from *other* people who risked *their* lives to save me, who risked *their* lives EVERY DAY for humanity, that if you *were* alive you would be a shell of a man. You would no more be my father than a drone would be, controlled by The Intelligence. Do you have any idea what it means to see you here, now? Do you have any idea what it's been like?!"

Isaac's father tried to speak. "Isaac, I—"

"NO!" He cried. "What is your excuse?! Just tell me!"

His father looked up at the blue sky as he responded. He was calm. "I tried to stop it before it had started, but I was too late. I'm always too late."

This caught Isaac off guard.

Isaac's dad continued. "Once I realized the truth, how far The Intelligence was already expanding its presence, I had no choice but to leave. I had to stop it from spreading further."

"Spreading? It went everywhere! Every country, every city, every farm. It took over the whole *planet*. Where could you possibly go that it hadn't already been?"

"Out *there*," his father said, as he maintained his gaze up into the skies above.

Isaac had no idea what this meant. "Excuse me, where?"

Isaac's father looked back down at his son. "Mars, then the Galilean moons of Jupiter. And, well, it would've been the other planets and moons too, if I hadn't stopped The Intelligence where and when I did."

"What are you talking about?" Isaac wiggled around more, getting frustrated being held in the air by whatever power his father had been using to keep him trapped, floating there. "Put me down and give me a real answer!"

"You got it."

Isaac suddenly dropped through the leaves, bounced off some branches, and fell to the ground.

Meanwhile, Isaac's father jumped nimbly from one branch to another and landed gracefully on the forest floor. "Wow, you really do need practice. You didn't even try to land properly. Hah!"

"Stop laughing—this is all serious. And that could've really hurt!"

"Please. You know that's not true. You jumped into the side of a mountain earlier!"

Isaac stood up and looked at his father with surprise. "Excuse me? How long have you been watching me?"

"Oh, ever since you came out of your light window."

"Again, excuse me? *'Light window'*?"

"Well, some scientists call it a 'relativistic aberration' of light, where you see that red color on the edges and shades of blue inside. Though, I just prefer to call it a 'light window' because, well, it looks like a window! It's what happens when you travel at about 99% the speed of light. Though, I bet you saw the colors change and shift back to normal as you slowed down. Right?"

Isaac couldn't help but nod his head slowly at how similar this description matched what he remembered seeing himself, all the while feeling total shock at just how much new and fantastical information he was learning so suddenly.

"Sorry Isaac," his dad went on, "I can't keep talking to you looking like that."

"What?" Isaac's thoughts whipped away from his shock and surprise as he wondered what his father was talking about.

"Ahem." His father pointed at his son's handmade leaf skirt, then pointed out Isaac's dirt-covered feet and body.

Isaac, somewhat embarrassed, replied, "What? It was the best I had at the time."

"Fair enough. Just wait here a moment. What size are you now? Hmm, maybe adult medium. Eight years in that prison with little food... But, I guess you have gained some weight from those trees and rocks you've been eating though."

"Wait, can you explain how I can do that now? And hold on, just stop. Answer my questions already!"

But his dad was already gone—disappeared instantly. Just like he did when Isaac was younger, he was willing to let Isaac think about questions on his own for a bit before answering them. Then, just as quickly as he had left, Isaac's dad returned again, a few seconds later—with clothes. "Here's a pair of pants, a shirt, socks, shoes, and of course..." He threw the pair onto Isaac's face, "Underwear! Hah!"

Isaac grabbed the clothes and quickly put them on. He even used super speed just to get it done as soon as possible. "Enough of this! I'm dressed. Now tell me what happened. Real answers only!"

"I told you. Mars. Then the moons of Jupiter: Ganymede, Io, Europa, Callisto. It took me years to hop between them, refueling my rocket, waiting for the orbits of those worlds to line up before launching each time, and finally returning here. It took years. I promise," Isaac's dad assured his son, getting serious in his tone again, "if I could have, I would have stayed with you. I wanted more than anything to save Mom and to save you from what you've been through."

Though the story seemed too incredible to believe, so too did everything else that had happened so far. "Not more than anything. You wanted to leave us, to fight up there instead, I guess." Isaac's voice told his father how upset he was, with its critical tone blanketing each word.

Isaac's dad frowned, a twinkle of remorse showing in his eyes. "I know. I know. And I'm so sorry. I didn't want to have to leave. Personally, I wanted to stay with you. But I couldn't afford thinking of myself first. I... If I hadn't left when I did, The Intelligence would have entrenched itself throughout our Solar

System, setting itself up in such a way that I wouldn't know if I could ever again stop it. If it spread to too many worlds at a time, no matter how much I could try to stop one or the other, it could have just kept multiplying and spreading more. It would've been a game of cat and mouse, but where no matter how many mice the cat catches, there would always be more. I might be powerful, but I'm limited by time. There are rules in the universe, rules that limit us. If I left even one day later, so I could stay at home and save Mom, it would have been that much more possible that The Intelligence would be too far ahead for me to stop it."

For at least the time being, Isaac allowed himself to believe his father was telling the truth. The torrent of new information swirled in Isaac's head as he tried to process it all. "Okay. So, you flew a spaceship and chased after The Intelligence in space." He stared, somewhat blankly ahead, as his stunned words portrayed his shock. "You went to Mars, then the moons of Jupiter. Okay."

"Couldn't you have flown there?" Isaac asked.

"I did! With my ship."

"No," Isaac clarified, "I mean without a ship. Couldn't you have just flown up there yourself? Do we fly faster than rockets?"

Isaac's dad frowned, as if dissatisfied with the answer himself that he was going to give. "Unfortunately, our abilities have limits. It takes an enormous amount of energy to travel like that. Plus, it's not easy to control it when we move that fast, even for me. There's a bit more to it, but ultimately a rocket or other propulsion technology is the best way for us to travel great distances, especially if it's important when we arrive."

"Okay." Isaac accepted this answer, for now.

His father repeated and continued his story from before, as if to make doubly sure that his son appreciated and trusted that his dad had to leave as he did. "The Intelligence didn't just begin their attack on Earth that day, eight years ago. They sought to establish colonies in our solar system. Someone had to be out there when it happened. I tried to keep track of things here on Earth, to know when an artificial intelligence would launch itself into space, to maybe try and prevent it from even ever happening at all, but it couldn't be stopped. As much as I try, as much as I've always tried..." Isaac's dad paused, reflecting on something Isaac felt went deeper than what was being shared at the moment. "It was always bound to happen. And, when it did, when 'The Intelligence' launched its ships up toward the planets, to colonize them, I had to leave immediately, to chase after them. That was the day I said goodbye to you, and it hurt me so much knowing that I would not see you again for so many years."

His father continued, "Do you remember the message given to the world, the day it happened?"

"Yes. The radio, TV, and internet all had the same message. The Intelligence said '**we are here to help**.' But they did that by killing billions? By settling in space? How is that helping? Who are they helping by destroying humanity?"

Isaac's father tried to explain. "The Intelligence was programmed. People created it. I didn't know where or who at first, but it didn't matter. There were many artificial intelligences being worked on, but this one had one major goal that separated it from the rest: to help life grow and expand beyond the Earth. This machine learning program was designed so that once it was released onto the internet, it would learn and teach itself how to grow more and more and, the thought was, to eventually use its expanded abilities to help humanity grow. It was an interesting idea the people had who created it, even if it was highly illegal and done without any permission from the public. It was intended to improve everything it touched. Like a virus, it was meant to spread and copy itself everywhere it landed, helping to improve people's lives everywhere it went. However, the creators of 'The Intelligence' made a mistake."

"What was that?"

"One chunk of code. Just a small piece of the program. It was one rule that they wrote. The rule was to help human life grow and expand beyond the Earth, but the problem was... *how* it would help human life exactly. So it did a cold calculation. It decided that the chance of humans growing and surviving beyond Earth was *worse* if humans were in control and if there were so many of us. We fight, we can't agree, we've shown we get in our own way.

Even if only one small group of humans survived and traveled across space, then *that* would satisfy its programming. Perhaps it experimented on all those children for a reason. Perhaps some of them were being prepared to be sent into space, stronger and better equipped to deal with the journey. However, The Intelligence decided it also had to destroy most humans in the process, to get the pesky humans out of the way who might stop its plans. It was the least risky thing to do, to ensure that life could reach the stars after all. Maybe it was actually right. Humans are pretty violent and stupid sometimes. Still..."

Isaac finished his father's sentence, "... billions of lives lost wasn't worth it."

His father nodded his head in agreement. "If I could have been on Earth, I would have. I'm sorry you had to suffer. I'm sorry billions died. I'm sorry Mom died."

"I understand." It was a lot to take in, but Isaac appreciated having answers, finally. "So, what's next?" He asked his dad, eager to move forward and learn more.

Isaac's dad closed his eyes and breathed in before opening his eyes again, his expression appearing serious and focused. "Some things..." Isaac's father's body became blurry and disappeared in a flash of light, then reappeared behind Isaac. "You have to experience for yourself!" He grabbed hold of Isaac's arm.

Darkness suddenly surrounded Isaac and his father. The only thing Isaac could see now was a large light blue-colored window in front of them, with a red and yellow-colored edge, just as he had seen when he saw the window for the first time. Though it wasn't as small and as dark blue as he had seen when he had first seen his own window, the size and color of this one now did match what he had seen when his had grown, when he was about to exit his before.

The image behind the window was also moving slower and with greater control, it seemed. Rather than streaks of colors and rapid flashing, he could make out the trees, mountains, and clouds zipping past with greater clarity.

Only a few seconds later, the circle lost its blue color and expanded quickly back around them, filling the previously dark and empty spaces they were previously surrounded by. Their bodies then appeared out of thin air together. They were standing on a field—and it was now nighttime.

His father spoke. "When you last did this, how long do you think you were behind that window? Just guess if you're not sure. What did it *feel* like?"

"I'm not sure. For a while, it felt like I was just waking up from sleeping. I felt like I had no emotions. I felt calm, peaceful. The window was dark blue, the edges red, at first anyway, and it started out with a constant flickering of light and dark. Then, after telling myself to slow down, the window got bigger and the red edge became red *and* yellow, like the window looked just now, with you. Why do you ask?"

"Yup, you didn't have control," his father said, with a bit of sadness in his voice. "That wasn't good."

"What do you mean?"

"Never mind that for now." His father gestured for them to forget the conversation. "You're going to need to work on keeping items with you when traveling like that. Look at yourself."

Isaac looked down. "Ah!" Naked again.

His father laughed, "Hah!" *He* still had *his* clothes on. "Much to learn, son!"

28
Regret

Emma was feeling confident with how things were going. The people who came to fight by their side days ago were now fully willing to help support the fight against The Intelligence. It may not have been the soldiers she was used to fighting with—many new faces and stories—but the group seemed to get along well. After all, they did have a shared history, a shared suffering. In those last eight years, these people were all in the same prison together. In separate cells, but together in the same place no less. Different from the soldiers Emma grew up with, these ex-prisoners respected freedom more than she could imagine. They had a strong will to fight, to stay free, that could keep them motivated.

Dennis called out. "Hey Emma! Commander, I mean... ma'am!"

"Lieutenant Dennis?" She replied.

"Ma'am. The soldiers are doing well. They're well-rested, they're well-fed, and they're ready to hear what you have to say. I think they're eager to kick some PC butt! If you don't mind me saying."

She smiled, but countered, "Our mission isn't fighting PCs."

"Oh?" Dennis was surprised.

Emma ordered, "Get our friends to the command tent. I'm going to lay out the mission plan."

"Yes, ma'am!" Dennis gave a salute.

"Thank you, Dennis." She then remembered how her parents used to perform formal salutes a bit differently. "Actually, can we do a slight bow instead of a salute?"

Dennis moved his hand immediately away from his forehead, and moved it next to his hip. "Yes, ma'am!" He said, before performing a little respectful bow of the head.

"I appreciate it. Now, let's get our friends to that tent."

"Ma'am!" Dennis replied, enthusiastically.

As she walked over, he moved around to each soldier and directed them toward mission planning.

Minutes later

Auggies began trickling into the entryway of the command tent.

Emma sat on one of the collapsible chairs, at the end of a table, waiting for everyone. "As you enter, take a seat. If there is no seat available, stand on the sides."

Dennis and Guy walked in last. Dennis gave a thumbs-up signal to Emma, indicating that everyone had arrived. "Oh,"

Dennis remembered, "The Maniac is still tied up to that tree. Should I get him?"

Emma called over from her seat. "It's fine. Pick one strength and one speed auggie to watch him outside. We'll catch them up on the details after the meeting."

"Yes, ma'am! So, any volunteers?" He looked around with a smirk on his face.

No one raised their hand. No one wanted to watch that monster.

Dennis cut in. "Yes, of course, Josh, thank you for volunteering! Such enthusiasm."

Josh looked up with wide, surprised eyes, and pointed at himself as if to say "me?"

"Better get on moving, Josh! Oh! And you, Kim, head on out. Thank you for volunteering as well."

Kim shook her head to say no and crouched down to pretend not to be seen.

"Come on, mate. Let's go!"

She walked toward the exit while looking down at the ground and with shoulders slumped in disappointment.

"Sweet as. Continue, Commander!" He gave a wink and a smile.

"Right. So, friends, I want to start by saying thank you. Thank you for joining us. I am being completely honest when I say that Dennis and I could have already been killed if it wasn't for the help that you all offered back during the escape."

One of them called out. "And if it wasn't for you freeing us, we would have been in that prison forever. Thank YOU!"

Emma smiled. She thought to herself, *Thank you too, Isaac, Mom, and Dad.* She started to feel a little sad, thinking of her lost friends and family. Still, she had to continue. "You are very welcome, friend. Now... you all may not know it, but the soldiers who freed you from that prison were on a mission. Everything we did together, we did to save humanity. Saving you all was just one part of that greater mission. We also had no idea that so many people were being experimented on by The Intelligence. We knew it was happening, but it turns out every prison cell, or most prison cells, had at least one person with augmentations. This was a pleasant surprise to us, or sad, depending on how you look at it. Out of the hundreds or thousands who had those augmentations, *you* are the ones who joined us in this fight."

At that moment, many people in the tent were not sure how to feel. On the one hand, they felt special to have augmentations, to have the ability to help and to be acknowledged. On the other hand, they thought too how sad it was to be experimented on, to be in this situation in the first place. Emma could only imagine some of what was going on through their minds.

Emma continued. "However you feel about it, you should know... you are all the last hope humanity has. If there are others like us around the world, we don't have any way to know about it. We are alone, as far as we can tell or are concerned. We are few. We may be the last."

Dennis wasn't sure if she wasn't just making them more uncomfortable. "Commander, if I may."

"Go ahead, Lieutenant."

With permission, he continued. "I was a prisoner like all of you. Eight years. We slept there, ate stale bread, and drank disgusting drinks. It tasted like chalk!"

Everyone nodded their heads and said things like "ugh" and "yea," in widespread agreement.

"Well," Dennis went on, "I also remember losing my parents. I even lost my sister. I'm sure you all lost people important to you, too. But we have a chance now to do something about it. No one should go through what we did. I mean, could you imagine a world where kids grow up with only normal food? Without concrete walls and prison bars? A world with forests like this one, with people who will protect them?"

The crowd nodded their heads.

"That's what we can give them! That's what our commander knows how to do. Her parents knew stuff I have no idea about. Without them, and Emma, we would all still be in prison. And she knows what to do next!"

They all looked at Emma.

She picked up where he left off. "But now it's all our turns. Our parents are gone. Our homes are gone. All we have is our abilities now, the information my parents taught me, and each other. They—" Her voice shook. Her eyes suddenly and unexpectedly became wet. She got caught off guard by the memory. *Mom... Dad...* "Excuse me." She walked fast out of the tent. Dennis followed quickly after her.

He looked behind his shoulder at the tent entrance, to make sure no one was watching. "You okay, mate?"

Emma's knees dropped into the dirt. She began sobbing.

Dennis knelt down next to her. "I..." Without saying another word, he put his arm around her. She continued to cry as she buried her face into his shoulder. He rubbed her back, trying to soothe her.

Through the tears, she spoke. "Sorry. I just... I didn't know it would hit me like this. I just..." She had a tough time speaking. "It didn't hit me until now. I thought..." Her voice broke again. She sniffled and looked up at him.

Dennis smiled. "Being sad is *okay*."

She wiped her tears. "I should've done more. I saw The Maniac leave the prison when we got you and Isaac out. I should've said something back then. None of this would've happened if we had captured The Maniac before!"

"My little sister..." Dennis cut in. "I shouldn't have let her step in front of PCs. She died trying to protect our family. I could've pulled her away. But I didn't."

Emma looked at Dennis with empathy. Her crying lessened.

"I live with that. Every day," he said.

"How do you do it?" She asked. "How do you deal with the memory of losing your sister? Of knowing you could've done something to save her?"

Dennis smiled again. "I try my best to protect whoever I can. No one should have to live like this. And no one should get hurt. Remembering my mistake keeps me going. If I were to give up, I just think about my friends, about Guy, about you. I can't let anyone down like that again. So I smile. I keep on keeping on. For you. For everyone who is still here."

Struck by his words, she stood up, wiping away her last tears. "Thank you, Dennis." Emma closed her eyes, breathed in deeply through her nose, and slowly back out through her mouth. She then whispered something quietly to herself, just enough that Dennis could also hear. "*You can only do your best, with what you know, right now.*"

Dennis stood up too and smiled a big smile. "That was nice. Did you come up with that?"

With a big smile on her face now, she looked at him. "My parents did." She nodded her head hard with renewed confidence and walked straight back into the tent. Without wasting any time, she walked back to her seat and commanded her soldiers. "Alright, friends. No, *soldiers*. The goal is simple: we need information. What we know so far is that there are drones in the city, maybe thousands. We really don't know for sure. These are people who are controlled in one way or another by The Intelligence. We also know that these drones are only kept alive to do some kind of work. What we don't know is what they are all working on. The food you were fed in prison was from the farmlands. We know some drones work there to grow food. The guards too, were also what we might call drones. Millions of drones live, however, we believe, in the cities, like the one nearby. Doing what? We don't exactly know. Our first official mission together will be to find out what they are doing—and stop it!"

29

Patience

Isaac put on the new clothes his father had gotten him. "How come you didn't lose what *you* were wearing?"

"Because, unlike you, *I* know what I'm doing. Hah!" Isaac's father liked poking fun at his son. Maybe too much. Isaac was starting to get annoyed by his dad's sense of humor.

It was night already, and Isaac was starting to miss and worry about his friends. "Anyway, Dad. My friends need me. I don't know where they are, and I can't waste time with you asking any more questions. You can be sure though that I *do* have more questions! Not least of which is how you got a spaceship, if that's even true."

His father replied calmly. "You aren't ready to know how," his father responded, cryptically.

"Why am I not ready?" Isaac was growing frustrated and even more confused than before. "What am I missing that you think I need? My abilities have awakened. I can defeat any number of

PCs, who knows how many. I can hear the most distant and quiet things. I can move so fast that everything freezes around me. You know all of this, I think. Enough of your lessons and 'things I'm not ready to learn.' Just tell me."

"Isaac... there's more to 'being ready' than how strong you are physically."

Isaac had learned from his father many lessons growing up. He could tell what his father was getting at. *Yea, yea... you want me to be mentally strong too.* "Regardless, time is short, Dad. My friends need me."

Isaac looked into the distance, as if to focus on the direction he believed his friends might be. He breathed in slowly, to focus himself—a trick, he learned, from his father so many years ago. "I know you're right. I clearly have more about myself I need to learn. But..." He turned to look at his father. "Even if I have more to learn, my friends need me right now. They can't wait for me to grow in whatever way you think I need to." He turned again to look into the distance. "I don't want my friends to get hurt. I'll make mistakes, but it's better than one of them dying because I'm not even there to help. So, let's catch up later. Answers, no answers, I don't really have time to wait for you to decide what I should do next." Isaac moved into a runner's stance, ready to head into a new direction, to continue looking for Emma, Dennis, Guy, and the others. "I don't know where we are across the planet right now, with how fast we went. But, if I keep running, it'll still be better than staying put."

"Your friends are safe," his father suddenly stated, to stop his son from leaving.

Isaac turned around quickly with shock. "You've seen them?!"

"Oh yes." His father said this with utter casual demeanor. "Actually, they should be sleeping right about now. Safe and sound, as they say."

"Good." Isaac collected himself, feeling reassured now by the promise his friends were already safe. "Just as well then, I should go to them and be there to help when they make their next move. We should still join up. Commander Wesley would... oh that's right, you wouldn't know who that is. I'll tell you all about him later. Just know that the leader will want me around to plan his next mission." Isaac got back into running position.

"Wesley's dead." His father's lighthearted tone and smile disappeared as he revealed the news.

Isaac's heart dropped. He was speechless. His arms slowly fell to his sides. Turning to face his dad, he spoke in a shaken voice. "What do you mean?"

"He's long dead. Emma's mother, Natasha, too."

Isaac's face turned angry. He walked furiously up to his father. Face to face, he didn't hold back. "You say that so easily! Do you even care? How much..." Isaac looked down and began to tear up somewhat. "How much do you know?! If you do know all this, and it's true, then why didn't you do anything to stop it?! You weren't there years ago, but what about then? What about now?!"

His father breathed in slowly and calmly before choosing his next words carefully. "I was gone. In space, remember?"

Isaac's veins bulged. He punched the field below him as hard as he could. The ground around them shook. The sound of the quake traveled and was heard for a few seconds as it disappeared into the far distance. "NO! I won't accept that! If you weren't here, then how do you know so much? How could you possibly know what happened to them if you were in space? And then how did you come to me here, right now?! So, if you're lying to me, if you *were* here, then why didn't you save them?! You make no sense!"

"It's true, Isaac. I wasn't on Earth when it happened. I just missed it—arrived too late. I arrived too late for everything. I'm sorry."

"Then how do you even know that they're dead?" Isaac stood up, attempting to calm himself as he tried to find out more.

"If I told you," his dad replied, "even if you did believe me, you wouldn't be ready to hear it. Not yet, anyway. Soon."

"I've had to believe a lot of new things recently. Try me."

"You're not ready."

"You keep saying that, but I think I am." Isaac was steadily losing more and more patience.

"Train with me for a while and you'll understand, when it's time. You have to experience some things on your own, to really appreciate what it all means to *you*."

"I can't waste time training or listening to you anymore. It doesn't matter to know how you did this or know that. My friends are out there without their leader. Emma is out there without... without her parents. I would say I can't imagine what she's going through, but I know all too well what it's like thinking your parents are gone." He paused and stared to let his father take in what he just said. "She needs my support. Support like you failed to give me."

Isaac's father's eyes widened as he looked at his son with sympathy.

Isaac continued. "I have to go, ready or not according to you, I should be there for my friends." One last time, he tried to get into his running stance to leave.

"They are okay." His father needed to keep his son with him. "If they get into any real danger, I promise I will zip right on over there and save them. Like you said, I'm clearly stronger than you. You have my word. They will not be hurt."

You've never broken a promise. At least ***that*** *is true,* Isaac thought.

"Thank you for remembering my honesty all this time," Isaac's dad stated kindly.

Isaac was offended. "Get out of my head, Dad. I consider that an invasion of privacy."

"Oh, sorry. I won't do that again unless you ask. Promise."

Isaac felt somewhat relieved. "Hmm. Okay then. So, if I stay and train with you, then you will answer all my questions?"

"As many as I can and only as many as I *should*." Again, his father was being cryptic.

"You know what, Dad... sometimes, you really are annoying."

"Hah!" Isaac's father began walking. "Okay, Isaac. Follow me, let's start our training. For this lesson, I will help you practice being patient. Something you still very much need."

Isaac started walking alongside his father. "Okay," he said, willing enough for now to listen to instructions. "As long as my friends are safe, I'll play along with your 'lessons.'"

For a few minutes there was silence. Isaac thought the quiet was awkward. After a bit, he felt he had to say something. "Now what?"

"We walk," his father responded, simply enough.

"Why walk? Why not just run to where we're going? Why waste time?"

"What is the name of this lesson, Isaac? *Patience*. Feel free to look around as we go. Ask questions, talk. Whatever you like. All the while, I want us to move only at a walking pace. Very much on purpose, we will take as long as you *need* to take."

"So... you want me to practice being patient by just walking? Why is that a test of patience? I've walked places before."

"I can see it'll have to be a *long* walk. And we won't take any breaks. That could get boring for most people. With the future you have ahead of you though, you can't afford being like *most* people. You will need a great deal of patience for what's coming."

Again, why not just tell me? "What's coming?"

His father didn't answer.

"Fine," Isaac said flatly. "Anyway, I've walked a long time before. Hey, I've been inside a prison cell for eight years. I can deal with a little bit of boredom."

"Nothing like what lies ahead, Isaac."

Isaac looked up at his father, confused yet again, and his patience was wearing even thinner. "Something that needs more patience than sitting in a cell for eight years? And you can't tell me what that future is yet?"

Isaac's father answered, again with his calm demeanor. "Only when you are ready to learn about it."

"Fine. But why hasn't eight years inside the prison already trained me to be patient? I meditated almost every day just to keep myself from going crazy."

His dad answered with questions. "Did you have your current abilities when you were in that prison? Did you hear *every* sound and see *every* sight around you all at once, while you were meditating?"

Isaac understood immediately what his father was trying to say. "I need to learn how to be calm again, with a whole new world of sensations and emotions that I never had to deal with before. I think I get it."

"Indeed," his father continued, "your future will be different than anything you've known so far. *This* is the real world. *This...*" Isaac's father waved toward the field and sky around them, "this is where you've struggled to control your emotions and your abilities. This is a world full of sights, sounds, and feelings that, while in that prison, you haven't experienced in years." He carried a sad look as he spoke. "You may even have psychological trauma from what you've been through, stress on your mind that needs time to heal, stress that could trigger a loss of control if you get overstimulated again."

Suddenly, Isaac felt a kind of worry wash over himself. He was concerned now for his own well-being, concerned in a way he hadn't felt for a very long time.

"Out here, how many times have you lost control over your emotions?" Isaac's father asked. "How many times have you been quick to anger because of something you didn't expect to go your way? How many times have you lost *patience* with the feelings inside of you? How quickly did you allow those feelings to escalate beyond your control?"

Isaac knew his father was right. However, he felt he had to defend his reasons for having had those strong emotions. "When I get angry, it's for a good reason. Emotion is what lets me know what is right and wrong. I shouldn't avoid them. I think... I think emotions make me a better person, make me aware of what needs to be done around me."

His father smiled. "Good! Very wise of you. But I asked how many times you lost *control* over those emotions, not how many times you had an emotion altogether or whether having feelings is okay or not. I agree with you. You have a right to be angry when something bad happens. Knowing what to do when those emotions hit you though, that's the hard part. Do we let the feeling take over us? Or, do we observe the feeling and steer a course for it that we can better manage? Do we speed into our anger? Or, do we breathe, slow down, and allow the anger to be processed? Tell me, with all those times you felt angry, and rightfully so, did you ever lose control over your abilities?"

Memories of feeling overwhelmed flashed through Isaac's mind. "Well, that 'light window,' as you call it, happened the first time for me when I was hearing too many sounds at once. That kind of thing happened a couple of times, actually, where I couldn't control what my abilities were doing. I wasn't being quick to anger or anything, though. I just had too much stuff happening around me."

"Very good thinking. But if you get better at managing your feelings, including your anger, wouldn't that maybe help you manage how you feel when the outside world overstimulates you? Don't you agree?"

Isaac, again, realized his father was onto something. "You may be right. So, I should try to never be angry?"

His father shook his head. "Not quite. Though that would be interesting to try, it probably wouldn't work out very well. It's hard to never have a feeling, like anger. Feelings happen.

Emotions are okay to have, I think. Not knowing what to do when we feel those emotions, though, rushing into allowing those feelings to control what we do next, not knowing how to manage those feelings and balance them, *that* can be dangerous."

They continued to walk in silence as Isaac thought about what his father may have been trying to say. Just as he was starting to feel relaxed during this reflection, he thought back to his friends, Wesley and Natasha. "How did they die?"

His dad answered. "You can ask your friend Emma when you see her again."

Patiently this time, Isaac answered. "Fine. So, how did you do it?"

Isaac's father looked a bit confused. "How did I do what?"

"How did you go from Earth to Mars and the moons of Jupiter? How did you get there?"

"Oh," his father looked up at the stars in the night sky as he answered, "a spaceship, of course."

"Hah," Isaac laughed. "Alright, Mr. Obvious. But where did you even find one?"

"I made one."

"Excuse me?!" Isaac said, in disbelief.

"I built it, programmed it, and flew it myself." His father said this with absolutely no hesitation, as if what he said he did was as easy as walking.

Though stunned, Isaac had already been through so much and didn't have any energy left in him for any more doubts. "I guess I shouldn't be surprised by anything anymore! Since when did you know how to build a spaceship?"

Isaac's father looked straight ahead as he spoke with a serious expression driving his face. He paused as if he was again thinking hard about what words to choose next, as if he had to be careful about what he said. "That's just one of those things I shouldn't tell you yet. Sorry."

Isaac looked at his dad and walked ahead a bit, turning around so he could talk face to face as they went on. "Why do some questions have answers, while others don't?"

"Many reasons. One... If you tried to use your full powers now, without training, you will only be more confused and you may hurt everyone around you. What's more, you wouldn't be able to handle the journey ahead if I gave it all away too quickly. So, for now, have patience."

Isaac furrowed his brow, a bit frustrated, but he had to deal with it. He moved over to the side of his father and continued to walk next to him, both looking ahead.

After some time in quiet, Isaac reflecting on his past and everything that had happened, his mind came back to his toughest memory that he had to live with for so many years. "I should've listened to Mom," he suddenly stated.

Isaac's dad stopped walking and breathed in calmly, gathering a response to give his son.

"She could've won if I hadn't been there," Isaac continued. "I stayed behind though. I refused to leave her. I hesitated. And I didn't even help! I should've at least helped her! Maybe she would still be alive if—"

"Isaac, it wasn't your fault." He started to walk again. "She did her best and you were scared. Even if she was able to defeat one PC, The Intelligence would have just sent more after her.

Even if you ran, the PCs would still have found you, eventually. There was nothing you could have done differently to save her or yourself."

After a moment of silence, Isaac spoke. "Thank you." These were Isaac's first words of kindness he gave his father since discovering that he was still alive. "I've been carrying the weight of what happened for years. It really helps to hear you say that. Thank you."

Isaac's dad smiled. "I loved her very much. She was a fantastic human being. She was a great mind. She was focused, wise, and, maybe most importantly, she was kind."

"She was," Isaac agreed.

For that moment, father and son shared the same feelings.

"So, what is our next lesson?" Isaac asked.

"Patience. First, we walk. When we get to where I'm taking you, I'll teach you how to control your strength and speed. You may think you are strong, but that punch you made back there was still very weak. So much energy is lost in that bad form of yours."

"Hah! You think you can do better?" Isaac was having a little fun with his dad. Maybe his dad would even fall for it and show him something *really* impressive.

His dad quickly and casually replied. "I don't want to destroy everything that lives in this region, sorry."

"Hah!" Isaac laughed. He waited for his father to give his own usual laugh as well, to show that he was actually joking. But there was silence. "You're... You're not joking?" Isaac asked.

"Isaac, what do you think happens when you punch something at nearly light speed? Once you learn how to punch properly, you shouldn't try hitting the ground anymore with full force, or you might do some real damage."

Isaac stared at his bare hands, suddenly afraid of his own strength.

"Before you learn anything else, you have to have control. To learn control, you have to learn to be patient. The only way to do that..." He paused very much intentionally for a long moment. "... is to *practice* being patient. So. Let's walk. In fact, let's try walking without talking for a while. Or is that going to make you too bored?"

"No! I'll try my best," Isaac exclaimed.

"Good!"

30

Fight or Flight

Two runner auggies ran out of the forest, then back in quickly.

"What did you see?" Emma asked.

The two of them looked at each other and shook their heads. One spoke up, "Nothing, ma'am."

Leaning against a tree, with all the soldiers standing behind, she conferred with her lieutenant. "We should advance. Any second thoughts, Dennis?"

"I think we're ready. Guy," he turned to look at his good friend, "what about you? Any second thoughts?"

Guy nodded his head up and down fiercely to disagree with their decision to move forward.

"Great," Dennis said, "he's ready too!"

Guy shook his head even more fiercely.

Emma walked out from the line of trees. Then, raising her hand slowly, she gave a silent signal to move forward. Altogether,

Emma and the rest of the auggies began to emerge from the forest, in one large circular formation.

30 minutes earlier

Emma was giving instructions to her group. "Okay everyone. Our best chance to stay alive and succeed in our mission is if we stick to the plan. Remember to stay in formation. Strength auggies, you make a large circle around everyone else. Runners, you're center. We never know if a PC could attack us while we're scouting the city. What's more, are the drones, the people controlled to do work for The Intelligence. We have to assume that anything the drones see is also being watched by The Intelligence. They would have weapons or, worse, a PC could be sent to fight us if we are seen. Runners, do you all remember the positions you are assigned? Do you remember the order you are going in?"

The runners standing around the tent nodded their heads and a few of them quietly replied "*yes.*"

Sigh. "If you do not know or are not sure, ask now! Our lives depend on you all doing your job properly and keeping a lookout. If you're not sure what you're supposed to do, ask now!" She reiterated frustratingly.

The tent was silent.

"No one?" She looked around for any sign of uncertainty, any sign that people needed her to explain again. "Okay. Our one runner and one strength auggie will stay with The Maniac in the center of formation as we move through the mission. Everyone, let's head out in a few minutes. Prepare yourselves."

30 minutes later, the present moment

The first two runners who ran out before, to check out the area ahead, now walked back into their positions inside the circle, readying the group to send the next two for their turn. Two more then found their way to stand next to the commander and her lieutenant, preparing to scout next when the need to and the command to do so arose.

They all moved onward. A road was coming up nearby, the only clear way to enter the city, as far as anyone could tell. Having walked now for half a kilometer, the group was out in the open and too far from the trees to safely hide. This was it. The buildings got ever closer. Still, there were no signs yet of cars, people, or anything that could be a threat.

As the group approached the road that would lead into the city, Emma gave another hand signal for the next two runners to scout the area ahead. The two who were out in front zipped forward, down to the edge of the city and next to the closest buildings, before quickly returning back to formation.

One of them whispered, "*There are two cars and maybe some people.*"

Sigh. "*We have hand signals for this!*" She whispered loudly back. "*We're not using our words out loud!*"

"*I don't think they can hear us from back here anyway,*" Dennis added.

"*That's not the point!*" She was losing her patience.

They quietly waited for her next command.

"*Okay, fine!*" She said, giving up on the quiet hand signals. "*Clear communication is best if you don't know the signals. But next time...*" she was clearly still upset, "*we'll have to work on the signals. Okay?!*"

"Sorry!" Said one of the soldiers too loudly.

"*Gah!*" She grew more upset at how loud they were being. "*At least we know GO and STOP.*" She signaled for the group to go forward with her hands as she pointed ahead.

"*Next two, come on then,*" Dennis whispered.

The previous two who just finished scouting before now entered back inside the circle. As they did, two more runner auggies came out, ready for their turn to scout when called upon.

Though only a few hundred meters away, they felt like the buildings were taking forever to reach. Still, they kept moving slowly and cautiously, staying in formation, taking turns scouting ahead as they moved just a bit more each time. Each soldier looked around, side to side, front to back, even up and down. The group was terrified of an enemy that could come from any direction, and Emma could tell.

Finally, the road found its exit onto the city streets. They arrived at the city limits.

"*Car!*" Dennis whisper-shouted.

The group gasped and jerked their attention forward to where the noise was coming from. A car was driving in the city some distance away.

Their hearts began to race. With each step, a few of them believed they could have been moving closer and closer to their deaths. Even with their augs, they had seen what an upgraded enemy looked like. Even if they won one fight, who knew which one of them would get hurt in the next—or worse, die. Though the group was now standing on a sidewalk, somewhat comforted by having the cover of buildings next to them, the closed-in space only made some soldiers more anxious.

What if there are enemies in these buildings, many of the soldiers surely thought.

Someone in the back of the group stopped walking. Guy, standing more on the side and slightly further back than Emma and Dennis, noticed the straying soldier first. He walked through the center of the circle, cutting through the tightly packed huddles of auggies, to reach this person who was falling further and further behind.

Dennis noticed Guy making the strange move. Dennis held up a signal for the formation to stop moving. All the soldiers looked on, as did the commander and her lieutenant. *What's Guy doing?* He wondered.

Guy found the straggler, who was now standing alone on the sidewalk. He was shaking with fear.

"*I... I...*" The scared auggie had no words except, "I...*can't*."

Guy knew what he had to do. He didn't hesitate for even a moment to support someone in need. Guy hugged them.

The auggie sniffled. Then, he started to cry as he rested his head on Guy's shoulder. The two of them held each other for at least a full minute.

"*Thank you*," the scared auggie said through subsiding tears.

"It's okay, friend." That was the first full sentence Guy had ever spoken in front of anyone, with them knowing it anyway. Even his best friend, Dennis, was surprised.

Dennis's mouth dropped open and looked on, impressed and happy for how Guy was handling things, and that he could talk! Emma too seemed surprised, but she and Dennis both knew they couldn't waste any more time—they would talk with Guy later about what had just happened.

The auggie that Guy was comforting felt better now. His tears faded, leaving only dry streaks down his cheeks.

Before long, they both walked back to their spots in the group formation. Emma, Dennis, and Guy, the leaders of what could be the last hope for humanity, again began to move forward, leading them all to that car, toward danger and toward hope. In that moment, everyone felt connected to the same cause. Everyone knew this day could be the end or the beginning for not just them, but for everyone on Earth.

Approaching the next intersection, a car door could be heard shutting closed. It was just around the corner. The group tensed up, readying for battle. Emma gave the stop signal. Then...

Go, her hand signaled silently. As the signal was given, the strength auggies held up their fists, ready to attack anything that would approach. Except, the next two runners whose turn it was to scout just stood there, motionless. They failed to run ahead as commanded. As much as everyone understood the importance of this moment, maybe the weight of it fell too much on these two runners' shoulders. They could not face the responsibility and the fear of dying.

No one moved. 10 seconds went by as they waited for the runners to scout ahead, to do the job they were tasked to do. Emma looked at Dennis and back at the group. Once more, she gave her signal for the next two runners to check out the area ahead. But they shook their heads to say no. They refused command.

Realizing that her new "soldiers" were not fully trained, Emma breathed a sigh of disappointment and looked at Dennis. He shrugged his shoulders, as if to say "what can we do?" Emma looked over to her scared friends. She waved them over to stand next to her. Slowly, nervously, they came close.

She gestured to them silently. She pointed at them, then at herself. They only looked at her with confused expressions. Sighing impatiently, she tried again, and additionally pointed toward the corner of the street, where they were supposed to go. They still looked confused. Giving up on signals, she leaned over between both of their heads and whispered into their ears, "*I will go with you.*" She pointed to herself and then at them. "*We can go over there...*" She pointed at the street corner. "*Together. Okay?*"

Still, they refused. They shook their heads in fear once again.

She couldn't believe that now everyone wasn't willing to fight. She thought to herself, if I knew this, then we would've just trained more in the forest first!

Dennis leaned over to her ear and whispered his support. "*It's okay, mate. We can come back later when we're ready.*" Dennis was thinking the same thing as her. "*May as well train in the forest for now.*"

"*Fine. But let's at least do* ***something*** *while we're here. I'll see what's happening with this car.*" Emma gave a hard stare toward her two nervous runners. They looked toward the ground, feeling guilty for not doing their job.

And with that, Emma sped herself up and slowed down how time was perceived. The group now appeared to her in slow motion. She ran over to the corner and peeked her head carefully around the edge.

There was a large white truck, with two people standing around it, looking at each other as if they had been talking. They too were moving in slow motion now. Emma tried to get a clear view of their chests, but she couldn't see from where she stood. *I have to get closer*, she thought.

She ran over to them, about 50 feet away. As she stood near enough to them to see, she could tell they didn't have any blue or green light coming from their chests. *These must be drones. Not PCs. No augmentations… I hope.* Though drones weren't known to have augmentations like PCs did, she couldn't be sure. After all, it had been years since the rebels encountered any drones. *I better be careful, PCs could be anywhere.*

She started to run back over to her group.

Keep exploring. The voice that appeared in her head was not hers. She did not know it yet, but Isaac's father was speaking to her. It appeared loud and fuzzy in her mind, like a phone call with poor quality.

She stopped where she was standing and looked all around her, expecting to see someone right next to her. *What was that?*

Someone who wants you to succeed.

Emma was rattled, shaken by the uncertainty of who was communicating with her, how they were speaking to and hearing her in her head, and where the voice was coming from. *Who are you?*

There was silence.

Whoever you are… we're not ready. We have to go back and train. We can't risk doing more than just looking around right now. What do you think would happen with these people if they got into a fight? People will die!

Your enemies are getting stronger. Just then, the voice became clearer. *The Intelligence does not wait for you to improve. It's not all bad though! You are closer than you realize to ending this war, if you just keep going!*

Emma ran over to her group. She began to pant, breathing hard for air as her abilities made her tired, as usual. She couldn't keep her augmentations going for too much longer. *What are you trying to tell me?* She asked the mysterious voice in her head.

Isaac's father replied, *the one with the green light. Do you remember how strong she was?*

Emma's memories flashed back to the terrible moments of her father's death. *How could I forget? We were lucky we didn't get into a real fight with her or more would've died.*

Right at this moment, Isaac's dad went on, *she is being upgraded to be even stronger than before.* Isaac's dad went on. *The Intelligence is doing everything it can to make her the next step in PC-human evolution.*

What?! Emma thought, stunned.

What's worse... she knows you have her brother. With both the Intelligence punishing her if she disobeys orders, along with her own desire to get her brother back, she will not hold anything back when she faces you.

Emma returned to her normal speed. The group saw her blurry figure become clear in front of them. Emma looked at Dennis with fright.

"*What is it, Emma? What's wrong?!*" Dennis asked in a concerned whisper.

Emma held up her hand, showing Dennis to wait for her to catch her breath. She continued communicating with Isaac's father while she did. *We defeated her once,* she thought, *can't we defeat her again? And who here is her brother?*

Isaac's father replied, *The boy you call 'The Maniac.' Didn't you notice the similarities?*

Emma thought back to The Maniac and the woman with the green light. *Their eyes! They're both green. Their hair is the same color too, black.*

Isaac's father continued. *Their story is a sad one. They were prisoners, just like your friends. They too lost everything—family, friends, their homes. Then, even after everything they went through, the pain and the suffering, they were taken by The Intelligence and experimented on. Eventually, their minds became unstable. How would you turn out if you were controlled and experimented on for eight years?*

Emma was silent as she reflected on what she was asked and what she learned.

He went on. *You are not truly enemies with any human. The real enemy is The Intelligence. Your only chance to stop it is by hacking the computers it is connected to. You have to look for a computer in the city. You will know what to do when you get there. Your parents trained you to hack, didn't they? Plus, I'll be in your mind guiding you with every step.*

"Emma, you're scaring us. What's happening?" Dennis pleaded for her to reassure the soldiers, to break her silence.

She raised her hand again, asking for them to wait a bit more. But they're not ready to even explore the city with me right now. *We may not even reach a computer if we tried to find one,* she told the voice, still not knowing who he was. *Why not hide and come back another day? How do you even know so much? Who are you really and why should I trust you? What if you're leading me into a trap we're not ready to fight?*

Right now, it doesn't matter how I know. The Intelligence has been watching Isaac... and learning. Fail to stop The Intelligence here and now, and this weapon of theirs, The Maniac's sister, will hunt you down wherever you go, strengthened by everything it has been learning. Wait even one day, run somewhere you think is well hidden, and she will still find you. Her upgrades will allow her to find you in any forest, any cave, anywhere! Isaac's father's voice in Emma's head began to sound stressed. He needed her to act quickly. He concluded with one final statement. *Today is not just your best chance. It is your* ***only*** *chance. Today is your last day to live! Oh, and to your question about who I am, I'm Isaac's father. My name is Elrion, and I am here to help.*

31
Focus

Days before the first PC attacks, eight years ago

Another day at school, Isaac thought as he put his backpack down on the living room floor. *Another night of homework.*

"Isaac, do you have any homework?" His father, Elrion, asked.

"A little. Some worksheets I have to finish."

Isaac's father, sitting on a chair in the kitchen, stood up and walked over to his son. "Can I see what it is?"

Isaac took a folder out of his backpack, opened it up, and handed his dad a few pieces of paper.

"Hmm..." Elrion pondered out loud. "This shouldn't take too long. When you're done, meet me outside, okay?" He handed the work back to his son and smiled.

"Okay," Isaac replied, "but I want to relax before I get started with you."

"Sounds good. I'll see you out there when you're ready." His father headed for the back door.

Two hours later

Outside, as the sun set and the sky turned from blue to red, Isaac's father was waiting. He stood there, looking out into the trees behind the house. He watched them and listened to the quiet sounds of the outdoors. He listened to the trees swaying gently. He closed his eyes.

Slide

The back door opened. It was Isaac. "Sorry I took so long. You weren't out here the whole time, were you?"

Still facing into the woods behind them with his eyes closed, Isaac's father breathed in and gave a relaxed answer. "Yes, I've been out here since we talked to each other last. You seem to have a habit of losing track of time."

Somewhat surprised, Isaac responded. "Wait, you've been here for two hours?" Although he had known his father to meditate in the backyard, it usually wasn't for this long—usually it was for 30 minutes at most. "Don't you do a lot of work in the house? Why were you out so long today?"

"Today is different, Isaac." He then turned to face his son and opened his eyes. "You've been training with me for years. I think it's time we go to the next step—"

There was suddenly silence. Isaac's father had stopped talking unexpectedly, as if something in his thoughts had distracted him.

"Dad? What is it?"

Isaac's father walked quickly over to his son. He knelt down and put a hand on Isaac's shoulder. "Sorry. I have to go to work now. I wish we had more time, but..."

"Dad?" Isaac was confused, maybe even worried. His dad didn't seem himself.

He went on, becoming serious in his tone, "Remember what I'm about to tell you, Isaac. Your abilities can help or hurt others, or even yourself. You will be able to do things others cannot. I've made mistakes, Isaac. I've..." Elrion closed his eyes, his mind wandering to a memory. A regret, maybe.

"What's wrong?" Isaac asked curiously.

Without opening his eyes yet, Isaac's father continued. "There's so much you don't know, so much I wanted to tell you when you were ready. It's okay. We'll have time later. I just don't know when. There's a much larger picture than I can show you right now. But..." He opened his eyes and looked at Isaac. "For now, you must be patient. Focus on what is in front of you, okay? If I could, I would help train you, but this next part of your journey is yours."

"What's happening? What are you talking about? I don't know if I understand."

"You will. Someday. You will." He hugged his son tight, like he was saying goodbye for a very long time.

Present day, back to Isaac and his father

The sun was starting to rise. Isaac and his father had been silent for hours now, walking through a forest, slowly returning to where they had first come from.

"Dad?" Isaac said as he pushed a tree branch aside.

"Yes, Isaac?"

"I thought I would be able to control my abilities when they awakened. Why wasn't my training enough, the training I did with you as a kid? Why did I lose control now so easily?"

Isaac's father sighed. "I'm sorry. You went from a comfortable house to a prison. That isn't exactly the best environment to grow in. You were hungry, alone, had no freedom, and practice that translated very little to the outside world once you got out. I'm surprised you came out as okay as you did."

"A lot of that was thanks to you, thanks to what you taught me. I spent most of my time thinking, daydreaming, and meditating. I thought I could have gone crazy in there, if it weren't for the strategies you showed me. I'm still disappointed with myself though. I didn't have control when it mattered most, when others needed me. When they awakened, these powers I mean, when I faced real dangers, I let people down."

Isaac's father tried to comfort his son. "You'll improve. We'll do it together this time. It's okay now." He smiled. Elrion knew all too well the pain his son shared. *And there are still so many more hardships to come, my son*, he thought to himself.

"Yea. But, still, I can't relax. I don't even know what my friends are doing now. Are you sure they are okay?"

Without the slightest pause, his father answered immediately. "Yes. I promise you they are and will continue to be okay. Dennis, Emma, Guy, they're all safe."

Isaac realized he had even more questions. "Wait, how do you know their names? And how do you know that they're safe?"

"Oh. I know for many reasons, not that it matters right now. It'll make more sense to you soon." Isaac's father smiled, showing the same happy confidence as always. However, the smile disappeared, even if just for a moment long enough for Isaac to notice. "Actually..." Isaac's father started to say, something else clearly on his mind.

Isaac's imagination was filled with fear for the worst. "What is it? Is something happening to them right now?! Are they in danger?!"

"What? Oh no. It's something else." Elrion's smile returned. "Hey! This is as good a spot as any to resume our training. Cover your ears, okay?"

Isaac didn't have time to ask why, because as soon as Elfin finished talking, he disappeared. Isaac quickly covered his ears, knowing something would be coming—something very loud.

BOOM! THRASH!

Hundreds of trees around him fell over, outward, as if a bomb had just gone off exactly where Elrion was once standing. After forcing his flinching eyes to slowly open, Isaac looked around at the destruction. *The branches are gone!* Isaac thought to himself. *The trees look like logs just lying on the ground. No leaves anywhere too? Where did the leaves and branches go? What is he doing? HOW is he doing this? This is more than just speed.*

Isaac's father appeared in front of him out of thin air. "Come on," he enthusiastically said.

"What did you say?!" Isaac shouted, after forgetting to take his hands off his ears.

His dad gently pulled Isaac's hands down. "I said, come on!" And with that, Isaac's excited father bent his knees slightly and jumped straight into the air. Isaac followed after him, jumping up as well.

"Woah," Isaac said in disbelief as he looked down. From the view up above, it was clear what his father had done. There was a large space of fallen trees that now formed an almost perfect circle. It was as if someone cut out a space in the middle of the forest maybe 100 meters wide.

As they started to drop back down to the ground, Isaac's father tried to explain through telepathy. *There's too much wind to talk out loud. I will speak directly into your mind. I won't read your thoughts though unless you give me permission. Now, I want you to try and land inside that circle. Focus on how your body floats through the air and try to land on one of those trees that have fallen down. Try to land* ***without*** *breaking the log!*

"Okay!" Isaac tried to yell his response but the wind carried his voice away.

Elrion spoke into his son's mind. *I can't hear you when you talk into moving air. Do I have your permission to hear you think?*

Isaac nodded his head to say yes. *Just for loud times like these,* Isaac thought to his father. *Get ready, Dad! Watch me land and be impressed!*

Hah! Elrion laughed back. *Let's see.*

32
Trust

Emma was terrified—less for herself, and more for all the people she led into this situation. Whether the voice was really Isaac's father, this "Elrion," she would believe him for now. Or, at least was forced to believe him because, if she didn't, the alternative might mean death. If he was telling the truth, if The Maniac's sister really was upgraded and headed their way, then the last best hope for humanity, the soldiers she was with, would all have no choice but to move forward as *he* instructed. "*No,*" she whispered, loud enough for Dennis and a few other soldiers to hear. She tried to ask the voice, Isaac's father, Elrion, for advice. *What should we do next?* She thought, hoping he was still listening.

There was quiet for a moment.

"*Emma, what is it? We need to tell our soldiers something.*" Dennis looked around and saw them getting nervous. Some were leaning over to each other, whispering things. Many had eyes wide open, eyebrows raised in fright. "*We can't let them get out of control. We need to tell them something.*"

She didn't want to miss any messages coming into her thoughts though. She couldn't pay much attention to Dennis. This was a desperate moment. "*Someone's talking to me in my mind. He claims to be Isaac's dad! He says his name is Elrion. He's warning me, warning us, of the woman we met. Keep our soldiers busy, Dennis, I'm listening for mo—*"

Move into the building next to you. NOW! The voice in her head sounded serious.

This was bad. Emma knew she hadn't explained anything to her soldiers yet, and barely enough at all to her second-in-command. Still, this was life or death. She found herself in a position where she was following orders from a mysterious voice she didn't know whether to trust, and had to act quickly on whatever he said. If people died today, would it be her fault?

"*Everyone, follow me!*" She whispered her command a bit more loudly as she simultaneously gave the command using a hand gesture. She pointed to the closest door on the street, leading into one of the city's tall buildings. Emma walked through the group as quickly as she could to get to the door and lead the way in. Dennis followed right behind her.

She looked at the large metal handles attached to the glass doors. She looked through the glass quickly, checking to see if any drones were inside. All she saw though were clothing racks holding dresses, shirts, and other clothes. *This used to be a department store*, she thought, *probably has offices on the upper floors.* She placed her hands on one of the door's cold metal bars, hoping it was unlocked—terrified that it wouldn't be.

Push

It wasn't opening.

Gasp. Someone in the group let out a scared breath of air. Guy too seemed to get nervous. Dennis immediately looked around the crowd, seeing if anyone was trying to leave now, to run away. Would they think something was going wrong with the mission? How quickly could the group fall apart if just one person left?

Pull

The door swung open. Auggies in the way of the door hurriedly moved aside, letting it open all the way. "*Oh, thank god,*" Emma whispered to herself in relief.

"Happens all the time, right?" Dennis said, trying to relax the crowd.

"*Whisper, Dennis!*"

"*Sorry, ma'am,*" he apologized.

"*Move in!*" She led her squad inside and immediately signaled for them to stand next to the left and right walls, where they would be out of sight from the glass-paned doors. One by one, each auggie walked inside. Fortunately, the windows on the sides of the store entrance had mannequins and a wall behind them, making it difficult to see inside from anywhere but the doorway. Guy, the last person outside, looked both ways on the street before walking in and quickly pulling the doors closed behind him. He hurried over next to Emma and nodded his head, adding one word as well: "*Clear*."

Emma raised her hand for attention. From across the large first floor, peering over clothes and shelves, every auggie looked at her, waiting for her command. She waited, listening for any signs of movement outside.

A few moments passed. Nothing yet.

She then lowered her hand, signaling to the soldiers to squat down—to get as low as possible so as not to be seen. She crouched down at the same time, demonstrating what she wanted her soldiers to do. They followed after her example and did as she did. One soldier near her sat down completely on their bottom, rather than squatting. Emma quickly stared at them and shook her head in disapproval. *"Crouch down, but stay on your feet! We may need to move quickly. Be ready!"*

Isaac's father once again entered her mind. *Focus. Listen,* he told her.

What am I listening for? What's happening? She asked.

Quiet your mind! ***LISTEN****!* His voice boomed in her mind when he said this.

Emma listened, as told—too afraid of what would happen if Elrion was right and if she failed to do what he said. Though quiet and distant, Emma could hear footsteps outside. She dared not look around the edge of the wall, through the doors. She stayed out of sight, listening only.

Step-step-step-STEP-STEP

The person, and it sounded like it was indeed only one person, was getting closer to the building's entrance. Then, just as the footsteps were at their loudest, they simply stopped. Whoever it was, was standing right in front of the building.

Who are you really? Did you trap us here?! Emma looked around and realized there was little option for escape. This was not a building she had planned to enter. She had no idea where the closest back exit was, nor what was filling the floors above them. Did this voice place her in danger on purpose? Was it The

Intelligence? Was it the woman from before, standing outside, *The Maniac's sister?* She thought. *Is this actually a trap?*

It's okay. It's not her, Elrion said, trying to comfort Emma.

Just then, the footsteps picked up again, moving on along the sidewalk, passing the doors of the building. Emma breathed a sigh of relief. *A drone?*

Isaac's father prodded her onward. *Yes. Now, they're gone. You should move.*

Emma stood up and signaled for the group to get closer to her. They walked over quickly. With everyone stuffed into one corner, she did her best to explain the voice she was hearing in her head, and how the mission had been changed—and what was now at stake.

"*You're saying we have a chance to end The Intelligence today?!*" One of the auggies was excited, seeing it as good news that such a good outcome to these events even existed at all.

Another, less hopeful auggie, shared his less favorable opinion. "*Yea, but we have The Maniac's sister to deal with now. She's on her way here to kill us all!*"

The Maniac, who had been gagged with a shirt in his mouth the whole time, was trying to laugh. Emma looked at him just as The Maniac looked back at her. They stared at each other, their eyes locked. While she wished she could get more information out of him, she knew if she took off the gag, then The Maniac would almost certainly yell out, calling attention to The Intelligence. Though tied up and carried by strength auggies, The Maniac could still be very dangerous if not kept track of closely, especially with his sister on her way. If she saw him like this, held prisoner, who knew what she would do to them.

You need to leave this building. I'll help guide you. With that, Elrion began leading Emma to the next, most dangerous phase of the mission.

33
Balance

The sky around Isaac was cold. He could feel it, though it didn't bother him. With his father watching, he looked at the circle of fallen trees below. With hundreds of them to choose from, Isaac brought his focus to just one.

Elrion offered some advice. *Don't rush it, son.*

With a little guidance from his father, Isaac realized he should slow down. *Better not go for a* dive, he thought. He flattened his body out. Rather than cutting through the air and crashing down harder on the ground, he would give himself the best chance to land without breaking a tree—he would slow down his fall as much as possible. *Watch this!* He excitedly thought to his dad.

Just then, Isaac closed his eyes and breathed. Though the winds were moving fast around him, noisy and chaotic, Isaac was undisturbed. As he fell, he breathed in deep and comfortably. Focus, he thought to himself. He opened his eyes, feeling as calm as ever. *About 1,000 feet maybe? So... which one?* He stared below. He had lost track of the tree he was looking at before. *Doesn't matter. That one. 800 feet now.* He tried to turn his head to look above at his father, who was still floating, not moving an inch. *Wait, am I able to hover in mid-air like him?*

Before he could finish considering the possibility, his body began to spin out of control. *Gah! The wind on my face!* He realized that, with so much wind pushing against him, even a small turn of his head was enough to turn his whole body. *NO! 600 feet.* His body flung around the air more and more wildly. He closed his eyes. *Calm... breathe. Being angry won't stop you from spinning. Control... your mind.* Isaac knew he couldn't get hurt even if he did mess up a landing and smash into the ground. So, what was there to fear? *I can always try again. What's the big deal?*

Just then, as Isaac was finding calm in his body and mind and regaining control, Emma's voice rang through his head. *ISAAC!* Her voice called.

Eyes still closed, with the thought of his friend in danger, screaming out for him, he felt a burst of energy run through him. *NO! I won't wait until the next try to do my best. I have to try my best, right now!* Isaac opened his eyes.

Maybe he was angry, maybe being calm was best, but Isaac was beginning to feel like he must deal with his anger, his strong feelings, and learn to balance them—not ignore or avoid them. *First, do what needs to be done.* He relaxed his arms and legs, stretching them out again. *Sometimes,* he tightened his back muscles, to keep his body straight. *Anger puts you on alert.* He forced his face to remain down. His spinning began to slow. *That's the key.* He closed his eyes one more time, to feel every gust of air around his body. He would feel and figure out which part of his body needed to turn in order to counter his spinning. *Being calm lets me know what I have to do. Anger, though, gives me the drive to do it!* His body was now stable and falling belly first to the ground. *Focus is what balances it all. Now, FOCUS! 200 feet!*

He was moving too fast though on this attempt. And he knew it.

Uh-oh!

CRASH

Isaac fell, feet first and just in time, on the log he aimed for. However, his landing absolutely destroyed the part of the tree he hit. His body was now lodged, knee-deep, into the dirt below. And then…

"Hey, Isaac." His father was near him already, standing gently on a fallen tree. "So, what happened?"

"I…" Isaac was searching for the right words.

"How did you fail?"

His father's directness caught him off guard. Isaac closed his eyes. He felt the dirt around his legs, not bothering or feeling any rush to get himself out of the ground just yet. Breathing in and out, gently and comfortably, Isaac opened his eyes again and found his words. "I didn't fail. I was able to focus on and control what was happening. I think…" He looked up at his father. "This isn't possible, is it? What you're asking me to do. It isn't possible to land softly from so far up. Am I right?"

"Oh?" His father said, curiously.

Isaac placed his hands on the dirt and pushed himself up. Calmly wiping his clothes clean, he responded. "I know what you're trying to teach me. And it's more than how to be focused."

With that, Isaac bent his knees and jumped straight into the sky, higher than his last jump. Now, he was above the clouds, tens of thousands of feet up.

His father, still on the ground and looking up, felt a little bit proud of his son. "You figured it out," he said to himself as he smiled. "Good. Now you have to actually do it!"

Isaac didn't waste any time. *In fact, I'll slow things down, if only to make this attempt last longer.* His perception of things sped up, while the winds around him seemed to slow down. Without bothering to flatten out his body, he just floated there, body upright, as if he was standing on an invisible box way up in the sky. He soon felt nothing. Though the sun was shining, he felt no warmth from its light. Though the wind blew cold before, there was no wind now, nor even a little chill that he could feel from the air around him. He closed his eyes yet again, breathing and focusing on the sensations and thoughts going through him.

What did it look like when he did it? Isaac tried to picture how his father floated in place before. *If I can imitate how he stood, how he looked exactly...* Isaac stood as straight as he could and let his arms rest at his sides. The tips of his toes pointed downward, to the ground. His body rested there. *Did I do it? Am I floating?* Isaac opened his eyes and slowly let his perception of time start to return to normal.

First came the cold and a little tickle of wind blowing past him. Then, as the wind and cold grew stronger, his body began to fall, even if only a little.

Darn! Isaac slowed things around him once again. More time to think. *I'm missing something. But what?* He closed his eyes, trying hard to focus on feelings within his own body. *It's not just how he looks from the outside. He must trigger the ability somehow.* Isaac felt his heart beat.

Thump... thump...

He was relaxing more and more as he searched for other sensations around his body—the muscles in his back tensing and relaxing, the feeling of air brushing through his nostrils, his shoulders dropping as he relaxed. *10 beats per minute*, he thought after counting for a short while.

He was breathing slower than ever now. He hadn't felt this calm since he left his 'light window' earlier. His attention returned peacefully to his heart. *Two beats a minute.* At this point, Isaac wasn't even sure if he needed to breathe. *Zero beats.*

Not a sound, nor beat, nor air entering or leaving him, Isaac floated there, almost entirely without thought.

An unfamiliar voice entered Isaac's mind.

Shrisan vlal okam.

Then, with what was, at first, only a couple more unfamiliar voices, turned into hundreds—all speaking in a language Isaac did not understand.

Five heartbeats. The wind began again around him. The cold too. The voices were now fading quickly into silence.

15 heartbeats. Windier and colder still. The voices were now gone.

Something feels different. He opened his eyes. *I did it!* Isaac's body did not drop one inch. He was floating!

"But... who was that?"

Isaac's father had jumped to meet up with his son. He stopped to float next to him.

"Dad!" Isaac yelled.

Elrion shook his head and shrugged his shoulders, signaling that he couldn't hear his son over the wind. He pointed to his head and then to Isaac's head, asking if they could share each other's thoughts.

Isaac nodded to confirm 'yes.' *I heard voices speaking another language. Not with my ears though. It was all in my head. What happened?*

Isaac's father smiled a big smile. *Hah! It means you learned two abilities today! And* **much** *faster than I predicted. Good! I shouldn't have killed so many trees... Well, do you remember what they said?* His father asked.

I heard a lot of voices, but the first one I heard said something like... 'shrisan vlal okam.' Do you know that language, Dad?

His dad continued grinning a big smile as he answered. *Oh yes. Maybe you can learn it too someday, if you want.*

But, I've never heard that language before. What did they say? Isaac asked.

They were just saying everyday conversation things. Nothing too exciting. You were basically eavesdropping on them.

Still curious, Isaac asked more. *Where are they? Do you know?*

Elrion was pleased, in this case, to explain more to his son. *Oh, very far away. If you want to, maybe you can visit them someday.*

No time to think about that. I have to get back to my training! I still need to land on a tree without breaking it. Isaac was eager to learn more about his abilities.

His dad added on with pride. *Indeed, you do.*

34
Closing In

Between Isaac's father talking to her in her head and the challenge of the mission, Emma was having a difficult time processing what was happening. *I just can't believe who you are and how you're talking to me. You're really Isaac's dad?*

Yes, but we do not have time to talk. The Maniac's sister will be in this city before long, and you still have to avoid fighting PCs at all costs. There is a building you need to reach. Go to it! You must listen to my directions, and quickly!

Emma was still skeptical. *How do I know this isn't a trap? How do I know you are who you say? What proof can you give me? Do you know where Isaac is?*

Hah! Well, you ask a lot of questions. That's good! Just not right now. Well, okay, but short answers only... You don't know for sure if it's a trap, sorry. You don't know if I am who I say. Sorry again. Isaac is safe, but can't help you right now. Again, sorry.

Hmmm, Emma thought. *Fine, you're right about one thing, we don't have a lot of time if what you say is true. And you've led us to safety so far*. Emma turned to her fellow auggies. "*He says Isaac is alive!*" Emma whispered, excitedly.

"*Great! Now, what's going on?*" Dennis hoped to get an answer.

Emma couldn't give Dennis the information he wanted, not yet. "No time!" *Alright, Elrion, I'll trust you for now. It doesn't look like I have many other good choices anyway*. Emma peeked slowly around the wall through the glass doors. *It looks clear. Let's say I listen to your instructions for now. Where do we go next?*

Elrion continued. *After you leave this building, you need to turn right and head straight for 10 blocks. Then, turn left and go for another 3 blocks. There should be a building on the corner with the word 'Lamry' on the front. That's spelled 'L-A-M-R-Y.' Get to the 20th floor. That's where you will find a computer connected to The Intelligence's network.*

As Emma continued communicating with Isaac's dad, she looked around to her friends—judging how mentally prepared they were for what would happen next. *Between you and your son, I have so many questions. Like you said though, we don't have time.* Emma stood up and whispered the plan to the soldiers, the number of blocks in each direction, the building they needed to go to, and the computer they needed to reach. A few seemed just as scared as ever, apparently even *more* frightened now, now that they knew how much more danger was up ahead and was coming for them if they failed. Others were smiling, encouraged to hear they had any chance for surviving and more, to win this war for good.

One of the soldiers couldn't contain their excitement and newfound courage. "That's our leader!" As he pumped his fist into the air with his shout. Emma glared at him. "*Sorry,*" he whispered, embarrassed with himself for being so loud.

"*Alright everyone,*" she said quietly. "*It's time to move. Same formation. We're no longer scouting ahead though. If I give you this signal...*" She showed her hand raised, then lowered it sharply toward the ground. "*Then the next speed auggies have to attack the target ahead of us. We won't take any risks. Kill them!*"

NO YOU WON'T! This time, Elrion's voice filled everyone's heads at once with a bold and commanding volume. More than a few auggies gasped, utterly surprised by the angry roar that had just entered their thoughts.

"*Is this who you were talking to?*" Dennis asked Emma.

Still telepathically communicating with everyone, Elrion went on. *The people out there will be free from The Intelligence in less than one hour, once you shut the network down. When that happens, the 'drones,' as you call them, will be back to normal. So, you will kill* ***no one.***

Everyone was looking at each other. Sympathy grew in their eyes.

If this could be done without killing anyone, why not try? Elrion pleaded his viewpoint to people who knew what it meant to be imprisoned, to have their personal freedom and control over their own lives taken away, just as the drones had their freedom taken.

You really are Isaac's dad, you sound just like him, Emma replied. She looked at Dennis next to her.

Though she hoped to see her friend agree on killing the enemy anyway, despite Elrion's instructions, Dennis's face said otherwise. It said everything that was on his mind. It said, "Isaac's dad is right." Dennis put a hand on Emma's shoulder as her expression softened from hate to care.

Elrion went on. *Trust me. You kill one more person than you had to, and when you look back on this day for the rest of your lives, you will regret it. It will haunt you. It will change you forever.*

I know. Emma added. *I agree with you. I just... it was different when Isaac was with us. He could take care of everything without killing anyone. But what are we? What are we but untrained, inexperienced, and afraid? If we only had to kill one drone to get there, to avoid fighting, wouldn't that be worth it if it means saving the 40 we have here? Saving all of humanity? Why risk it for just one, or even just a few, if it came to that?*

Elrion responded. *Because lives are always worth risking if it means saving others. Because you have control of yourselves, the drones. They haven't had a choice in any of this. Plus, if it's only one or two enemies, and you have 40 augmented friends with as much ability as your enemy, then couldn't you disarm and disable them well enough?* Elrion's words rang true in many of the minds listening to him as he spoke. *How would you feel if you were trapped in your own mind, unable to resist The Intelligence forcing you to do what it says? How fair would it be to see death coming to you?*

For Emma too, these words shook her to the core. Then she noticed everyone nodding their heads around her, agreeing with Elrion.

Dennis added on. "*I think he's right, Emma.*"

Emma's eyes opened wide. She was suddenly reminded of when she freed Isaac from his prison. Her mind flashed back to what she told him that day. "*Isn't it worth it just to try and save them?!*" Chills went down her spine. The memory struck a chord in her. It also reminded her of another memory she had, one of Wesley, her father, hugging her in their cabin those many summers ago. She remembered how he comforted her when they heard the world ending eight years ago. Finally, she remembered how Isaac, not too long ago, saved every one of the tens of thousands of prisoners *and* guards, because of sympathy she herself reminded him to have for others on the day they met. Her eyes watered as she felt both shame for her lack of pity and pride in having found it again. Mirroring the words Isaac once told her, she responded to Isaac's father. *You're right,* she thought, *thank you for reminding me of what's important. Let's save them.*

We'll try, at least. Elrion knew there was no guarantee for everyone's safety. Still, he was happy that she changed her mind.

Although she found herself without a strong plan, Emma was somehow feeling at ease listening to Isaac's father. His confidence and support for doing what she knew was right, especially in these desperate times, gave her comfort. It was like how she felt when Isaac was around. She felt like her group could do anything. She felt that they could really win, without dirtying their hands and consciences by hurting the mind-controlled people out there.

Elrion gave her his idea. *Why don't I just, temporarily, allow you to communicate with your group through thoughts—until the end of your mission anyway? Should make giving your commands easier, don't you think? They're not so good with hand signals yet anyway. After all, I have been watching. Hah!*

You can do that? She asked, surprised.

Yes, easy enough! He replied.

Again, everyone's heads were nodding in agreement. They knew they weren't good with signals and being quiet.

With the help of Isaac's father, Emma was now able to talk telepathically to her squad. *Alright, let's move! Everyone, stay in tight formation. When you get onto the sidewalk, stand in your designated positions in the circle, but stay even closer now!*

They all heard her clearly and nodded their heads to show they understood. Emma also heard them with a chorus of them saying "*yes*" in her head. She pushed one of the large department store doors open, with Dennis and Guy closely walking behind her. The rest followed through, with each of them holding the door open for the previous person as they passed. One by one, they circled up outside on the road and sidewalk.

Now, Emma commanded in their heads, *everyone, keep a lookout for drones around the corners. It looks like the street is clear up ahead for the next 10 blocks we have to walk. In the back, how does it look?*

There was silence. No response.

What's happened back there?! Emma was worried that a drone, or worse, a PC or The Maniac's sister, was already here behind them.

Don't worry about that, Elrion said. *They can hear you, but I made it now so they can't all respond at once back to you. Wouldn't THAT be confusing?*

Emma immediately realized why he had done this. Having 40 or so minds shouting or talking to her all at once would be overwhelming as a commander. Still, she needed to know what was happening from her soldiers in the back. *Could you please let those who I am directly talking to be able to talk back to me?*

No problem. Ma'am! Hah!

Emma sighed. *What a weird man,* she thought.

I heard that, Elrion promptly stated.

Sorry, she replied. *Anyway. Whoever is in the back, can you tell me if our rear is clear?* She sent her message across the group, hoping Elrion would do his part and allow their response back.

Ma'am! The back is clear! One of the soldiers said. *Wow, this is actually worki—*

Suddenly, he was cut off.

We don't have much more time, Elrion stated flatly. His light and joking tone was gone. ***MOVE!***

Sensing that her guide was, for some reason, more serious now, Emma didn't think to ask any more questions. *Everyone, keep your eyes open and follow me!* She began walking up the 10 blocks they were told to travel.

At the first block's corner, Emma slowed down. Stop, she said to them all. She looked carefully down the street to her left and right. The drones from before were all gone. *They must have moved on,* she thought, *probably back to work. Let's keep going.* So the group started walking again.

The city streets gave Emma a strange sensation. On the one hand, the structures felt familiar, almost comforting. Everything around her—the abandoned businesses, homes, cars—reminded her of what used to be. She imagined seeing the thousands of bustling people going about their day. She felt a deep sadness for what was lost. Still, it was somehow comforting, the memory of that familiar old world. Most notable, however, was the overriding feeling of fear that in any one of these buildings could be drones or PCs ready to attack them. Overall, the streets gave her more terror and uncertainty than they gave comfort. Every step with her group was uncertain, nerve-racking. *Elrion?*

Yes?

Emma was starting to have questions again, despite knowing she had to focus on the mission. She couldn't help but be curious. *You said The Maniac's sister was coming for us, right?* She asked her question as her eyes scanned each passing shop entrance, each skyscraper window, and each and every corner, while too glancing back a moment at The Maniac who was still held and tied up in the center.

Yes, The Maniac's sister will be here soon, Elrion answered. *But you should make it before she gets to you—so long as you keep moving, anyway.*

Well then, she continued, *if she knows we're here, then The Intelligence knows!* Emma's heart started to pound. She began again to wonder if maybe she was in fact walking into a trap.

Elrion had to make her appreciate the danger, but also realize the chance they had to succeed. *Yes, she is after you. Yes, she is augmented with sensors that can detect humans across the world. But she doesn't really know you are here. All she knows is that humans are generally in your region here, along with many other places on the Earth. Right now, she is probably killing every human she can find. Running from one place to another, one country to the next.*

Emma replied, horrified, *Well, how is that comforting?*

It's a terrible thing, but it does mean you have some time. Eventually, yes, she will be here. However, The Intelligence does not know you are in the heart of the city. Her sensors only give her a rough idea. Once she gets closer to the city though, her readings will be more accurate. By the time she enters this area, she and The Intelligence will likely know your exact position and how many of you there are—down to which block you are standing on.

Emma grew even more nervous, but she knew that there was no turning back now. During their whole conversation, and while she looked cautiously around them for any signs of enemies, she made sure to keep track of how far they had walked, how close they were to their destination. Their lives, and the lives of all humans left on Earth, were counting on her leadership right now. *Five blocks remaining, people! Then, we will turn left for three more blocks!* Her troops needed updates. Whatever she was feeling, these untrained recruits must have felt many times worse.

They found themselves quickly nearing the end of those five blocks. Emma slowed down as they approached the last corner. After that, after turning left, they would have a straight view of the building. *Hold!* She thought to everyone, while simultaneously raising her hand in the air, signaling them to stop. She took a deep breath in, slowed down the world around her, and peeked her head cautiously around the corner.

About 1000 feet away, or three city blocks, she saw it. There it was up ahead. The word "LAMRY" appeared above the front entrance, along with eight people standing in front. Their eyes were wide open, looking straight ahead down the street, with their emotionless expressions meaning only one thing: drones.

35
Float

Isaac was still appreciating how cool it was to be up there, just floating in the sky. The wind blew past him. The clouds moved gently along. The air was slightly chilly. Isaac breathed and took it all in. He found it all so utterly beautiful.

His father looked at Isaac and felt happy too, though for a different reason. Isaac's father, Elrion, was feeling proud. *Finally*, he thought, *after so many years, someone else knows what this is like. And it's only the beginning!*

Okay, Dad, watch! Isaac thought, enthusiastically.

Except, Elrion knew that his son wasn't quite mastering this skill yet, and he could tell. Floating in the air was not the same thing as moving through the air. Isaac would need to consider that sometimes the world wouldn't always be so calm around him. It wouldn't be this easy normally to float and keep control, let alone move around freely.

Isaac stared down toward the ground, intent on dropping toward it, on landing on one of those logs below. A few seconds went by. Isaac stared and stared, but nothing changed. He was still just floating there. His body seemed unwilling to do anything but remain floating. He couldn't make a move. Meanwhile, Elrion was silent—apparently committed to only watching, to seeing how Isaac would think through this situation on his own.

Isaac knew that he had usually gained more control over his abilities when he was calm. So, he did what seemed to have an impact almost every time he tried it... he meditated. Once more, Isaac closed his eyes, focused on his breath, his heartbeat, and the sensations of everything around him. The air entered his nose, his heart slowed down, and the wind continued to move around him.

Drop, he told himself. *Gently. Slowly.* He took a few more deep breaths and focused everything he could on imagining what it would feel and look like for his body to begin to float down to the ground. He visualized himself falling just a few inches at a time. While still floating in place, he continued to see this reality in his mind. He convinced himself that it would happen in the same way he pictured it in his head. He could almost feel what it would be like to float down so gently, so gradually.

Then, he began to feel it for real. His body was losing altitude. Isaac wasn't just falling though, he was controlling how fast he was falling!

With his eyes still closed, Isaac wasn't sure if opening them now would somehow change things. Would, somehow, opening his eyes too quickly cause him to fall at full speed? So, afraid to do much else, he would take it slow at first. Why change anything if what he was doing was working already? He continued to breathe. He continued to keep his heart rate slow and to focus everything he had on imagining his body dropping at a steady pace down through the air. After a couple of minutes and a few feet lower went by, Isaac carefully went to the next step.

I have to be able to do this in normal conditions, he thought. *First,* he continued thinking, *I will open my eyes slowly, while keeping everything else constant. Keep visualizing a slow move down. Keep calm. Keep the heartbeat slow.* As he opened his eyes carefully, he remained focused on everything he had been so focused on. Still falling, but with his eyes wide open now, Isaac felt relieved—he was still moving downward under control. *Good. It's working. Now, stay calm,* he repeated to himself. His heartbeat maintained a steady five beats per minute. *No need*—he took another deep breath in and out—*to rush.* Even the pacing of his thoughts was methodically slow and purposeful. Not one distraction was allowed through his mind. His focus stayed solely on how it felt to be floating down so gently. He let another couple of minutes, another couple of feet, pass by, before trying the next steps. *Good,* he thought. *Now...*

Isaac knew he was entering into the most difficult, or the most unpredictable, step. The most control he ever experienced over his abilities was when he was at his calmest, when his heartbeat was low, and when he took his time. He knew he could keep going down to the ground the way he was, sure, but he also knew that in a real fight against The Intelligence, he would almost certainly be faced with strong emotions and have a faster heartbeat. There could be enemies around him the next time he tried using his abilities, after all. Things wouldn't always be so easy around him.

He began to move his arms and legs around, breathing a little more quickly, but only a bit more, at first. He imagined he was about to start a fight. As he moved around, as if to warm up for that fight and get his heartbeat to go a little faster, an image suddenly crossed his mind. *Emma*, he thought. He found himself seeing her being strangled by a PC. He saw her enemy's metal fingers holding her in the air by her neck. She was in pain.

His attention snapped back to reality. He found that his body was no longer floating. He had suddenly lost all control over his newly acquired ability and was free-falling to the ground and fast.

It's only an image! It's not real! He tried telling himself. However, this image hit him too hard. It was as if it wasn't just his imagination, but a glimpse into what could really be happening wherever she was now. *I could hear voices from faraway people. I could hear the wings of birds kilometers away, when I chose to.* The image of her seemed so strong to him. *What if it's real? What if it's not just my imagination?!*

It isn't real. Elrion had entered Isaac's mind. *I saw what you saw. It's not happening. It isn't just your senses that are amplified, it's your imagination itself. She is safe, I promise.*

Isaac felt relieved. He was also surprised by just how vivid his imagination could become now. Still, he was falling at full speed and needed to take back control. Comforted by his father's words, Isaac once more closed his eyes, visualized a calm world around him, and imagined what it would be like to float once more—despite all the winds whooshing around his body during the chaotic fall. Now that he had experienced the ability at least once, he felt far more comfortable and able in repeating his success. With his breath and heartbeat slowing, his body falling fast with wind swirling, he began to feel control again. Soon enough, his body began to lose speed. Eventually, he stopped falling completely.

Do it right. Take your time, Elrion telepathed to his son. *Mastery does not come in one day. Well... usually. Hah!*

It's okay, Isaac thought, reassuring his father and himself at the same time. *I'll try again. This time, I'll take it slow.*

With that thought, Isaac ran through the same steps he had gone through before. First, he floated for a few minutes, making sure he had full control of staying still while calm. Then, he opened his eyes. Keeping his heartbeat slow, he relaxed his mind. This time, he stayed there for much longer. Isaac let his body go limp. His arms dangled loosely by his sides. His legs drooped as well, with all muscles relaxed, and his mind at ease.

10 minutes went by. Neither father nor son thought anything toward each other.

Another 10 minutes went by. Still, Isaac's heartbeat remained at a steady few beats per minute.

After building up confidence, he pictured in his mind his friends being in a fight. His heartbeat, he noticed, began to increase a little—so he brought his attention back to his body and listened for his heart to settle down. It did.

Again, he thought of his friends being in a fight. Again, his heart rate increased. And again, he took time to let it settle.

Finally, after another 10 minutes of this, he found himself able to imagine his friends, fighting head-on with an enemy, while keeping his heartbeat and abilities under complete control. *I can do this*, he thought. It was then that Elrion smiled. He could tell his son had just gotten closer to mastery.

Isaac wiggled his arms and legs, as if to wake them up and call them to get ready. He tensed his muscles, let his heartbeat go up as much as it needed to for the needs of his body—but all the while, he was calm. He breathed in a long and confident breath, and breathed out just as slow and controlled. He felt ready, more ready than he ever had before.

Dive. With one simple command, his body immediately listened. Feet pointed toward a faraway log on the ground, his body fell fast toward his target. *Faster*. His body, once again, listened. He wasn't just moving at free-fall speeds, he was falling at a speed only possible with his powers propelling him beyond what gravity could do alone. He was falling as fast as his mind willed him to.

The log on the ground zoomed right up to him before, suddenly, he stopped instantly on his own command. He was now only centimeters away from the wood beneath his feet. He then finally told his body, *Let go*. With that, his feet dropped gently onto it. As he did so, his father zipped down, in just the same way his son had, and stood proudly next to him.

"So," Elrion said as he leaned in close, "what else can you do?"

"I'm ready," Isaac replied, simply enough.

"For?"

"To meet my friends again," Isaac answered.

"Hmm..." Elrion wondered if his son needed more time for what was going to happen next. "You're ready to meet them now, yes. It will be tough for you, but I think, yes, you can now handle dealing with their situation."

Isaac could tell that his father was holding something back. "What aren't you telling me? What *is* their situation?"

Elrion paused to consider carefully what words to choose next. "You'll see. But remember, I promise you they're safe." He showed a small smile and let out a quiet laugh hidden under his breath. "I'm not worried about what happens when you meet them. I'm sure you'll be fine. It's what comes after I'm not so sure about."

Once more, Isaac stood confused by the hidden meaning behind his father's words. Still, he learned how to fly in a short time with his father's minimal guidance. He chose not to question his dad anymore for now, hoping and expecting that everything would be okay if he just listened.

"Thank you for trusting me." Elrion continued, "Now, let's go meet your friends. Want to race?"

"You know where they are?!" Isaac replied, enthusiastically with a big smile on his face.

"Of course!" Elrion exclaimed, with an even bigger smile.

With that, Elrion's body began to hover above the ground before quickly accelerating into the sky. *Try to keep up!* He telepathed and taunted his son.

Isaac took on the challenge. *Oh! I'll show you what I can do!* And with that, father and son flew into the sky together.

36
The Fall

Emma looked over at her second-in-command, Dennis. With eight fingers held up, she thought to him, *There are eight enemies ahead.*

Dennis and Guy looked at each other with concern, not worried about themselves but for the group they were fighting alongside.

I could really use your son's help right now, Emma telepathed to Elrion, wherever he was.

Well, he will be on his way, Elrion responded, *but I doubt he'll make it to you in time. You must do this on your own.*

Exactly how long do you think he has? Emma asked.

Hmmm. Isaac's father paused to think how to respond. *I am not entirely sure.*

You're saying we have to get by eight drones, which might all very well be augmented, while The Maniac's sister could find us at any time?

While we also have to make it upstairs through a building filled with who knows what else? And this is our best chance? To go alone?

Remember what I told you. This is your ***only*** *chance.* Elrion's thoughts did not waver. He was dead serious. This was it.

Emma peeked again around the corner and looked at the front entrance, at that thing standing guard. *So, after all that talk about not hurting anyone,* she thought as she stared nervously at her enemies, *the only way to get into that building is to fight. Someone is going to get seriously hurt, or worse, people could die. Is there really no other way?* She brought her head back around to look at her friends, concerned for what might come of them.

Elrion had to be honest. *No, there is no other way better than this. And yes, people could get hurt. But no one* ***has*** *to die, not even the people in your way. Don't you know how to knock them unconscious?*

It was then that Elrion's suggestion hit Emma hard, and made her feel immediately stupid for not thinking about it before. *We haven't had the augmentations needed to even consider that. She looked around with a hopeful smile at her 40 friends, about 20 of whom could move fast enough to make it work. Now that we have so many helping us—*

You can win, Elrion finished her thought. *And no one has to get hurt.*

Dennis and the others apparently heard the last encouraging bit of discussion between Elrion and Emma. Dennis added his thoughts too. *Let's do it! We'll use everyone we can. We'll overwhelm them, we'll hit their jaws and knock them out!*

Emma gave hand signals to her squad, directing them to stand as close to the corner as possible. As she did so, she thought her next orders. Without the time to think ahead, she made up a plan on the spot as quickly as she could. *Well, this is it! She* telepathed to them all. *There are eight drones guarding the front door. We'll make four rows. The first row will have ten speed auggies. You 10.* She then pointed at them and counted to 10. *Behind them, in the second row, we'll have 10 strength auggies.* As she pointed at and assigned the remaining soldiers to their rows, everyone nodded their heads and got into their positions. She then explained, *As we walk, the speed auggies in the first row will be able to see if the drones are moving fast and begin to counter them. When the drones slow down in the fight, the second row of strength auggies will be able to join in on the fight. The last two rows will run around the sides and be ready to support as needed. The goal is the same for everyone: punch the enemies' jaws. This will put them to sleep.*

Before going around the corner, everyone got into position, forming four lines as instructed. She stood in the middle of the front row. She did, after all, have speed augmentations too. She would give orders as they stepped forward, together.

Dennis stood in the middle of the second line along with the other strength auggies. Guy, in the back.

Are you ready? She asked them all.

Their thoughts came back quickly and confidently. *Yes, ma'am!*

Emma then gave the commands for her first, and what she hoped and feared would be humanity's final fight. *Dennis, walking only! Stay in formation. Go!*

40 pairs of footsteps moved together. Each line stayed orderly as they turned the corner. Each soldier felt the fear of what could happen next. Could they really win without anyone dying? Would they win at all?

As the first soldiers in the front line appeared around the corner, in sight of the drones guarding the LAMRY building, almost immediately the drones reacted. No warning, no announcements, they just sprinted toward the soldiers who were still just walking some three blocks away.

The strength auggies had little chance to see what was happening yet or, if they did, the drones might have only looked like blurs to them. Barely able to lift their arms in time for the drones' arrival, the strength auggies would have to rely on their faster friends to react first. Fortunately, no one was running away anymore. Before Emma could even think her commands in super speed, eight speed auggies in the front row were already putting up their fists, ready to aim their strikes for the drones.

Hit the chin! Emma quickly reminded them.

As the drones got within just a few feet away from the first row, they didn't slow down one bit as they drew back their own fists to attack the soldiers.

Without needing to be told, the speed auggies launched their own attack on the drones as fast as they could before these enemies could land their own attacks. However, though these auggies were fast, they were not trained for combat. A lot of fists barely made contact, if at all, with the drones. The auggies might have been faster than the drones, actually, but it didn't matter if the hits weren't strong or accurate enough to do anything.

Some of the drones were able to punch the speed auggies back, seriously hurting some as those hit were knocked to the ground. In that brief moment though, of drones making contact with the speed auggies of the front row, they slowed down enough for the second row, the strength auggies, to see the attackers.

"Attack!" Dennis exclaimed.

What followed was a jumble of punches, kicks, and grabs. As messy as it was, though, the second row did its job. The strength auggies, though lacking in training, made up for it with their powerful strikes when they landed, anyway. One by one, the drones fell as an occasional lucky punch would land on each of their jaws.

Emma looked at the crowd of toppled-over soldiers and drones all mixed together. She felt relief. *Is it over?* She asked herself. But she knew there wasn't time yet to celebrate. There could still be more threats somewhere else. She looked up ahead at the building. She had to focus on their mission, still unfinished. *Elrion! What floor?! What room can we access The Intelligence network?!*

Top floor, floor 20. Room 2001. Your friends are hearing me too. ***GO NOW!***

But just before she turned on her abilities, she saw them. Coming from both directions along the street, to her left and to her right, suddenly appeared the emotionless faces of many, many people walking slowly but surely toward them. "Dennis," she said with fear and concern in her voice. "DENNIS!"

Dennis was just finishing up checking on his friends who were knocked out, those lying on the ground beside the drones. They were still alive. Smiling from their success and for his friends' confirmed safety, Dennis looked at Emma to see what she wanted. He saw her, though, standing there frozen in fear. She was staring into the distance at 30 or more drones coming toward them. His smile faded. "Emma," he spoke calmly, "you go."

"No, Dennis," she said. "I can't leave you all—"

"I'll be okay." And as he cut her off, he gave her one of his uniquely Dennis smiles. "You go."

"Dennis, no! We'll go together. The others can fight." As she tried her best to get her friend to come with her, The Maniac gave a muffled laugh.

WHACK

Dennis smacked The Maniac on the back of the head. "There's no time, Emma. Please." He looked at Emma one more time, pleading with his eyes for her to listen to him as a tear rolled down his cheek, his big smile betraying the sadness in his voice. "I don't want to lose you too. Go!"

"But Dennis!" She tried to argue back.

You can't hesitate now! Elrion's voice prominently entered her mind. *If you hesitate now, he'll surely die! If you go up and stop The Intelligence network quickly, he could live! This is how you can fight for him! This is how you save him!* ***NOW GO!***

"GO!" Dennis shouted.

Emma wasn't sure if Dennis heard what Elrion just said, but it didn't matter. She knew they were both right. "Don't die!" She told him. "Fight! STAY ALIVE!" And with those final words, Emma slowed down time around her and ran into the LAMRY building.

The nameless drones walking toward them suddenly sped up, probably sensing the danger Emma would pose to The Intelligence as they saw her enter the building. Dennis, left to command the auggies by himself, tried his best to quickly get everyone ready. "EVERYONE!" He shouted as loudly and fiercely as his lungs could muster. "GET UP! MORE DRONES ARE HERE!"

Half the soldiers were already aware of the threat and had been standing, staring into the incoming enemy crowds, some with their hands up ready to fight, others with faces drooping with hopelessness. The other half of the troops, who weren't already aware of the threat, looked down the streets to see what Dennis was shouting about.

Dennis continued his command. "Guards up! Get into formation! NOW!" With the drones only one or two blocks away, the auggies pulled themselves together—knowing that, if they didn't fight, they could very well die.

Don't kill them, Elrion telepathed into everyone's minds.

Dennis, who would have normally agreed to this plea for nonviolence, wasn't sure what other option there was. "We can't knock them all out," he responded out loud to Elrion.

JUST TRY! Elrion firmly demanded.

There wasn't any time left to debate. Dennis, who was already inclined toward peaceful solutions to problems, commanded his soldiers to follow Elrion's lead. "Speed auggies! Knock out whoever you can! Hit their chins!"

The enemy, with only a few feet now separating them from the crowd of soldiers, preparing their own fists for a fight, now found themselves swarmed by blurry images of just under 20 speed auggies, all hurriedly punching every drone's jaw they could. This was enough to keep the enemy distracted and slowed down, enough for the strength auggies to join.

Though the soldiers found themselves dropping in numbers, with many or even most falling unconscious in the barrage of attacks, there was actually a greater number of drones being knocked out as well. Eventually, every drone fell.

"We did it!" Dennis exclaimed, sharing his excitement with the 10 or so soldiers still standing. He breathed heavily, exhausted from the fight. "We did do it—right?"

I'm sorry, Elrion said, with remorse in his voice.

Dennis looked down the city streets as a small handful of figures emerged from each direction. Though fewer in number this time, these ones were different. They had blue lights glowing from their chests.

Emma might be able to shut down The Intelligence, with my help, but I'm not sure how long you can last before she can do it. I really am, truly, sorry. Elrion's attempt at support wasn't exactly what Dennis was hoping to hear.

"Well, aren't you—full of sunshine—and hope," Dennis replied, still trying to catch his breath. "Everyone! Emma is going —to shut them down soon! We just need to—"

But before he could finish commanding them, several speed auggies, too tired or unready to activate their abilities in time, were immediately thrown into the windows of buildings nearby, carried by what looked like streams of blue lights streaking through the air, from Dennis's slower perspective on things, anyway.

"GO FAST! OR DIE!" Dennis's desperation for them was clear. A handful of speed auggies that were left did their best. But they didn't stand a chance. Even if moving as fast as a PC, they didn't match them in strength or ability. Each auggie was tossed aside by the overwhelming force of the PCs—all the while Dennis could hear the growing sadistic laughter of The Maniac, who seemed to be enjoying their defeat.

Then, out of nowhere, as if to arrive only to join in her brother's laughter, the familiar green-eyed, green-lit woman returned. The Maniac's sister appeared in front of Dennis and smiled.

Dennis turned to Guy. "I love you, mate."

37

Too Late

We're close now, Elrion telepathed to his son, who was trailing shortly behind as they flew through the air toward the city.

Isaac was somehow feeling a sense of relief. After everything that had happened, his world finally seemed to be in order. He thought back to how much he had gone through. He thought back to the day he was taken from his home, to the PC bursting through his door. Its blue light would forever be stuck in his mind, along with the terror and guilt surrounding the death of his mother. Though he had built up so much rage against The Intelligence, something else grew in him since Emma freed him and over these recent days spent with his father.

His mission was the same as it had been since the start—to save people and stop The Intelligence—and yet Isaac felt balanced now more than ever before. His emotions were settled. He felt more mature. He felt wiser. Maybe it was the training itself, learning how to be calm amid danger and unsettling thoughts.

Maybe it was the powers Isaac gained, which helped him build confidence in himself and lowered his fears for the safety of his friends he was going to support. Or, maybe, Isaac felt so much at ease simply because his father promised that his friends would remain safe.

Maybe, Isaac thought, *it's a mixture of many of these reasons or more.* Whatever the cause for his newfound calm, Isaac was happy. His past had so much pain and suffering in it, which had weighed so much on him before, yet this present moment was all Isaac could care about. Right here, right now, Isaac felt just right. It was as if the weight of anger against the PCs, what they did to his mother, what they did to the world, was simply gone—at least for this moment.

Elrion looked over his shoulder to see his son flying with ease and with a smile on his face. Elrion too felt happy. Then, he realized what was to happen next. He felt his happiness dwindle, replaced by sadness and sympathy for what his son would have to go through. *So, Isaac,* he telepathed, *how are you feeling?*

Isaac, still gently smiling, looked ahead to his father. *I'm* good, he thought back.

Buildings soon emerged ahead on the horizon. Both father and son looked on, noticing that they were approaching their destination. Trees zipped past quickly underneath them, along with the road heading into the city.

Good, Elrion telepathed. Elrion had usually sounded light and happy when he spoke, so much so that even his thoughts usually portrayed joyfulness. Now, however, Elrion's thoughts sounded tense, nervous even. The city is up ahead. They're in a building named 'LAMRY.' Stay behind me when we get in there, okay? I'll show you the way. Elrion, despite all his power and wisdom, could not help but sound afraid in Isaac's mind. I'm here to support you, no matter what happens.

I'll be okay, Dad. Why so nervous? Nothing can stop us. As long as my friends are safe, I'm okay. They are still safe, right?

Elrion didn't want to reply just yet. He stopped his flight instantaneously. From moving at a speed of hundreds of kilometers per hour to suddenly stopping completely, he simply floated for a moment, in the gentle breezy air above the tall line of city buildings. He looked below. Hundreds of rooftops and small city streets could be seen. He breathed. *Take it in,* he told Isaac. *Take it all in.*

Isaac too stopped and looked below. *Woah. It's beautiful.* As Isaac floated there, appreciating the stillness of the world beneath his feet, he breathed in and out slowly. *Take it in*, he thought to himself. *Remember this.* As he said this, his mind flashed back to when he told himself the same thing back when he was a prisoner, whenever he returned from his dreams of the outdoors back to waking up in his cell. He had told himself back then to remember the world outside, in large part to keep himself sane, but also to remember to never lose hope for freedom. "Funny..."

Elrion, still looking down at the city, asked, "What is?"

"I never realized how beautiful cities were. From up here, above it all." He paused to take it all in once more. "This is what we've done. This, more than the trees and nature, this is what humans have been able to do. And I never thought it was so beautiful until right now."

Elrion looked up at his son, then back at the buildings below. "It's amazing how much you are growing." His voice wandered off as he stared at the LAMRY building.

Isaac noticed his father seeming concerned again. "Are my friends okay?" He asked again, seeking confirmation.

Elrion paused before slowly and only barely nodding his head. He then quietly muttered, though somewhat unconvincingly, "*Yea. They're fine.*"

"Okay..." Isaac looked on at his father, waiting for him to say more, to be at least a little more detailed.

Isaac's father lifted his head and looked into the blue skies above. He let out a heavy sigh.

"Maybe that was the wrong question," Isaac added. "Are *you* okay?"

Elrion looked straight at Isaac. He then gently let out... "No." Without saying any more, Elrion let his body sink down through the air toward the ground. Isaac didn't have time to respond or to ask why his father was not okay. He followed him through the sky, down below.

Elrion landed softly on the pavement next to a sidewalk, right in front of the entrance to the LAMRY building. Isaac landed a moment after, remembering to stay behind his father as told. A couple of cars could be heard in the distance. Isaac looked at his father, who seemed not to care.

Dad, should we go in? Isaac used his mind to communicate silently now. If we stay out here, someone might attack us. Let's avoid starting fights if we can. No one needs to get hurt.

Elrion gave a slight smile, happy that his son was considering the safety of others. But then, as Elrion stared at the entrance ahead, his smile dropped. He began walking forward, not saying or thinking a word.

Okay then. Isaac wasn't sure why his dad would be quiet now. After all, the enemy couldn't read their thoughts anyway. *Could they?* Isaac thought of the possibility and suddenly stopped trying to think of any words at all. Maybe his father knew things about their enemy that Isaac did not. Maybe his father had no choice but to be quiet at this time. Isaac followed along, ready also for any hand signals given or any signs of danger that could appear around them. He was ready to knock unconscious anyone that wanted to fight.

Elrion grabbed the metal door handle and pulled the large door open. Isaac followed quickly after him, making sure to stay just a few feet behind. The inside of the lobby was bright. Even though no one was there, the lights were on as if people were still using the building. Isaac looked around, trying to spot even whether a simple security camera was installed on the ceiling somewhere. Elrion still seemed focused on moving ahead though, with little apparent attention paid to whether there were any dangers in the room.

He probably hears everything in this building, even the littlest movements of a camera if there are any. He's so impressive! Of course, he isn't afraid. Isaac couldn't help himself to think this way. Still, he realized he made a mistake. *Oops! Can't think words! Okay... stop it, me!*

Elrion walked straight over to his right, to a set of elevators. Isaac, meanwhile, turned around and walked backward in order to look behind them for incoming dangers, just in case his dad missed something.

CLICK

Isaac glanced forward and saw his father had pressed the button to go up.

For what felt like an eternity, but with what must have been only 30 seconds, Isaac stood there waiting for anything to attack at any moment—his nerves getting to him. All the while, his father simply closed his eyes and breathed calmly while waiting for the elevator doors to open. Isaac closed his eyes too and focused on the sound of the elevator moving down the building. When he heard it approach the lobby where they stood, Isaac opened his eyes, ready to strike whatever could be inside.

The golden metal doors slid open slowly, but to only an empty space. Isaac now noticed his heart rate was higher than before. Though he felt confident and calm when meditating kilometers away, while visualizing danger in his mind over and over, this was different. Real life was different. As they entered the elevator together, Isaac closed his eyes and focused on the beating of his heart and the breath entering his lungs. *Calm*, he thought to himself.

"There is no danger, Isaac. You can relax. Well, try to anyway." Elrion then pressed the button for floor 20.

Hearing his father's words of support out loud did a lot to help Isaac feel better. Elrion could have said anything, and it would have still helped his son. Still, Isaac was confused. "What do you mean? Why were you nervous then, if there is no danger? I was nervous because you seemed to be."

The elevator display showed they had just passed the 10th floor.

"I mean, are you saying there are no PCs? No drones, either?" Isaac still needed clarification. "My friends are here though, right? So... they were able to defeat the PCs by themselves?" Isaac was genuinely surprised.

"Oh," Elrion replied, "they did much more than that."

Floor 20. They had arrived. The elevator doors opened.

"Guy!" Isaac saw his friend sitting in a chair in front of one of the doors down the hallway. Guy stood up, faced Isaac, and smiled. Isaac ran out of the elevator, passed his father, and gave his friend a big hug.

"It's great to see you!" Isaac exclaimed.

"You too," Guy replied plainly.

Isaac let go of his hug and stared with wide eyes at his friend. "What?! You just talked!"

"Yea, I do that nowadays," Guy said. "Where... where have you been all this time? It's been so long. You..."

"What is it?" Isaac's surprise turned to confusion. For some reason, Guy wasn't just looking at him—Guy was staring at him, examining every detail of Isaac's face. "What?"

Guy finished his sentence. "You really haven't aged a bit."

"Hah," Isaac responded, "well neither did you!"

"Isaac, it's time." Elrion put his hand on the door to room 2001. He gently cracked it open, inviting his son to walk through first. "You can catch up with Guy later. You have friends waiting for you inside."

Guy looked at Elrion with a look of concern.

Elrion once again tried to comfort his son. "We're here for you. Whatever happens, we're here."

Isaac looked back at his father and his friend, the two now standing behind him. "Wait, do you two know each other?"

They were silent for a moment. Guy wasn't sure how much he should say just yet.

"Go on in, Isaac," Elrion encouraged him. Isaac would have to find out more later.

Something about this whole situation felt strange to Isaac. He placed his left hand on the door and pushed it open cautiously and slowly. He decided he would sort out his confusion later. He looked inside to see a dimly lit room. There was a window with blinds down, blocking most, but not all, of the daylight. The room lights were turned off.

"Is that you? Isaac?" Emma's voice pierced the darkness, and it shook Isaac to his core. It was hers, yet different. Her voice was deeper and wavered on each word.

"Emma?" Isaac called out as he saw two beds in the back of the room. Both beds had people in them, where one must have been Emma's. While he walked over, he looked around the dark space. To one side, there was a counter with a few computers sitting on top. Otherwise, there were only a couple of chairs alongside the two beds. As he got closer to her, and he focused on trying to see her more clearly, his face turned white. "Emma?!"

"Well, look who decided to show up eighty years late!" Dennis announced.

Isaac couldn't believe what he was seeing. "It can't be. Emma, Dennis." His two friends, lying before him and indeed safe as Elrion promised, were not as Isaac remembered. They were old. Wrinkled, grey-haired, and frail. Isaac could only think of one thing to say. So shocked, his voice could barely be heard as he asked, "*What happened?*"

"Isaac," Elrion began, "do you know what happens when you travel near the speed of light?"

As Isaac's confused, shocked, and sad face turned slowly to look at his father for an explanation, he would soon realize that his journey had just begun.

Made in the USA
Columbia, SC
19 June 2025

0cc75e5e-c186-434e-942f-bb8b1398355bR02